Praise For

BEASTS & CHILDREN

"With her hauntingly perceptive and deeply honest voice, Amy Parker transports readers into the astonishing and often calamitous minds of children. *Beasts and Children* is a dazzling debut to be celebrated."
—**Ruth Ozeki,** best-selling author of *A Tale for the Time Being*, *My Year of Meats*, and others

"Reading *Beasts and Children*, I was struck not only by Amy Parker's incisive and skillfully crafted sentences but also by the depth and integrity with which she treats every one of her characters. A beautiful and engaging debut."
—**Molly Antopol,** author of *The UnAmericans*

"It isn't often that we encounter a writer who presents us, as readers, with a new-new style, a new way of looking at our beleaguered, battered world. But Amy Parker is that kind of artist. *Beasts and Children* is utterly original and true-hearted, a clear-eyed exploration of the natural world and our own delightfully flawed human relationships. The spirit of Flannery O'Connor resides in this collection of stories; *Beasts and Children* is the literary debut of a major talent."
—**Nickolas Butler,** internat̶ ̶ ̶ ̶ ̶ ̶ ̶ ̶ ̶ ̶ ̶-
ning author of *Shotgun Love*̶

"*Beasts and Children* is a beautiful, haunting collection of stories whose deeply flawed and yet deeply human characters weave and wind themselves around your heart. As we follow them from childhood to adulthood, from old age to death, we learn that in the midst of all of life's tragedies, love comes from unexpected places."

—**Chinelo Okparanta,** author of *Under the Udala Trees* and *Happiness, Like Water*

"Intense, beautiful, and true, the stories in *Beasts and Children* speak to that catastrophe known as childhood: the loneliness and fleeting camaraderies; the perilous gaps of adult attention and soul-saving intimacy with the natural world. In her remarkable debut, Amy Parker proves herself an unflinching, passionate, and profoundly humane writer, even as she holds a knife to your heart."

—**Michelle Huneven,** author of *Blame* and others

"Amy Parker's stories are intensely interested in the human heart, and in particular the way it is often laid bare by the perpetual crises of childhood and family. As the stories twist and knot into what we understand as the characters' full, complex lives, the reader is taken again and again by the alacrity of Parker's narrative vision, her radical empathy for person and animal alike, and her touch with language. This collection rejuvenates and fantastically engages a classic preoccupation; it is fiction that does justice to the complicated joy and sadness of being alive, in a family, in this world."

—**Arna Bontemps Hemenway,** author of *Elegy on Kinderklavier*, winner of the 2015 PEN/Hemingway Award

"Amy Parker's stories are thrillingly self-possessed. They stand perfectly poised, like balancing artists, between the lyrical and the no-nonsense, the impassioned and the restrained. She has a gift for uncloaking the mysteries of her characters, particularly the children, who themselves struggle to uncloak the mysteries of the great big world of other minds into which they've been born: friends and grown-ups, strangers and parents, humans and animals alike. I was moved and fascinated by this book. I'll be first in line to read her next."
—**Kevin Brockmeier,** author of *The Brief History of the Dead* and others

"Zestfully inventive. An electrifying, daring, and magical debut collection sure to appeal to fans of Karen Russell and Lorrie Moore." —*Booklist,* starred review

"A vivid kaleidoscope of narratives. Characters appear as children and then reappear, later in the book, married and with children of their own. Their stories are told and retold from varying perspectives, which provide new insight into their histories in the same way that a mystery can be pieced together from new details. This riveting collection executes a grim autopsy on American family life." —*Kirkus Reviews*

BEASTS & CHILDREN

BEASTS &
CHILDREN

Amy Parker

A Mariner Original
MARINER BOOKS
Houghton Mifflin Harcourt
Boston   New York
2016

For information about permission to reproduce selections from this book,
write to trade.permissions@hmhco.com or to Permissions,
Houghton Mifflin Harcourt Publishing Company, 3 Park Avenue,
19th Floor, New York, New York 10016.

www.hmhco.com

Library of Congress Cataloging-in-Publication Data
Parker, Amy, date.
[Short stories. Selections]
Beasts and children / Amy Parker.
pages cm
ISBN 978-0-544-37013-5 (paperback) — ISBN 978-0-544-37016-6 (ebook)
I. Title.
PS3616.A7434A6 2016
813'.6 — dc23

Book design by Greta D. Sibley

Printed in the United States of America
DOC 10 9 8 7 6 5 4 3 2 1

To Katherine and Michele

My arms
fit you like a sleeve, they hold
catkins of your willows, the wild bee farms
of your nerves, each muscle and fold
of your first days.

—Anne Sexton, from "Unknown Girl in the Maternity Ward"

Contents

THE WHITE ELEPHANT

*The dust that Pancho bit down South ended up in
Lefty's mouth.*

Carline and I sat at the breakfast table dressed as the dancing
ostriches from *Fantasia*. It was Halloween morning, 1967—the
last year of my family's unbroken life—and my older sister and
I were having a fight with our mother. She had made these out-
fits for our schools' costume parade.

"My beautiful ballerinas," Daddy said. "Both of you. Miss
Cissy and darlin' Carline the Pageant Queen."

"We're not ballerinas," Carline retorted. "We're freaks."

To eat, we wore our papier-mâché beaks shoved up on our
foreheads. My tummy strained against the waistband of the
ostrich-feather tutu Mother had stitched; Carline, lithe in her
plumage, batted irritably at the huge black hair-bow Mother insisted each of us wear.

"Nobody but Minnie Mouse wears a giant goddamned bow on her head!"

"Language, Carline."

Carline's eyes, lovely and blue and huge, blazed under false eyelashes. My own eyes burned from envy and eyelash glue.

"Carline looks better than me."

"Better than I," said Mother. "Don't compare, Cissy."

"If you didn't want her to compare, you shouldn't have dressed us alike," said Carline.

Unfortunately for us, Mother was a woman of powerful imagination.

"You wanted an animal costume, Cissy," Mother told me. "Carline wanted to go as Odile. It's easier to make one costume twice."

"You always say never do something simply because it's easier," I said.

"A mother can't survive without some double standards, Cecilia. And besides, no one will know you're dressed alike; you go to different schools."

She took a prim sip of her coffee and with maddening composure returned her attention to her halved grapefruit.

"Mama, this getup is about as far from Swan Lake as the moon!"

Carline had just turned twelve and still danced ballet. Most girls had given it up by then. (Mother had already let me quit and I was only ten.) Carline at least was built like an ostrich, long neck and all, so her costume suited her. Except for the beak, she looked gorgeous. I was, Carline pointed out, built more like one of *Fantasia*'s dancing hippos.

"My tutu's itchy," I complained.

"Clothes impart discipline," said Mother. "Look at your father."

Daddy wore his pilot's uniform, which might as well have been a Halloween costume. He flew for Lonestar Air—a trans-Texas airline company his own father had started back in what Pawpaw called the golden age of flight. Daddy was airforce-trained, saw action in Korea. Someday, Pawpaw said, he would run the company, if he kept his nose clean and his whistle dry. Tee-totalitarian, Daddy called him.

The heavy navy blue uniform gave Daddy square corners. His white shirt made him look crisp and alert; the knotted tie dignified his poorly shaven neck and lifted his chin. When he set his heavy captain's hat on his head, its shade lent his features an expression of cheerful seriousness. In his pilot's costume, he looked like someone you could trust.

His uniform perked us all up because it meant he'd be gone from the house. His absence from home was like a pulled tooth, a hole to explore, gingerly, but with deep relief.

"There won't be any fighting during your Aunt Loretta's visit," my father said, and lit a cigarette. "And you girls best get home from school right quick and clean my trophy room."

"I wish you wouldn't smoke at the table," Mother told Daddy. "Carline, you eat two more bites of that egg."

Carline cut the bites and pushed them around on her plate. She didn't like to eat. She used her mouth for sass, mainly.

"It's not our *job*," Carline announced. "It's her job to clean Daddy's morgue."

"I'm standing right here," said Mother.

Carline pinched me.

"Caroline Louise Bowman," snapped Mother. "You are excused from this table." Carline smiled. She'd gained her point; she handed her plate to Mother, egg uneaten.

Mother stacked the plates noisily. When she leaned over to clear Daddy's, she inhaled deeply and said, "A little more aftershave, Mark. And you might want this."

She slipped him a packet of Sen-Sen to clear up his breath.

"Shoot, Grace, you got a nose on you like a bloodhound," said Daddy. "No one else can smell a thing. Right, Cissy?"

I leaned in and sniffed.

"No sir," I lied.

"I don't see why we need to clean up for old Aunt Loretta," said Carline from the doorway. She looked over at Daddy to gauge her effect.

He sat turning his pilot's cap over in his hands, putting off the moment when it would weight his head. He had one last Starliner run to make to El Paso—a trip that would bring him back to us by the late afternoon. Fortunately, he hadn't caught Carline's remark. Daddy was a great talker but a bad listener; he tuned in at the wrong times and to the wrong things. If we pitched our voices right the odds were good that he'd miss half the meaning of anything we said. It was safer that way. Daddy had moods.

Usually any mention of Aunt Loretta brought on a tirade about how far away his sister lived or a hymn to her praises. He took hops out to see her in Big Spring because it was on his flight route, but we had never met her. We were pilot's children, but we had never been up in a plane.

"What's this about Loretta?" said Daddy. "You girls ready for the sweetest woman that ever lived? You ready to meet your little cousin? Loretta says he's pure Bowman. I ever tell you girls my sister's nickname?"

"Only a thousand times daily from birth," said Carline.

"Can I call her Aunt Pistol?" I asked. I hoped if I loved Aunt Loretta as much as Daddy did, I'd get on his good side.

"It's 'may I. ' And say *aunt,* not *ant,* Cissy. She's not an insect," said Mother.

"She sure as hell ain't no insect! My big sister," said Daddy, "is a pure pistol; one hundred percent red-blooded Texan—wild, wild, wild. Sure is cute as a bug, though."

He winked at Mother. Mother looked away. She couldn't bear it when Daddy got folksy.

"Ever since we was kids," he said, "I called her Pistol and she called me Gunn. Can't wait for you girls to meet her. She's a true Southern lady. She's a Belle Starr bombshell. She's—"

"Getting a divorce," said Mother.

"Don't you start, Grace. It's not for you to pass judgment on my family's affairs."

"*Affairs* would be the operative word," said Mother.

"Damn right," said Daddy, so busy lighting another cigarette that he didn't catch her meaning.

"They're staying for how long?" I asked.

"Not long, sugar," said Mother. "Loretta never stays anyplace long."

"I want that trophy room clean . . ."

"Then you better do it yourself," said Carline, "because I'm not going in there. Those animal heads," she said, "are just wrong."

Three generations of Bowman males had shot and stuffed

a whole herd of bucks, a bull moose, a buffalo (bison—*dammit, girls, the proper term is* bison). On the trophy room's walls hung a mountain goat, a bighorn ram, the tusked, ugly head of a wild boar, the sprouty-whiskered sneer of a javelina, the head of an antelope, pronged as a barbecue fork, a caribou, even a churlish badger with inky black whiplashes down his neck, and of course, Great-Grandfather Bowman's infamous black rhino with its tiny piggy eyes peering out above its great and terrible thorn. The family trophies were all male. Females, Daddy explained, made worthless trophies. Except as wives. *Your mother has no sense of humor.*

I stared at my yolk stains on the tablecloth and tried sister-telepathy. *Oh, leave him be, Carline. Why do you always start something? Let him leave so we can breathe.* Carline was too busy looking in the mirror to read my mind.

"Your great-grandfather started out shooting jackrabbits with a slingshot for food, he was that poor."

"By the time he was twenty-five he'd earned his first million dollars and bagged a black rhinoceros," Carline chorused.

I watched Daddy deciding whether or not to be pissed off. But he was too happy about the Pistol coming to waste his energy.

"Well, you girls just know everything, don't you."

"Killing animals for sport is barbaric, Daddy."

"Carline, I never took you for a peacenik! It doesn't suit you, darlin'," said Daddy. "Tell you what, you go in there and clean my trophy room and maybe I'll let you stick flowers in my gun barrels."

He left the room.

Mother picked up his abandoned cap. She touched the

heavy gold badge, traced the seraphim wings that strained around a map of Texas as though God himself were hauling our state off to heaven.

"Well, *sugar,*" she said. "Silver liners and silver clouds!"

That was the family airline's motto. Our grandmother Gigi came up with it; it sounded grand until you unpicked it and realized it didn't mean a thing.

Daddy designed the trophy room without windows, to protect the trophies from sun damage. The room had no overhead light, just standing lamps that cast pale amber puddles and created deep shadows in the corners of the room. With their fringed shades and skinny, old-fashioned poles, the lamps had the effect of palm trees leaning over tiny lagoons. When I switched one on, the heads on the walls leaped and loomed.

I was ten years old before I realized that all the heads in Daddy's trophy room weren't alive. I used to believe they were only pretending to be dead. I kept their secret. In reward for my silence, they looked at me. No one else in the family did. Carline spent most of her time looking in mirrors. Her breasts were very new; she couldn't get over them. Also, she was beautiful. Mother looked at Daddy, or read her books, and Daddy looked off into space.

Until I was ten I believed in everything: fairies, witches, magic, god, the future and the present, though I was old enough to know which beliefs to conceal. I also believed in cleaning my plate, which all my life was crowed up as a virtue, but then I turned ten and that, too, changed. Heifer, elephant, buffalo, pig—I became them all. The trophies taught me to focus on the head and drop all sense of body, and for that I loved them.

When I looked in a mirror I pretended my body was plastered up behind a wall. I had big fringed eyes and a steady gaze. I could still be someone's prize.

In the corner across from the piano, Daddy's glass-fronted gun cabinet made a ghost of me, golden and distorted, frisking across its reflective surface. Inside it, the guns, too, hummed. I didn't doubt they were alive. Anything that could kill you had a life of its own.

"You ever notice," Carline said, watching me from the doorway of the trophy room as I wiped the dust out of Mickey Moose's eyes, "how worn the heads are getting? Like they're dying all over again?"

She cracked her forbidden gum. (Mother said it was uncouth.)

Carline leaned into the room, reeled out a long grey-pink string of chewing gum, and fixed one end of it to Buffalo Bill's nose.

"I hate this room," she said. "Mother hates it too."

"Maybe," I ventured, stating my own suspicion, "she is afraid the heads are alive."

"Ha! She hates it in here because everything is dead."

Carline went on. "Other kids have pets. We have Daddy's heads."

She leaned farther into the room, crooked her leg in an impressive *attitude*, then extended it in an even more impressive *arabesque* and pressed her gum more firmly onto Bill's nose.

"You don't even have a tail to wag, mangy old cuss. You don't have a buffalo butt like Cissy, and you haven't got a leg to stand on."

As part of my pact with them, I had never touched the heads.

If I touched them, I'd know for certain—alive or dead? But that day I broke faith with them. When I scraped the gum from Bill's nose and wiped the film off Xavier the javelina's teeth, it felt as pointless as any other dusting.

"You know," I said to Carline, "I guess I hate this room too."

That night Cousin Danny and the Pistol arrived in a big red convertible with fins on its back side and crushed bugs on the windshield and dollops of bird doo scattered like dripped pancake batter on the dirty hood.

"Trick or treat!" sang Aunt Loretta. They weren't wearing costumes.

Carline sloped over to the car and held out our bowl of candy. Aunt Loretta grabbed a fistful of Baby Ruths. She wore dark glasses even though it was deep twilight and tied her hair tomboy-style in a bright red kerchief dotted with white paisleys that looked a lot like the bird doo dabbing the car. Our cousin Danny hugged close something wrapped in a baby blanket. At first I thought it was a doll but that made no sense because no nine-year-old boy would have a doll, except maybe a Howdy Doody. Then I guessed it might be another cousin, but it turned out to be a monkey.

They'd been on the road a long time—through Arkansas all the way up to Wisconsin, and then out to California and back, he said.

("Chasing that man," I overheard Mother sing to Carline. "Might as well try and catch the wind."

"Mother, I never knew you liked Donovan."

"There's no law against it," said Mother. "Even if I am over thirty.")

Cousin Danny looked like a Campbell's Soup kid—wide, smackable cheeks, and round eyes. Danny's monkey wore a tiny diaper fastened with a blue diaper pin, and flashed its teeth in a way that just told you it bit, and it had tiny hands with little gray nails and dark brown palms.

When Aunt Loretta waved up from the car calling "Gunn! Gunny!" our daddy ran over to her like a boy and called, "Here she is, girls! Don't she look purty?" He sounded extra Texan when he said it, and I knew this annoyed Mother, who said that real Texans have no discernable accents and that his hill-country drawl was a hick affectation.

"Here she is, here's my Pistol!"

Daddy always raved about how beautiful his big sister was, but in the porch light Aunt Loretta looked like the bad side of fifty—her face gray and rubbery and pulled into skewed witch lines, though she wore lipstick like a beauty contestant, a blossom of red all wrong on her old-lady face and her hair under the red bandana dyed black. The Pistol hopped out of the car. She wore tight dungarees and open-toed wedges, and her toenails were chipped bright red.

"Mark, honey, I'm in love."

"Let me look at your eyes," said Daddy.

She trembled in the heat, and when she whipped off her sunglasses her eyes looked like dead lightning bugs at the bottom of a jar.

"Take a look, Cissy darlin'," said Daddy. "Loretta has the Bowman eyes. The prettiest eyes in the world."

If those were the Bowman eyes, I was sorry that I had them too. I envied Carline, who took after Mother. Mother was ten times as pretty as Aunt Loretta in or out of makeup, and she didn't stand there lashing her tail like a cat, letting off a sweet sick smell of nerves. The Pistol was so thin and ugly, I felt sorry for her and kind of also for Daddy, for being blind about it.

Cousin Danny inched out of the car carrying the monkey in the baby blanket. One hairy arm snaked out of the blanket and hooked its fingers in Danny's belt loop. Danny hooked a finger in the belt loop of Aunt Loretta's dungarees, so the three of them—monkey, cousin and pistol—latched together like burrs. She just unhooked his fingers and said, "Honeybunch, why don't you show the girls your monkey."

Daddy guffawed and the Pistol swatted him. Daddy strode up the porch steps, his boots booming. He poured them each a bourbon, rattled a glass out over the railing to entice Aunt Loretta. Danny reached for her again but the Pistol was already halfway up the porch steps.

I hated her. The Pistol.

But I wanted her to like me, so I said "Come on, Danny," in my best company voice and took him to the trophy room, where I thought maybe the monkey would feel more at home. With a real live monkey scrambling around the walls the room felt bigger, less frightening and more alive. The monkey wiggled out of its diaper and pooped on Mother's grand piano. Then it climbed up between the moose's antlers and refused to come down.

An hour later we wandered back out to the driveway, where Daddy sat at the wheel of the convertible, contemplating an empty glass smeared with worms of red lipstick set insecurely on the dash. Aunt Loretta lay in the back seat; her chipped toes peeked over the side of the convertible. Danny ran over and jiggled her foot.

"Momma," he said. "Momma!"

"Leave her be, son."

"I thought she was dead."

"Shoot, she's just sleeping. Go on inside."

Mother came out onto the porch and put her arms around Cousin Danny.

"Mark, she should leave him with us. He shouldn't be out of school. And that man she's chasing—"

"I don't like it neither. But she's in love."

"It's no life for a little boy. First his daddy and now—"

"That's my family's business. I won't have ugly talk, Grace."

Daddy caught the monkey with a pool net and told us they'd be leaving in the morning.

"Your poor Uncle Jefferson. His tire treads weren't even cold before Loretta started chasing Nestor Roche," Mother said to Carline.

"Uncle Roach?"

"He's not your uncle. Jiminy crickets! Cockroach? The man is a cockleburr. Saved your daddy's life in Pusan, my eye. More likely he enticed him into some foolishness and then 'saved him' to make an impression. He's a Heep! Heep!"

"A heap of what?"

"Don't you read anything, Carline?"

I retreated behind the kitchen door.

"If Loretta had any character she would have stood by her own husband, stood up to that talking macaroon who runs their lives, and not let him go. And your Uncle Jefferson's no better. Any man who loved his wife and son wouldn't let himself be run off or even paid off. I have no patience for them."

Carline spotted me behind the door and gave me the hairy eyeball. She clattered the plates to cover Mother's voice, but I heard anyway.

"Our money's like blood in the water. Your Aunt Loretta's too smitten to know Roche for a shark, and she's dragging Danny to hell and back chasing that piece of worthless trash. If my parents were still here, God rest them, you girls wouldn't be so overrun with Bowmans. The women in this family have no character."

Carline said, "But aren't you a woman in this family too?"

Mother turned on the faucet, hard, and called out to me.

"Cissy, come on in here and help your sister dry!"

Mother started talking brightly about a window display she'd seen at Neiman Marcus—dreadful, no style—and I dried and put the plates away.

Aunt Loretta sat on the porch steps with her chin on my daddy's knee. She wore his flight cap wobble-cocked over one eye. They passed a bottle back and forth. She looked up into his face and he looked away, off to the side, at the trees where the bagworms had turned the branches into dim racks of webbing.

"Think what you're doing, Loretta."

"Mark, you know me—when I fall in love it's like a firework going off in my head, a burning dahlia that says 'mine' and weeps hot petals and sends out roots of flame that take over my heart and burn up the foxtails that grow there. Sometimes my heart feels like a vacant lot and I lie back in the weeds on hot nights waiting, just waiting for them fireworks."

He tutted, pulled on his cigarette. Loretta staggered to her feet. She stood like an actress, like Elizabeth Taylor, all gritted teeth and fire. I thought, She's wonderful. I thought, How could anyone be so phony? I pressed my cheek against the screen, feeling sick and strange.

"Thailand's halfway across the danged world, Loretta. It's practically Vietnam."

I blew little puffs of dust out between the gridding, scratched it with a nail.

"Udorn's an air force base—safe! He has a government contract! *Humanitarian*, Mark. Roachie's crew performs rice drops and I don't know what all. It's good money."

I was a bug, scaling the screen. I could see with eyes that looked in all directions, a million facets. I didn't have to face anything head-on.

"Stay here, honey."

"I can't," Aunt Loretta said. "Gigi cut me off."

"What about Danny?" Daddy threw his cigarette on the lawn.

When she didn't answer, he stood up and shuffled over to the door. Aunt Loretta just stood there, looking out over the lawn at the trees in their shrouds, rubbing the back of her head and shivering.

"Hey, bubba!" she called finally, "you could come too. Come with us! Roachie says they could use more pilots."

Daddy shook his head and pulled at the screen door. I spilled out onto the porch.

What Mother said when Aunt Loretta died was: "Maybe now at least she'll stay put." She gasped and clapped a hand over her mouth. "God forgive me, Cissy. I didn't mean that. I always said she was a few sandwiches shy of a picnic, and Danny spoileder than the mayonnaise on them. All that acting up, the crazy scheme to leave the country—and it wasn't even her fault. She was sick the whole time and I couldn't see it. I just hated her."

The week before Christmas, Gigi phoned to ask if our cousin Danny could come live with us.

"I'm worn out," Gigi quavered. "Sheerly done in. He is a sweet boy but not at my time of life."

I listened on Carline's princess extension and heard Mother, steely-soft, say, "She should have left him with us in the first place."

"Put my son on, Grace," said Gigi. "Let me talk to Mark. I never can talk to you."

"Cissy, hang up," said Mother.

"You got to breathe through your nose if you're going to eavesdrop, Cissy," Carline poked me.

"Hey, Cissy," said Gigi. "You all are going to get a little brother."

"We haven't decided that," said Mother. "Cissy, hang up."

After the phone call, Daddy got loaded and Mother sat with her head in her hands all day.

Carline and I painted each other's nails up in her bedroom and chewed off the polish and ate the bitter flecks and painted them over again.

"When Aunt Loretta came," I asked Carline, "she seem crazy to you?"

"I don't know, Cissy. No. Maybe. She did buy Danny a *monkey*."

"She seem like she was gonna die?"

"She was younger than Daddy."

"How do you get a brain tumor, Carline?"

"Your brain pushes against your skull or something. It's like you hit your head on the ceiling, only the ceiling is inside your head, and you die."

This was so awful, I dropped a gobbet of polish on the rug. I glugged acetone onto a cotton ball and swabbed at it.

"You're making it worse," said Carline. "Dab, don't scrub." She stroked another perfect ruby line on her pinky.

"Mother says Danny's spoiled," said Carline, "and with a dead mama he'll be worse."

"You be nice."

"Shoot, he's got my sympathy. Crazy mama, dead mama, and he might have to come live with us. You're no bargain, Cissy."

"Neither are you."

"The hell I'm not. I'm a peach."

"You're something that nearly rhymes with it, Carline."

Cousin Danny looked just the same except he'd shot up a couple of inches and he wouldn't make eye contact.

"He's wearing floods," I whispered to Carline, pointing at the dirty inch of pale white ankle showing below his pants cuff.

Danny wore a red bandana cowboy-style around his neck. When Daddy came out of his trophy room to greet Danny, he saw the bandana and said, "That was Pistol's." Instead of hugging Danny and taking his suitcase, Daddy pulled the bandana up off of Danny's head, which must have smarted considering how tight Danny had it tied. Daddy yanked it off and absconded with it to the trophy room. He left Danny standing there with his big betrayed eyes watering and a clean white ring around his grimy neck where the bandana had been. His skinny arms strained at the suitcase. I grabbed it from him and Carline ruffled his hair and we took him up to my old bedroom.

Carline plugged her portable record player into the wall and set it up on my old dresser. She spun Harry Belafonte singing "Day-O." "You know when they sing 'Six foot, seven foot, eight foot bunch'? They're measuring the size of his tallywhacker," Carline said. "And guess what's really the hairy black tarantula? They mean a lady's—"

Danny popped the latches on his suitcase and it sprang open, revealing dozens of wrapped Christmas presents.

"But where are your clothes?" I asked him.

"Gigi packed for me."

Carline upended the suitcase. Boxes slithered out onto the carpet. Carline picked through them—rattled the biggest present experimentally. "Erector set, comic book, comic book, regular book. And not a single damn thing for Cissy and me. Gigi getting senile?"

"She was sad," said Danny.

One item remained in the suitcase, squared carefully in the hard frame and wrapped in a ratty Snoopy pillowcase. Danny unveiled, reverently, a Disney LP of Halloween sound effects. He hugged the cardboard sleeve to his chest briefly and set the record on the rug. I picked it up.

"*Chilling Thrilling Sounds of Halloween*? What on earth, Danny?"

"'The Haunted House.'" Carline grabbed it and read from the track list. "'The Very Long Fuse.' 'The Unsafe Bridge.' 'Chinese Water Torture'? Groovy tunes, man. 'Cat Fight'? 'A Collection of

Creaks.' 'A Collection of Crashes'—bet you can dance to that one—"

"Give it!" Danny said, rising to his feet.

"Oho, he's ALIVE!" Carline groaned, and waved the record out of reach. "'Drips and Splashes.' 'Things in Space'?" She jumped to her feet and did the Monster Mash.

Day me say day me say day me say day ay ay oh.

Lately she'd been subject to these fits of frantic meanness, laugh attacks, dance crazes. I started laughing; I couldn't stop. Danny jumped for the record, but Carline stood a head taller and held it high, fanning herself with it, flicking it back and forth like a flamenco dancer, whoooing like a ghost.

I rolled red-faced, laughing until I hiccuped, which made me laugh more. Danny's distress only fed our frenzy. The worse he raged, the harder we laughed. Incandescent with meanness, drunk on its champagne fizz.

Danny's Christmas presents lay under me, crushed and creased. The inside of my mouth tasted terrible; tears smarted my eyes and my ribs hurt as though they'd been kicked. Danny sat vacantly scratching a mosquito bite on his anklebone until it bled.

The record hissed on the turntable. Carline lifted the needle.

"Want us to play your record?" she asked.

"Y'all's house is haunted," Danny said. "It doesn't need sound effects."

"It is not." The hair stood up on my neck.

"I heard things in that trophy room," said Danny.

"I have too," said Carline.

They turned on me, Danny pale and serious, Carline glittering with spite.

"Things moving behind the walls," he said.

"Those heads might be dead, but something in the walls is coming to life." Carline was grinning.

"You lie!" But I believed her.

Carline was always Daddy's favorite. Before he quit paying attention to her. When she was little, he treated her like a son, which is funny because she was pretty. He liked that, too. It made her tough and dangerous; she would become the kind of woman he admired, beautiful, but someone you could tell things to. When Danny came to live with us, Daddy abandoned all interest in Carline. Danny was the Pistol's boy.

"What do you all talk about?" asked Carline, as if she couldn't guess.

"Momma," said Danny. "He tells his stories."

"Let them be," our mother said. "Maybe between the two of them they'll settle her ghost."

"Danny's his favorite now," said Carline. "It's not fair."

I was nobody's favorite—not Mother's, not Gigi's, not even my own. So I had less to grieve over when Daddy turned his attention to our cousin. Neither Danny nor Carline could see that when Aunt Loretta died, Daddy died too.

The new year turned over. The airline company fired Daddy. There was nothing even Gigi could do about it. Carline claimed he'd been drunk and sheared off a wingtip taxiing before take-off. Scraped it against a traffic control tower. He lost his pilot's license. He'd seen Aunt Loretta waving to him from the runway. He saw her everywhere, I heard him telling Danny.

Once Daddy started favoring him, Danny never uttered a

single original word about his mother. He just repeated Daddy's words, verbatim, telling the same stories over and over, offering them up like novenas.

"Jeepers. Daddy might as well be Edgar Bergen and Danny his dummy," Carline complained.

As kids we grew up in a thicket of talk. Daddy sprouted words up into a briar fort of stories that nothing—certainly nothing as insignificant as our own experience—could contradict. Daddy's certainty never let anyone else get a word in. We lived in a chamber of echoes. Daddy's voice could bounce and reverberate, collide, and contradict, but women were supposed to whisper.

"I bet astronauts could hear Daddy from space," Carline said to me.

I suspected Daddy's stories leached the words right out of Mother. She was always telling Carline and me to hush now, shush now, quiet down, don't run on like those mendacious Bowmans. She told us that Daddy's family stories were worse than lies, worse than secrets.

"Silence is clearer than speech."

"You hate stories, so how come you read so much, Mother?" I asked.

Most stories bear as little relation to reality as Daddy's trophies do to the warm and living animal, she told us. You girls can stare at those heads as long as you like, but their eyes are just shiny marbles. An animal looks back at you, but a trophy's gaze never offers anything but a distorted and diminished reflection of your face. Most people's stories, when you lean in close, serve as aggrandized self-portrait, confirmation bias, and wishful thinking. (Mother could out-rant Daddy, if she chose.)

To be the exception that disproves the rule, keep mum, but if you must, tell the truth and shame the devil and at any rate go to sleep.

Tell us just a little one, we'd beg. Mother, just one story.

She'd stand over our beds and say: "I'll tell you a story about Mary Morey and now my story's begun. I'll tell you another about her brother, and now my story is done."

Then she'd switch off the light and leave.

I lay in the dark and wondered about Mary Morey and her brother. Mary with her near-mirror name and her brother who didn't even rate a proper noun—who were they? What happened to them? Why did Mother open and shut the book of their lives with that curt/pert little rhyme?

I'll tell you a story about Mary Morey, and now my story's begun.

Aunt Loretta died of fireworks to the brain.

I'll tell you another about her brother.

Daddy shipped off to the Udorn air force base, in spite of the war, in spite of his children, way off across the world. He left a stock of tales, like a bolster hidden the under bedclothes, to take his place.

Roche says he'll hire me, no questions asked . . . Hellfire, it's a paycheck, Grace . . . I've got to go, I've got to take it . . . a man provides for his family.

That isn't why you're leaving us, said Mother. *You're going after Roche.*

A man pays his debts.

I'll tell you another, about her brother.

Daddy came back. He lost everyone's money, he lost the family company, he lost everything.

There's your story, begun and done.

"Mother," I called to her one night, "what was the name of Mary Morey's brother?"

"Mark," she said.

"That's Daddy's name," said Carline.

"Well, there are such things as coincidences," said Mother. "Go to sleep."

After Daddy left, Mother aired the trophy room, scattered lavender on the carpets and vacuumed it up, flung the door wide, kept the lamps burning, and played Bach preludes on her piano to sweep away the gloom. She misted the heads with Hermès perfume and made us run under them performing wild ballets with vetiver fans. The trophies stared in mute reproof.

In June of 1968 Daddy returned from Udorn. He'd been gone for six months, sending us postcards Mother didn't bother to read, and then he was back and bivouacked on the front porch, where he refused to drink anything but bourbon and ginger ale. He called it his porch wine; it was a mixture he and Aunt Loretta had invented when they were kids, and he clung to it like he was missing some essential component in his blood that could only be set straight with that transfusion.

When he drank porch wine, Daddy never got high or tight—he got loaded. Like a question, or a silence. Like a gun.

Mother ignored the drinking—retreated behind a wall of thought. She stopped planning our meals, fired our cook, and kept a vat of collards aboil on the stove, a food she had never before permitted us to eat, because it was low-class. Whenever we felt hungry she expected us to come and spoon the ham hock up out of the pot without bothering to turn off the burner. She had bigger problems than feeding us, or cleaning dishes, she said.

"Mother, you told us yourself: she who eats from the pot will never be rich."

And Mother grimaced and said, "Superstition won't save you from any real disaster." She slurped pot liquor pointedly from the ladle and returned her attention to her copy of *The Snows of Kilimanjaro*.

"What does she *think* about?" we asked each other.

"Not us," I said bitterly.

"What does he drink for?"

"Not us."

Mother's book roosted on her wing chair. A postcard that had been marking a page fluttered out, paper-clipped to a photo. Carline separated them, and scanned the postcard. I picked up the photo.

It was the first shot of Daddy I ever saw where he wasn't smoking a cigarette or holding a drink. He stood with an arm slung around the neck of a water buffalo. He grinned into the camera, looking a little like Hemingway on the back cover of Mother's book: working blues, brilliant black hair, black mustache, solid torso. Our handsome Daddy, standing next to an animal that was upright and wholly alive.

> Dear Gracie,
>
> It's like the Wild West out here. No laws and no interference. I feel free. Some air force boys trapped a blue-eyed black panther down in Cambodia and made

him their mascot. He's a big ole cat, name of Eldridge
(as in Cleaver, there's that "hippie" sense of humor!),
and they take turns patrolling him around the base on
a leash. They swear he's tame. I've looked in his eyes
and I got my doubts. I miss you and the girls, Mark

The postcard lied about everything but the panther.

When I try to imagine what really happened in that jungle, I am certain Daddy hated it. He hated its fervid monot-
ony. Something always pulpy and dying underfoot. Something
always blooming. In this country a huge studded fruit with
flesh like corpse-cheese was considered a delicacy, though you
couldn't bring it aboard any bus.

Everything the jungle produced was fleshy, sweet, flow-
ery, rotten. His feet caught some fungi and dropped white wet
flakes. It had all been a mistake.

He must have written this postcard sitting at a desk in a
small oven of an office where a Thai official in a short uniform and a rifle slung over across his back smoked cigarettes
and toyed with his passport. The official rubber-stamped a piece
of paper printed with curly shapes Daddy could not read, the
ink red and smeary, limping a trail down the document. He
couldn't read the letters, but all the same, he knew it meant
"Denied."

Denied.

Denied.

Denied.

He tracked the stamp's bloody progress. He wanted a drink.
He was not a criminal. It wasn't like he was trying to smuggle
goddamned hard rice to the Viet Cong. He tried to make himself

understood. A mistake. Where he came from you didn't lock up a white man up for his mistakes.

Roche's pilots flew private cargo planes through Thailand and Cambodia. They made air drops to remote villages—hill tribes the war had cut off from food, equipment. Daddy told us a long, rambling story about some hotshots air-lifting a live elephant to help a village with its plowing. He'd seen a lot of elephants.

Why he ended up in those jungles so far northwest of Udorn he never would explain. These stories always begin at a bar somewhere. Nestor Roche glad-handing a de-enlisted NCO with a bragging voice and split-veined nose, some Yankee grown fat and shady, alongside his tiny, tough wife. Lots of girls, colored lights. The kind of talking that men do when they are far from home and can afford to fictionalize. That far from their real lives, it's all dreaming. *Best friend, you're my best friend, Roach.* A plane dipping over the mountains. *Ah, why'd you leave her? Why didn't you tell us she was sick? I'll kill you, Roach.* Smoking black gum in a pipe. *Don't you leave me too.*

My father lying alone in a house on stilts beside a river. Cockroaches on a bare floor. A gun at his side. He wanted to kill Roche. Had he killed him? Something needed killing. He can't think straight. He's not even awake.

When he opened his eyes and saw the moving shadows of moonlit leaves, he knew that something big waited out there. The bull elephant: a king come to meet him. He knew it would come to him and take whatever he offered it, a ripe mango, a snapshot of his daughters. It would bend its domed head and then pluck, with perfect trust, the offering from his palm. He watched the moonlight glitter in the cracks between the floor-boards. He heard a weird lizard's cry—*tokay, tokay*—that Roche claimed was a harbinger of ghosts, and he felt the long breath of the river. Sweat crawled off of him and crept away to join the roaches. He sat up. The river smelled rank, but he caught, too, a cool drift of jasmine. Yesterday's garland still hung from his neck.

He stood, and the rosebuds on either end of the garland knocked against his chest. It was out there, the bull elephant, waiting to meet him by the river. He bent, shook out his shoes to check for scorpions as Roche had taught him—*You ever hear the one about the scorpion and the frog, Roachie? Which one are you?*—and then slipped his feet, raw and slimy, into his shoes. At the threshold he stopped. He'd forgotten the gun. He had it in his hands. He was terrified.

The smell of jasmine wafted up to him, so sweet and cool, his heart ached. The gun hung heavy and lean in the crook of his arm. Loretta had leaned on his arm in the old days, leaned in her high heels. The jungle's heat softened the starch of her full skirt; he felt its limp folds brush his leg.

The moon made the trees hold still. It shone on the river, grained as teak. He saw the elephant bathing in the river beneath the white tusk of the moon. It emerged from the river, dripping.

And, sure he is dreaming, he asked it, "Loretta, honey, is that you?"

The white elephant approached. My father trembled in its presence like a woman. His sister, his Pistol, lay an ocean away, and deep in the ground. If it would only reach out, if it would bless him, then all would be well. All manner of things would be well.

Daddy tried to stifle the cry that escaped him as *"Please."* The elephant simply brushed its trunk in the dust. No half-stifled plea has ever moved a white elephant. It sloped off toward the river and left him alone with his full-broken heart and his half-stifled *Please,* he who had never begged any man for anything.

"Please," cried Daddy, hurling the word, unstifled, a command.

No will has ever compelled a white elephant.

So his gun spoke. That single report that stills. The moon hung over the river, and the elephant's blood ran into the moon's track on the water, black as tears.

When our telephone rang I ran to the entryway to answer it. I loved to snatch up the gold and ivory receiver, raise its weight to my ear, and say, "Bowman residence, Cecilia speaking."

My father's voice: hoarse, familiar, calling forth love I didn't realize I felt. The connection was terrible.

My mother wrenched the receiver from me and curled herself, as stony as an ammonite, around the phone.

I waited on the staircase. It surprised me that I missed him.

"Let me get this straight, Mark. You want me to wire Roche our account numbers?"

"What did you do?"

"He better take care of everything."

"How much?"

"Silver liners!"

I watched her writing things down.

(Don't go, she had said. Come back, she'd said. Why? she'd

said. Don't do this, she'd said. I love you, she'd said. We'll be waiting, she'd said.)

Son of a bitch, she said now. How could you she said I hate you she said Goddamn you she said. Mark honey she said I'll do it she said. Don't worry she said. Stop crying she said. You bastard. She said. What choice do I have? You bastard. She said. Let me go.

It was a Saturday. Daddy had been back a full week. His duffel, still packed, slouched on the porch like a carcass he had slain. Mama wouldn't touch it. All Daddy did was sit on the porch and smoke. But he and his neglected duffel took up all the space in our minds. We couldn't talk about it, not even to ourselves. It was a silence you sort of got used to, but like before a thunderstorm, there was constant pressure. You waited for the heavens to break.

Danny and I played dead under the cottonwood tree. We had to let the snowy seed drift onto our faces. Whoever moved or sneezed first lost the game. I watched Daddy to see if he noticed us. But he just sucked at his relay of cigarettes, peering into the crevices in the cottonwood bark like he was searching out a face in its wrinkles.

A car door slammed: Mother and Carline back from ballet class. Mother clipped up the walk and around the side of the house past Daddy with no hello. Carline still wore her ballet clothes, even her toe shoes, ruining their cameo-colored satin on the driveway. She didn't bother to change because she wanted Daddy to tell her she was pretty in her regalia—and she was pretty, so pretty. Cottonwood seeds fetched up around the satin throat of each shoe and overlaid the vamps with glittering white fur. And in her leotard she looked sixteen with those brand-new bosoms—a cute figure, that's what Mother called it; she was coming into such a cute little figure if only she didn't get any taller.

Carline dashed splay-footed up the porch steps, her toe shoes knocking the boards.

"Girl, you sound like a woodpecker's artillery unit running in them things."

"Want to see what I learned in class today?" She stood in front of Daddy, shaking the cotton off her feet. She even leaned down and gave him a little kiss.

"You're too big to be doing that." He flicked a glance at her bosoms.

She crossed her arms swiftly over her chest and looked away.

Daddy flicked a fall of ash onto her ballet shoe. It left a grey blur on the pink satin.

Carline rubbed the ash out on the back of her knee.

"I learned a double tour. I'm the only one in class who can do it. Want to see?"

"All right, honey," he said. "After this cigarette."

Carline waited. Daddy finished his Marlboro and immediately lit another. Smoke fled his nostrils and he tapped ash.

"Daddy!" said Carline.

She flexed the pointes of her shoes.

We hung on his every drag, hypnotized by the cherry. When he inhaled it blazed as open and red as an animal's eye but gave a grey wink when he exhaled.

By the fourth cigarette, Carline drooped like a warped birthday candle.

"Daddy?" she said in a very small voice.

"Go ahead."

She did a preparatory *plié,* then straightened up and surveyed the porch. Daddy had been drinking so much porch wine that he commanded a full militia of bourbon and pop bottles. They besieged the porch, mustering on the stair treads, standing in formation on the floorboards and at attention along the railing. Under the swing a company of reinforcements waited for the call of duty. Carline might have been the best dancer in her class, but she wasn't so good that she could get her pointes between the necks of all those dead soldiers.

She flicked her ponytail over one shoulder, Carline the Queen, and said haughtily (*there's a reason* haughty *rhymes with* snotty, *miss*), "I can't do it. Not until you clear all this crap out of the way."

"Don't say crap—say carp, Carline!" I hissed from under the cottonwood.

"Can it, Cissy! Lord."

"And don't say lord! Say lard because it's all right to take the name of pig fat in vain, but not Jesus."

"You should know about lard, fatty-two-shoes."

"Daddy!"

"You kids give me some peace."

His eyes hooded. He lit a fresh cigarette.

"Looks like a white trash party out here," Carline said.

She perched airily on the swing and unwound the satin ribbons at her ankles. She eased her stocking feet out of the shoes and stood. Casually, she knotted the ribbons together, as though to string the pointe shoes over her shoulder. Instead, she let them hang from one hand, idle and pink, swinging above the litter of bottles on the steps. Her elaborate insolence terrified me, but not nearly as much as Daddy's persistent mildness. Anger coiled in him like a sleeping snake, and he never rattled before he struck.

Carline cut her eyes at Daddy, gauging his reaction, and then swung the shoes gently, almost as an afterthought.

"Trash," she said, and flicked the nearest bottle.

It tipped over and drooled a half-hearted trickle of liquid.

"Trash," she said, and pendulum-struck more bottles, *whap whap whap*. These rolled off the steps and thudded in the grass.

"Trash!" she screamed, and lashed at the bottles on the railing, whipping them so hard that they ricocheted off the porch and shattered in the chinaberry bushes near Danny and me.

She whirled the shoes harder, and I swear to God she whipped the cigarette right out of Daddy's mouth (later, she showed me the black plantar's wart it had burned on the shoe's sole). Ballet Carline became a rodeo queen, Oakley Carline, flogging Daddy as hard as she could.

He had left us, wounded, trailing blood into the jungle, and he had come back more absent, but more dangerous, than before. Carline was a Bowman too, she had that berserker's rage, and so did I, and so did Danny, but Carline had been our father's favorite, and she was screaming *trash, you're nothing but trash.*

Beyond the pink blur and her spinning shoes, I swear I saw a red chrysanthemum bloom around Daddy's heart.

So far astonishment had kept Daddy bolted to his chair.

Then Carline's satin bullroarers caught Daddy square in the face, smacked him hard enough to leave rosin-prints on his cheek, and the spell holding Daddy broke. He lunged, caught a shoe on its descent, and hauled on the ribbons, trying to saw the other shoe from Carline's grip.

"You know what trash is, Carline? Trash is what folks heap on the heads of their friends."

Carline staggered back and stepped in Daddy's ashtray.

"I don't see any trash 'cept what's standing here wearing a tutu."

The ribbon drew taut between them.

When Daddy got mad he trembled all over. His nostrils turned white and his eyes went red and he breathed hard and blew the porch wine smell of anger in your face.

The knot snapped. Carline swayed but kept her balance, one foot planted in that puddle of ash.

Daddy tested the weight of the shoe he held, bouncing it on the end of its ribbons. He reeled it up again, bound it in its own strings, and slapped the hard toe box thoughtfully against an open palm.

"You're as ugly as your mother, Carline."

Her tutu had wilted around her colts' legs, and patches of sweat came out under her arms.

"What should we do with you?"

The blood drained from Carline's face. She tried to swallow, and her dry throat made a tiny sound, a chirp, a click.

"Go ahead. Say trash again," said Daddy.

"Don't hit her!" shouted Danny. He rushed for the stairs, tripped on a tread, and fell backwards into the broken glass at the bottom of the steps.

The blood blazed back into Carline's cheeks. Eyes full, but no tears falling, she let go of her shoe.

"Trash," she whispered.

"Lucky you're ugly, Queen Carline," he said. "Since I won't have ugly girls in my sight. Get out of here, all of you."

Carline cleared the steps in one leap and landed by Danny. She caught his hand and pulled him up and together they ran.

I stayed hidden in the hot shade under the cottonwood. Daddy slopped more bourbon into his ginger ale. With every drink he fled further out of range.

"Goddoggit—Carline. Sugar-pie. Honey. Come on back. I didn't mean that."

He flipped his Zippo—*snick, snick*—and fell into the muttering that was more frightening than his shouts or his smoky-wet silences.

Potted, Daddy was potted. He called it loaded, but my mother always said potted, like meat.

"Cissy, darlin'! I know you're there. Get up here, girl."

I went and let him pull me onto his lap. My legs hung awkwardly, and his kneecaps dug into my backside. He blew sickly breaths into my neck and squeezed my stomach so that it hurt, but it felt good, too, to be held. Scary and good.

Then Daddy told me how big prey fights to the death. How the end is grace. Time slows to a mercy. A shot, the prey falls, bleeds out, goes still. If flies light on it, it won't flinch. When he shot he could feel every flex of muscle, every bone, the strength that rose up his back and beat in his blood. Even the points in his eyes screwed tight to see clear—a rock in the dust, the rill of blood, and each sound so sharp against the fact of the wild beast turned thing.

His cigarette wagged above my ear. I felt its heat and I worried that he would set fire to my hair.

He didn't shoot to act brave, or to feel like a man. He hunted to feel sharp and still. And when he hung his trophies up on the wall, he held that stillness for good.

His sister did not once hold still. Look where it got her. Dead in the ground. No man dreams of a thing like that.

With his gun he made a place of peace. Where things could abide. Where love behaved. Grace could not break him. He would not let her.

What did it mean to be a man? Disown what's soft. Hold fast what moves too much. And take dead aim.

"You think I don't know what I did? It's not my fault. I got boxed in."

He buried his mouth in my hair. I squirmed on his lap.

"Let me down, Daddy."

"No, I did not let you down!"

I tried to bear his hot breath on my scalp, but unlike my sister, I let myself cry.

"Won't none of you girls hold still?"

Daddy suffered no one's tears but his own, so he shoved me from his lap.

Then, like my sister, I ran.

On the back porch there were no bottles except for the ones that held bluing and bleach. Carline sat in a pink tulle heap, picking at her cuticles. Danny squatted next to her, chewing on the neck of his T-shirt.

"I just wanted him to look at me. But he just sits there!" said Carline.

"I know," I said. "I hate it."

"Maybe he's sad," said Danny. "I get sad."

"That porch wine. Why's he call it porch wine? It's not even wine! Who the hell drinks whiskey and soda pop?" I said.

"The smell makes me gag," said Carline.

"I kind of like it," said Cousin Danny.

"Makes my eyes water," I said.

"How can he stand it?" asked Carline.

"Imagine how it tastes," I said.

"It tastes okay," said Danny.

"That smell," said Carline, "holy carp, I despise that smell. What's it remind you of?"

"Furniture polish," I said.

"Nail varnish," said Carline.

"Momma's perfume," said Cousin Danny.

The back porch led into the kitchen. Gradually we became aware that Mother was hollering into the kitchen phone. This was impossible, since ladies, when hard pressed, merely spoke with emphasis. She even had a little rhyme for it: *Jezebels raise decibels but Texas belles speak low.*

"All of it?" she hollered. "Yes, I know that, but Mr. Roche must have left us something. When I wired those numbers it was my understanding that—"

"He couldn't have! Those shares were held in trust for our girls."

"I am not shouting. No, I will not lower my voice. And Mrs. Greta Bowman's stock? Hers, too? All of it. What about my nephew's?"

"I see. Well that's something. But what do you propose that I do?" her voice dropped.

"I wish I could go away," said Danny.

"Shhh, Danny, we're trying to hear," said Carline.

"It's way too hot out here," I said, because I felt certain our mother was weeping.

"Let's go play bank menagerie in the trophy room."

"Thought you were scared," said Carline, but so mildly that I could tell she heard Mother crying too.

I drew a barnyard in the green nap of the trophy room rug and we assembled our menagerie. Carline and I owned an assortment of ceramic piggy banks: a white Cheshire hog named Wilbur and his black and white twin, Lucy, both fine-legged English porcelain; Juanita, also called Piggy, a hideous Mexican porker made of terra cotta and painted with crude flowers; Ferdinand, a longhorn who ate the grass-green babysitting bills I fed him; Winona, a yellow West German ceramic duck; her brother Sammy, a seal; and a china poodle that no one liked. She was flocked with pink velvet, and we decreed that her sit-up-and-beg pose and lone rhinestone eye made her too pathetic to deserve a name.

Danny lugged a big china dachshund with a long slit in its back and a broken tail. Someone painted its smile on crooked—one side of his mouth turned up and the other turned down.

"What's its name?" I asked.

"Doxie," said Danny.

"Did you name her after your mama?" asked Carline. "Do you know what a doxy is?"

"Danny, first you introduce the new member to the assembly," I said, smoothing over Carline as usual.

"Take Doxie and present him to all the trophies."

Danny paced the room, stopping at each head. He raised the dachshund bank carefully, using both hands.

"This is Doxie," he said.

"Jingle him. That's the signal."

Danny jingled his bank.

"They accept him," I said.

"Now we take out their babies and count them."

Most of our banks had rubber stoppers in their bellies, easy to unplug. Sammy and Winona were fancier—they had metal stoppers that fixed with a lock. Carline kept Sammy's key in her ballerina box and I hung Winona's around her neck. Unstopped, all it took was an index finger to tease out the coins or rolled-up bills from the bellies of the banks. We said we were taking out babies.

We never spent our money, just counted it. The animals conducted alliances and rivalries, and belonged to factions based on their denomination. Sammy and Winona, because they could be locked, ate the big bills, the tens and the fives. Ferdinand and Juanita swallowed ones and heavy coins—silver dollars, half dollars, quarters, Wilbur and Lucy were our great joys, but like many beautiful things, neither had much functionality. They ate the light change—the dimes and nickels and pennies. As for the poodle bank, we only put pesos or plug nickels in her. We also consigned to her innards any fortune cookie slips with fortunes that displeased us, and we fed her stray bobby pins, buttons, broken barrettes, trash.

Our goal was to convert the contents of each animal's stomach into coins or bills that would feed the animal ahead of it on the food chain. Ultimately we hoped to empty all the menagerie into Sammy and Winona, who would be stuffed so full that we could exchange the contents of each pig's stomach for a one-hundred-dollar bill.

"When I get mine," I said, "I'm going to frame it and hang it on my wall."

"What you want hundred-dollar bills for?" Danny asked.

"Just to have," we said. "Just to show people."

Mother, limping a little, watched us from the doorway with a claw hammer tucked in the waistband of her skirt. She took a long look at all our banks lined up on the rug. Then she strode over and crouched down to stroke each animal.

"Forgive me," she said.

She clubbed Sammy on the head with the claw hammer. All the tightly rolled bills in his body erupted and shot between the legs of the piano.

We held ourselves as still as china animals kiln-fired by fear. Our loose-nickle hearts rattling.

"Pick it up," said Mother to Carline.

Carline crouched and scraped the shards that had been Sammy into a pile.

"Not the pieces," said Mother. "The money."

Carline's shoulders shook as she dug more splinters from the nap of the rug.

Danny crawled under the belly of the piano, plucking up bills from the carpet.

Mother moved to Winona.

"Mama, there's a key!"

I knelt beside my duck, fumbled with the cord around her neck, but Mother's hammer smashed the smiling beak, and Winona was nothing but a litter of sharp yellow feathers on a nest of green bills.

"Why are you doing this?" I asked her.

"Ask your father," she said.

Mother's hammer brained Ferdinand, knocked his head off clean. Not satisfied, it pounded his body into powder. Coins cannoned the rug. The hammer turned on Juanita, split her cupid's bow, gashed open her coin slit. Then Juanita, too, was rubble—her broken edges bright red. The piano strings vibrated in sympathy.

"Carline, save Wilbur and Lucy!"

Carline grabbed for Wilbur, but the hammer was faster. It smashed past Carline's knuckles and broke Wilbur's pink and white snout. Lucy went too.

"But why?"

"We need the money."

Amid the ceramic carnage the poodle sat up and begged. Her red tongue lolled. I realized how much I loved the slick feel of her cheap patent leather. How I loved her flocked back and her missing eye. The hammer nosed forward.

"Mother, there's nothing in her! It's just trash!"

Pink fuzz on the nose of the hammer. A cheap blue jewel whizzed past and landed on the piano, where it lodged between the C-sharp and the C.

Danny lay on his stomach, pressing the pedals of the piano with his chin. Eyes vacant, chin on brass: soft pedal, sostenuto pedal, damper pedal. Mother had named them to me.

"We need money," Mother said. "Every penny."

"None of us even saved our hundred dollars," protested Carline. "It's not enough to matter!"

"Take it up with your Daddy," Mother said.

She hadn't spotted Doxie behind the piano leg, but Danny trotted him out.

"No, darling," said Mother. "Doxie belongs to you."

"It's okay. He's already broken."

Danny rubbed a thumb over Doxie's stump. Mother's hammer finished the dog.

When I was very small, the trophies frightened me—their size, their teeth. Daddy set me on his knee and said I had nothing to fear from those heads. Because man was a dangerous animal. Look at those heads, any one of them could have taken you down. Then how did they get so harmless, why were they hanging up on our walls? Because man is the most dangerous animal of them all. And the trophies knew it. Daddy turned his victims into emissaries of his strength.

"They'll watch over you, or they'll answer to me," he said.

I had come to doubt their protection. When Mother smashed our piggy banks, something behind the paneling mocked and capered. It echoed her hammer-blows. The heads hung cold and impassive. *Just what did you expect,* their blank eyes asked, *when you nailed us to the wall?*

Mother tucked the hammer into her sash. It clashed with her pink pique skirt. The weight of that heavy anvil-claw pulled her waistband askew and revealed a small, angry cut, still bleeding, on her back.

"Carline, get the dustpan."

"Wait," I said, "we can fix them."

Carline swept smithereens into the dustpan. I stole shards from the heap and sorted them. A chip of yellow tail feather. Atom of wrinkled snout, orange fleck from a beak, a flake of

carnation flank, a curl of brittle periwinkle that might have
been Sammy's fin. Mother left us nothing whole enough to
mend. Carline ranged the biggest pieces on the carpet: a red-
brown ear that belonged to Doxie, an intact steer's head, two-
thirds of terra cotta flower. A cracked black trotter, a suppliant
pink paw. On the rug these fragments fit together like a map of
all the vanquished countries we would never find again.

One day a large crate arrived on our porch, its splintered lid
tacked down with industrial staples.

"God bless the diplomatic pouch," said Daddy.

He dollied the crate into the trophy room. He crowbarred
the lid and moved it aside, avoiding the splinters, and dug out
ringlets of excelsior.

The thing inside the crate was too heavy for him to lift because it was the head of an elephant. And it was white.

Pure white. The wrinkled white of bacon grease left to cool
in a pan. A curl of excelsior clung flirtily to its brow, and for
a moment the bull elephant looked coy, like a contestant in a
Shirley Temple contest. Like Juliet at her balcony, Daddy leaned
over the edge of the crate, besotted.

"I read about them, Mark. The white ones are sacred. It's a
capital offense, to kill a white elephant."

"Help me get him out."

A perverse, nervous smirk flickered under Daddy's mustache.

All five of us heaved together, even Mother. Daddy had
crushed us once, she said. She wouldn't have him crush us again.

The weight of the thing, on its teak mounting—*I nearly
carped my pants,* Carline whispered to me later. We leaned the
head against the wall. Taller than I was. And white, white. Just

as Mother's face revealed its pure planes when she put on her cold cream, so the whiteness of the elephant's skin, pure as bone, made its beauty even more apparent, and somehow doubly naked. The white an eternal shock. This elephant would have nowhere to hide. It would flash beaming limbs among greenery. It would shine in the darkest thicket. It would be impossible to miss.

"So this is what you were ransomed for," said Mother.

I caressed the swoop of skull and counted each pore and dimple of the powerful, delicate trunk.

Daddy roped the tusks and we all hauled them out together, sweating and green-faced from the effort.

He laid the tusks like creamy parentheses around the head. I bent to caress one—I'd never felt a length of uncut ivory before. I expected it to be cool and smooth, like stone, but fine ridges rippled under my palm and it gave off a peculiar warmth.

"Don't touch. It lowers the value."

He ran a chamois along the tusk to wipe away my fingerprints.

"I thought I'd display it over the fireplace for a while, until I find a buyer," he said. "Isn't that a good idea?" All my father's questions were coercions.

What happened to the elephant's body, Mother wanted to know. Was the great snow hill left to melt beneath the trees?

"That's not the point, Grace, scavengers ate it, I don't know—the point is the head."

The point. Always the point. A buck was said to be such and so many points. The more points, the bigger the prize. If you didn't have a point, not a single one, or worse, if someone questioned your point, you could be sure you were no prize.

I pictured the elephant's big white body lying pointless, bleeding in the mud. A fist of sun tossed handfuls of flies at the body. Black pips on a white die.

Mother picked free a fleck of foreign grass that had been trapped in the elephant's eyelashes when it died.

"These animals with their eyelashes," said Mother. "Elephants. Giraffes. It kills me."

Daddy bent into the container and brought out a foot.

"Umbrellas."

It, too, was white, a perfect plinth, and the pink toenails, each the size of a baby's fist, were, like the eyelashes, a reproach.

A white body lying desecrated in the foreign grass, just backbone, ribs, pelvis, and four stumps hacked off at the knee. What had been the point?

I gentled a hand along the bull's white balustrade of a trunk, fingered the torn lily ears. Why did my father shoot it? There's no questioning why a gun wants to shoot—a fashioned thing does what it is made to do. But for what task are men fashioned?

"Worth a king's ransom," Daddy said. "Once we find a buyer, this'll pay for everything, Grace. Roche knows people. He'll make us an offer."

"My God. He made you do this."

"I shot it," Daddy insisted. "Me. I finally got something big, and it just kills you, doesn't it?"

Later I would hear her in their bedroom, crying hard enough to make herself retch.

"Yes," said Mother. "Yes."

• • •

I waited at the door to the trophy room. When Daddy sidled by, I blocked his way.

"Why do you love Aunt Loretta more than us?"

"She was my blood," he said. "You don't get over your blood."

He pushed me aside, strode down the hall, shut himself in the bathroom. I heard water running. Faker. I knew for a fact he'd peed into an empty bottle earlier because he had not wanted to leave Mother alone with his white elephant, not even for a second.

"Why do you love Aunt Loretta more?"

He was stooped over the sink and drinking from the faucet.

"Hellfire, you startled me." He wiped his mouth on the back of his hand.

"We're your family."

"A sister's different. There's no one closer to you in the world. You know that."

"I hate Carline."

"Don't say that. Nobody else will know your life, Cissy. Carline's your spare memory, a spare you. Once she's gone, a whole heap of you will die with her."

He tried to slip past me again. Drunk, he was lithe as an eel. I dove for his boots and grabbed him around the legs the way I had as a very small girl; I knew it was risky—but I hugged his legs, burrowed my head into his shins. My head ricocheted off his kneecaps as he walked but with every step I clung harder. If I could just hold him with all my weight and all my questions and all my love, the love I still felt for him even though I hated him, I hated him.

"Come back, Daddy," I said.

I was certain he'd forgotten. But astonishingly, Daddy laughed.

"Ten Roger, Sweet Thing."

When I was six he taught me CB slang—*because anyone with your initials should be fluent, Sweet Thing.* He hadn't used my nickname in years.

He raised me up and for a minute, a full minute, I know because I counted the ticks of his wristwatch, my father held me. He held me and he held on.

His moods could shift so quickly; all his strings went loose and his belt buckle bit into my cheek and suddenly he was crying, shuddering and shaking me off.

Mama's agony sounded through the house.

Your mother, he said, shifting into anger, and it was dizzying, how his face flashed from the droop of woe to the rictus of anger—he didn't know who she was anymore.

"Do you know what Grace said to me? She said Carline isn't good enough to make it as a dancer. Without a college fund she'll marry someone on the strength of her face and be helpless, like Grace herself was helpless, if disaster came. And as for you, Cissy, she said you listen at doors and have no life of your own. You, Cissy, are a person who feeds on other people because she can't feed herself. She asked me what I was going to do about that? Without money, what can Cissy do, she asked me.

"Well your mother doesn't know anything," he told me. "Carline will be a ballerina. Cissy, you'll be happy too, when you outgrow your puppy fat and get out of Carline's shadow.

You'll lose weight. And one day I'll tell you everything, my side of it, I'll tell you what it all meant. But now I've got to get some peace."

He stumbled into the trophy room. The lock clicked.

"You understand me," he said to the bighorn ram. "You know how it is."

He raised his glass in a toast. The bourbon slashed his throat. He heard a keening, high and wild, behind the paneling. Grace again. He strode to the door to make sure it was locked, and blocked it with the heavy Pullman davenport.

On his weave back to the chair he stumbled against the umbrella stand and stubbed his toe hard on the toenails of the elephant.

"Goddammit!"

He flung out all the umbrellas. A snap holding one of them shut popped and the umbrella unfurled and cartwheeled across the carpet. Lifting his feet high, Daddy stepped fully into the elephant's foot. He raised his boot and brought it down and stomped violently. "Goddamn you!"

He caught his reflection in the glass panel of the gun cabinet—the weak curve of his back, his sag of belly, his eyes like sumps, the prissy hole of his mouth. The cylinder of the elephant's foot swallowed his legs so he looked like a deranged jack-in-the-box. Cissy and Carline would find out what he'd done to them.

His pores stank of the shame that flooded him, and for one horrifying instant he felt how much he hated himself.

He grabbed an umbrella and smashed every panel of the gun cabinet's glass.

"Goddamn you, Grace," he said. "I'm not ashamed."

He retreated to his chair and lit a cigarette but could not think what to do. The guns hung close to hand, offering their answers, as always. Instead he drained his glass, poured himself another. But the bourbon, which should have spread protective wings and enfolded him, took off, and a raptor settled in its place.

And then the stag's head moved.

It twitched an ear and swiveled its neck to crop the tip of the television antenna, but Daddy felt no surprise. Nor did he when the buck lowered its antlers and scratched at the plaster on the wall where its chest would be. Daddy let it scrape white chips from the wall. He watched the plaster sift onto the floor. He listened to the creaks in the paneling.

A hoof stamped. The buck lifted his jaw and sounded. Then, straining, he broke through the wall, shaking white dust from his flanks. He turned his scut to Daddy and calmly, almost insolently, went back to eating the rabbit's ear on the television. The hole he made in the wall gaped, black as velvet.

When the bighorn bleated, Daddy's heart began to pound. The stag stepped delicately over to the section of paneling below the ram's head. He lowered his rack and rushed the wall. His antlers punched holes in the paneling. The wall began to buckle as the ram butted at the lathing. Daddy remembered hefting the ram's head, the feel of the thick horns in his hands, blunt and tough.

The ram charged out of the wall. The mountain goat, of his own accord, broke through.

The animals circled Daddy's chair, the stag bugling, the ram and goat bleating, their tongues rattling hot breath in his ear.

More and more animals cracked through the walls. The javelina bent his head and knuckled through. Antelope bucked, deer scattered, and a cougar padded out of the paneling. The badger pelted past on the heels of the elk. Their feet thundered as they circled the room, a multitude. Buffalo, ancient rhino, bewildered moose. They galloped the tour of the room, seeking a way out. Finally, the stag bolted back into the wall, and the animals followed him, racing each other out through the secret channels of the house.

He heard them gain the lawn, braying, bleating. They crossed the gravel drive, their horns tearing at cottonwood branches. He heard them faintly lapping water from the drainage ditch. They stampeded down the road, leaping fences, dashing in every direction, galloping wildly. Eventually, the sound of hooves died out.

Dust on the jewel green rug. Pink guts of insulation gasped from punctured walls. Drafts whistled through the holes in the paneling. One wall remained unbroken, over by the piano. The white elephant's head floated there like an iceberg on an arctic sea. It raised its trunk and knocked. Behind the wall the pulse of a skin drum answered the knock. *Thump, thump* knocked the skin drum behind the wall. *Thump, thump* banged the heavy trunk on the plaster.

The wall swelled and contracted as the elephant drew breath, then burst like a nova when the elephant wrenched free. Plaster rained down radiant legs that had been lopped at the knee. The elephant's back breached the ceiling. His tusks uncrossed and flew from their mountings to take root in the wise, grieving head. For it seemed to Daddy that the elephant wore a look of deep grief.

It touched a piano key, *plink, plink, plink,* tapping that note repeatedly, as Daddy might tap a cigarette.

The bull turned and its rump knocked over a lamp. In the sudden darkness the white mass of the elephant shone like a moon on a pond.

Plink, plink.

The elephant ran its trunk over Daddy's face, across his eyelids, over his cheeks, and up to soothe his forehead. It caressed Daddy's ears and his mustache and it stroked the crown of his head. It smoothed Daddy's hair. It swept over his shoulders, across his chest, touched him even between the legs, found the bottle and the empty glass at his feet, and patted his knee consolingly.

Daddy could not say what was the elephant and what was its light, but he knew the elephant wept. The elephant touched its trunk to an eye, caught a tear, and offered that bright mercury to Daddy's lips. I hope that Daddy drank it.

To give in to such sweetness would have unlaced Daddy's heart. When the elephant tried to take Daddy's hand, Daddy refused. Daddy wasn't afraid. When the elephant tried to pull Daddy to his feet, Daddy dug in. When Daddy cut his eyes to the cabinet where he kept his guns, the elephant sighed. As it moved aside it seemed to shrink, though its light intensified.

It wasn't that big, really, the size of a Clydesdale, maybe. Its wattage fooled him, fiendishly bright. But Daddy wasn't afraid. When Daddy reached for the gun, the elephant bowed its head. When Daddy grasped the gun, he heard the elephant's heart. The elephant is afraid, thought Daddy. But Daddy wasn't afraid. He'd already killed it once.

• • •

Mother heard him smashing things all to hell in there and pushed me away from the door.

"Cissy, you take Carline and Danny and get! Go on! Down the road to the neighbors'. I swear to God if you don't move it now I'll whip you!"

We stampeded off into the night.

Then the trophy room fell quiet, and Mama listened to Daddy play one high note on the piano over and over again—*plink, plink*—and she tried the handle of the door then, but it was locked.

Light poured from the cracks around the door. The silence swelled, turned her cold and she knocked on the door, gently at first, because she was so frightened that she could barely raise her knuckles to the wood. She knocked. Silence. Then a tinkle of glass, and the sound of breathing, heavy and huge. Terrified, she hammered at the door, calling Daddy's name.

Gracie, she heard him say, *that you?*

It would be hard to raise the gun, trapped as he was by the bulk of the elephant, hard to set the stock in place with the white beast blocking the way. It would be hard to aim for the knowing eye in that massive head, blinded as he was by the elephant's redoubled light, and hard to steady his hands when the throb of the elephant's heart shook the room. It would be hard to curl himself around the body of the elephant, a body, which, he knew, would fight him at the last. He kicked off his right shoe and carefully, not breaking the elephant's gaze, stripped the sock. He inched his bare foot along the stock, until his long second toe, his Morton's toe, the toe his mama told him meant he'd always be the head of the house, stretched up and, without any difficulty at all, found the trigger.

After the funeral, when we kids returned from our month at Gigi's, all the trophies were gone. I passed the last few weeks of that summer holed up in books. Mother yielded and sewed Carline her first miniskirt. Carline found herself a secret boyfriend and spent her time either with him or in concocting alibis. And Danny—I still don't know how Danny coped. We lived like castaways on our individual islands of grief.

And then it was autumn, and time to shop for school clothes, although we couldn't possibly afford them. Mother hauled us up to Dallas Northpark Center and brought us up short in front of the Neiman Marcus window display. There they were, Daddy's trophies, even the white elephant, bearing down like a god on some headless ladies in shantung silk. It was Mother's first window display. It had earned her the job.

RAINY SEASON

The maids are leaving the compound on their scooters. Maizie and Jill watch from the tennis court. The red clay is still hot, and when Jill closes her eyes the white fault lines linger behind her eyelids. Jill lobs a ball, and Maizie misses.

"There's Neepa!" yells Maizie. Their maid's nightly transformation—from a self-effacing shadow who sweeps the floors with a handleless broom to a glittering sexpot with flying hair and high-heeled feet—thrills Maizie.

The guards roll back the gates and the maids shoot out into the heat and noise of the city, their laughter high and bright as they perch sidesaddle behind their boyfriends and grip the seats when the scooters go over the potholes, catching air, fishtailing a little before regaining traction on the uneven street outside. The guards wave to the maids; the guards never salute them. Jill and Maizie stand there silently until the gate clangs closed.

"Where do you think they go?" Maizie asks.

"I don't know," Jill says. "To nightclubs. The way they're dressed."

"Do you think Neepa has sex?"

"Don't be tacky, Maiz."

Jill hits another ball, and Maizie ignores it.

"I just want to know."

"It's too hot to talk," says Jill. "Go chase that ball you missed."

It's the rainy season in Chiang Mai, but the rains haven't arrived. Songkran, the New Year's water festival, has come and gone, and the mountain has yet to pull the stopper from its bath of cloud. Jill hates tropical heat. The heat's intimacy drives her out of her thirteen-year-old skin.

Jill and her little sister, Maizie, have been in Chiang Mai for three months. Their father works at the consulate; his job is classified. Jill knows it has to do with drugs; they're close to Burma and the Golden Triangle, and he goes north all the time. But Jill is too self-involved to care what her father does. She's never had a boyfriend. She wonders what a kiss feels like. Not that she'll find out here. Not on this compound, where she and Maizie are the only kids. They spend afternoons swatting flies and feeding them to Maizie's turtle. Evenings they play tennis, sending the balls wild and high, sometimes over the compound gates, where they roll into gutters and are lost in the street.

Jill looks up at the darkening sky. Maizie crawls into the oleander to pick up balls. She's lithe and her movements are purposeful. At eleven, she has no idea how pretty she's becoming. In a year or two Maizie will be the pretty one. Her calves are smooth and tan and dusty, and she rattles the bushes, rolling balls out between her legs so that they come at Jill from all directions. Jill doesn't bother to corral them. "I'm so bored!"

"Dad says only boring people are bored."

"Easy for him to say, he gets to travel. And maybe it's true for grownups. If you can do whatever you want, it's your own fault if you're bored. But when you're younger, you're a prisoner. You can't do anything. If I could do whatever I wanted, I wouldn't be bored."

"What would you do?"

"I don't know, go places. England. Italy. Someplace nice, with old buildings and museums. Oil paintings. Fountains. Someplace where Americans go to be creative. Not diplomatic. Like Paris. I'd stroll. See things. Go on rendezvous. I wouldn't stay here."

Through the netting enclosing the court, Jill can see their entire compound. It's a box enclosing more boxes. It has high concrete walls tipped with barbed wire and glass, and a square metal gate on rollers. Weird pink flowers spring out at wild angles from the square clipped hedges, and crewcut lawns fight weeds that want to grow into tall flame-tipped trees. There are flippant palms, rosebushes, banana plants, jackfruit, lychee trees, and a strange, spindly bush with leaves that fold shut when you zip a finger down the central vein.

When their father goes away on government trips, Maizie and Jill stay up all night watching *Gone with the Wind*. They can't sleep. They usually live with their mother, in various embassy dwellings in various nations. Australia most recently. They still have slight accents. But their mother's in language training in D.C. for six months, and the government pays for housing only if you live overseas, and she can't afford an apartment for the three of them. They'll join her in Georgia (the country, not the state) later. Jill says they got sold down the river, abandoned in the jungle. The horror.

They're supposed to be lucky. A chance to see the world! Broaden their horizons! Jill is sick of it. She feels dizzy, like a cartoon character treadmilling on a spinning globe. She's never lived anywhere longer than two years. She's never gotten used to the gates, the guards, the language she can't read. Their father learned his parenting moves out of some ancient 1950s handbook. He's needlessly strict and has blind spots you could parade an elephant through. Maizie and Jill aren't allowed to pierce their ears until they're sixteen, he says. But he goes on trips to the Golden Triangle and leaves them alone in the house.

He's been gone for a week. He's due back in a couple of days. The kitchen is stocked with sodas and commissary boxes of Tuna Helper. The house has a VCR and plenty of toilet paper. But Maizie and Jill can't sleep, hence repeated viewings of *Gone with the Wind*. Jill reads the book on airplanes. It's the right length for international flights. It blots things out, and there's no danger of coming to the end of it, of being stranded with no place to escape. You can board a flight with Scarlett and the Tarletons and be reassured that no matter how fast you read, you won't hear Rhett not giving a damn until after you land. It'll get you through unexpected layovers, even an eight-hour layover in the Bangkok airport, where a trumpet version of "The Impossible Dream" plays over and over.

The movie of *Gone with the Wind* is good too, nice and long. They have it memorized, and Maizie imitating Prissy makes Jill laugh. When the video ends, the two girls sneak out of their house and hop the pool fence. They turn off the pool lights and go skinny-dipping, pretending the guards care enough to enjoy being flashed. The girls' father, even if he knew, wouldn't care. There's nowhere they can go. Maizie says, "Let's go visit Moon-Face."

Moon-Face is their favorite guard. He likes Maizie to sit with him in the guard box at night. She's taught him to play double solitaire. They wait until his partner dozes off, and then they play well into the night. Jill usually comes too, sitting behind her copy of *Jane Eyre* and peeking over it at the guard intent on his cards. Jill loves his crescent eyebrows and smile, loves the creases at the edges of his eyes and the playful snap-salute he gives them when they leave through the gates with their father. Maizie salutes him back. "Kap!" he says, and she says "Kap!" And that breaks him up, though the other guard glowers because it's inappropriate for a little *farang* girl to use a masculine term of respect, and it's undignified for a guard to laugh at a consulate car.

Maizie gets away with familiarity because she's young and cute. Her hair is still blond. Jill feels too tall for Thailand, too dark, and too chunky and uninteresting. Out in the markets, people smile at Maizie and press little gifts on her—embroidered felt vegetables, *durian* candies, tiny silver rings. The same people point and laugh at Jill, whose feet are so big that the only shoes that fit her in Thailand are men's.

Just wait until you're older, Maizie, thinks Jill. You'll see.

Jill sits with them in the guardhouse, listening to the slap of the laminated cards and the sound of the night frogs. A tokay lizard calls from the bushes, and she counts the hiccupping cries—seven in a row is unlucky: you or someone you know is going to die. She looks at the hat Moon-Face has laid aside. She imagines sniffing the groove of the sweatband where it pressed against his forehead. She drums her fingers. She feels sweaty and her legs itch from a million bug bites. Nothing ever happens, unless she picks a fight with Maizie. Jill sighs. She thinks she hears a rumble of thunder. She sits up—maybe it will finally, finally rain. She can run out in the warm downpour, screaming into the wind. She can lean backwards into a wind so strong, it will hold her up like she is its fainting lover. She can let the rain drill her skull, part her hair, and flay her until she is wet and shining.

The thunder rumbles again, louder this time, but metallic, backed by drunken voices. Not rain, but people banging at the gate. It sounds like they're kicking it, hitting it with fists. Moon-Face's partner rubs his nose, pulls himself slowly to his feet, and goes out with a flashlight. Moon-Face follows with a fistful of cards, and Maizie and Jill come after. Every once in a while groups of plastered tourists, usually Japanese, mistake their compound for the whorehouse located a few miles down the road. Both are brightly lit all night and have heavy steel gates that give out onto the street and high white walls tipped with broken bottles and razor wire. Moon-Face opens the pedestrian door, and Maizie and Jill crowd against him to get a good look.

Three men lean against one another, tripod style. Their business suits are sopping wet, and their ties are askew.

"Songkran ended two days ago," Maizie says to Jill.

"Not for these guys."

Two of the men look old; they have little bellies and their faces are lined. The third, a young man, appears the least drunk. One of the older men raises his head, unhitches a water pistol from his waistband, and squirts Moon-Face's partner in the eye.

Moon-Face goes through the formalities, explaining the men's mistake and giving them directions to the whorehouse. They don't appear to understand any Thai. The youngest keeps bowing sheepishly, and each time he does, a blunt lock of his black hair falls into his eye. The two older men prod him impatiently with the noses of their water guns.

"English?" he asks Moon-Face hopefully.

Maizie muscles her way forward. Jill follows her out.

"He only knows how to say 'We named the dog Indiana,'" Jill says to the men. The third episode of *Indiana Jones* is the only English-language movie in theaters. Jill and Maizie have been to see it eleven times, and that line about the dog tickled Maizie so much, she taught it to the guards.

The two older men straighten up and clap the young man on the back. One of them points to Maizie's blond hair and grins. Jill moves closer and can smell the ferment on the men.

Up close she notices that one has a long, straight nose and a face shaped like a melon seed. The other is worse; his ears stick out and he has bad teeth.

"Wrong place!" shouts Maizie. Her white cotton T-shirt sticks to her back. She pushes a strand of hair behind her ear.

"Yes, please?" The young man turns to Jill.

"This American compound. No hookers," says Maizie.

"Hooker?" he asks Jill.

"No . . ."—Maizie hesitates—"pussy."

"Maizie!"

"What? He gets it." She speaks loudly and distinctly, sweeping her arm in a broad arc. "Pussy down the street!"

The two old men vociferate—apparently the one word they catch is "pussy." The young man's face lights with comprehension. He looks directly at Jill and says, "Please forgive, I have shame."

"Oh . . ." Her tongue feels thick and gawky. "It's okay."

He turns to his cohorts and explains. They look at Maizie, laughing, and their eyes gleam.

Melon-Head steps forward and takes Maizie's hand. She twists away, wiping it on her cutoffs. Bad-Teeth says something to the young man. And then the young man looks at Jill.

"You come with us, please?"

Tuk-tuks hung with garlands and colored lights buzz past on the street. The young man's hands are pale and tame. She looks up at the sky. Clouds race. The moon is a dim smudge.

"Okay."

"Jill! Are you crazy?"

The air outside the compound seems fluid—not cooler, exactly, but less still, and filled with exciting smells—alcohol and motor oil and the lingering smokiness of the fields.

"Drink, some boogie, we not bad men, please."

He has a way of working his upper lip with his bottom teeth. The teeth pull and release in a slow drag that brings red to the well-cut wave of his lip.

"Okay," she says.

"Jill, no!" says Maizie.

The young man's shirt sticks to him, transparent against his chest. Goose bumps stand out on his neck. He looks at her, and it makes her dizzy.

"I'm going."

"We're not supposed to go out alone!"

"So? Dad's not here. Are you going to tell?"

"They think we're hookers."

"No, they don't. I'm going."

"Jill!"

"You can stay here like a baby if you want. I don't want you to come, anyway. Go home, Maizie."

Maizie looks at Jill, and then at the young man.

"Just because you want some guy to kiss you."

The businessmen giggle. Jill sees the long red shape of a songtao and flags it down. It pulls up and she scrambles aboard, defiant. The men follow.

"Jill!" Maizie stands in the doorway of the pedestrian gate. Her face is white and drawn. She looks very small, and so pretty. Beside her, the guards consult each other. One of them picks up the gatehouse phone.

"You're so selfish, Jill! Why are you so selfish?"

Jill closes her eyes so she doesn't have to see the anguish on Maizie's face. For as long as Jill can remember, Maizie has embarrassed her by being—what's the word for it? Better. More pure of heart. If Jill is Scarlett, then Maizie is Melanie. She doesn't tell lies. She never pretends to be someone else, doesn't change the way she talks according to who is listening. She's better at everything than Jill and never does anything wrong. And it's so easy to hurt her. It isn't fair. Jill grits her teeth.

Moon-Face runs forward, waving his white-gloved hands at the driver. The driver answers back. The Korean men pound on the glass, bounce in their seats, urging the driver to go. The engine revs.

Moon-Face frowns, shouting at the driver. Jill's dad told her once that if a Thai person shouts, which is almost never, violence is sure to follow. Thais never show anger, he said, unless they're about to go berserk.

Jill can't remember how to say *stop* in Thai. She feels sick.

"Wait for me!" Maizie runs out of the gate and hurls herself into the back of the songtao. The old men clap with glee and reach for her. She holds her hands out like a shield. She's shaking.

"I hate you, Jill. You're getting us in trouble."

"I don't care."

Jill is almost relieved when the songtao starts to pull away.

"Dad's way north. Even if they call him, what can he do? He's not here. Besides, we're Americans. Dad says Thai people assume all Americans are immoral, so for all they know, we're allowed to go out."

"Moon-Face chased us. Didn't you see him chasing us?"

"Whatever. The guards probably think we're both whores waiting to happen."

"They're my friends!"

"Not anymore. Now they think you're a slut, because you came with me."

Jill hates herself for being cruel to Maizie, but it feels good, too.

They sit on the benches in the back of the red songtao. Every time the truck hits a rut they all bang knees. The two older men hold on to each other and laugh. They're very drunk.

"This Mr. Yoo. This Mr. Lim," says the young man. The two older men, Melon-Head and Bad-Teeth, bow.

"My name, Kyung Moon. You know *moon*?"

Jill nods.

"Someone will come for us," Maizie insists.

"I doubt it," says Jill.

"Do you think Moon-Face will get fired?" asks Maizie.

Jill hadn't thought of that. "I'll say it's my fault," she says. "They can't fire him if it's my fault. Can they?"

Maizie settles back with a frown. "They better not. I'll really hate you, then."

The songtao hits a rut and they are lofted. Jill feels the rush of her insides—a swoop of stomach, a flush in each breast. The hairs all over her body tighten, as if she's stepped into a hot bath.

"Are you Japanese?" Jill asks Kyung, turning away from Maizie as brightly as possible.

Mr. Yoo makes an offensive gesture. Mr. Lim blows a long horse breath through his rubbery lips.

"Korean!" he says.

The conversation jolts along in the careful bad grammar of international English. They piece together that Lim and Yoo own an electronics company and want to set up factories in Thailand. Kyung is an engineer. They live in a sort of bunker in the foothills. Eighty Korean men, sleeping in shifts, working eighty hours a week. They get three days of leave every six weeks. This is the last day of their leave.

Maizie sings under her breath the way she does when she's nervous. The wind butts through the vents of the songtao and lifts tassels of her hair. It blows Jill's hair into a sheep's nest.

"Why are we stopping?" Maizie whispers.

Mr. Lim and Mr. Yoo go to a white gate and negotiate with a guard. They hand over a wad of baht mixed with U.S. dollars. A woman comes out wearing a shiny yellow dress and a boa of blond fur. She squeezes into the truck between Maizie and Jill.

This woman is exactly the same size as Maizie. The woman notices this and taps Maizie on the chest conspiratorially. She perches as far forward as she can without falling off the seat. When the truck hits a bump she flies into Mr. Lim's lap, laughing.

The fur thrown around her neck opens its eyes and bares black gums in a yawn. It's a monkey, a golden gibbon. The woman unwinds it from her neck and makes it sit on the floor at her feet. It closes long fingers around her ankle while she burrows into her purse and pulls out a miniature diaper. She leans down, showing little breasts that sway inside her dress, and pins the diaper on the gibbon.

"*Ich heisse Heidi,*" she says to them. "*Das ist meine Nico.* My baby."

Heidi knocks on the cab window and speaks to the driver. He makes an abrupt U-turn, and they drive past a field of sunflowers under the moon, a huge field, acres deep. Jill recognizes that field: it's next to their favorite billboard near the compound. It's hand-painted, sometimes advertising bloody Chinese movies, but this month it's painted with hypodermic needles and skeletons, a frieze of dancing condoms, erect cocks, and skulls.

"We could hop out right here," Maizie whispers to Jill. "Please."

Jill's tempted. They could just walk back to the compound and watch *Gone with the Wind* again. But Kyung catches her eye and smiles, and Jill shrinks. She reaches for Maizie's hand and squeezes it.

They pull into a dark driveway and stop. Heidi slithers out, Nico knuckling after.

"What's this?" says Maizie.

The men shrug and follow. Jill hops out and sees light glimmering on greenery—moonlight and shadows. Bamboo rustles.

They're in a sacred grove. Candles twinkle from a spirit house set up on a stilt. Next to it, life-size, sits a black iron statue of the starving Buddha. Candles gutter at the statue's base. Broken incense sticks lean at drunken angles in little pots of ash.

The statue shouldn't be beautiful, but it is. Buddha is skeletal, his sinews caved around curving bones. His ribs stand out, his sternum juts below his corded neck. The expression on his face is one of infinite weariness and pity, but so tender that Jill catches her breath. Visitors have pressed tiny squares of gold leaf onto his body. The gold leaves tremble in the air, bright gold against the black iron, so that the statue appears to vibrate.

Jill ignores her sister, ignores the men. She steps closer. She wants to touch the knob of Buddha's knee, run her fingers over the concavities of his stomach, chest, and cheek.

Heidi hands Nico to Maizie, and Heidi's posture changes—she becomes graceful, reverent. She slips off her high heels and glides forward. She drops into a prostration, rises, lights a candle, dips a stick of incense to the flame, touches it to her forehead, and places it in the cup of ashes in front of the Buddha. She puts her palms together, bows, and stands in front of the statue. The men hang back. Maizie strokes Nico's head. The gibbon hooks one arm around Maizie's neck and picks through her hair.

Jill, too moved to keep silent, has to spoil it. "I thought Buddhas were fat," she says.

"Before he Lord Buddha, he no eat, long time, long time," says Kyung. "He try, try. Old way. Many days, he no eat, and he look like this."

"Was he on a hunger strike?" Maizie asks.

"He close to dying. Still he sit, no eat. Then a girl come." Kyung looks at Jill. "Like you." He smiles. "She give Buddha ice cream."

"Ice cream?"

"Ice cream. For respect. He holy man, she give respect."

Jill shakes her head. She can't follow what he's saying.

"Lord Buddha not want to hurt feelings, so he quit starving and decide to eat."

"Why was he starving himself? What was he doing?"

Kyung looks puzzled. "I do not understand."

"Can you explain what he was doing? Why wouldn't he eat? Why did he eat ice cream? Why did they make a statue of him starving? Don't you think it's kind of sick?"

Kyung frowns. "He eat ice cream. He sit under tree. He awaken. This show determination."

Mr. Lim and Mr. Yoo squirt Heidi with their guns. She turns on them, furious. But she draws a smile around her fury and leashes it with painted lips. The gibbon chews an incense stick, swinging from tree to tree. Heidi whistles for Nico. They all get back into the songtao.

"Love time!" shouts Mr. Yoo.

"Happy time!" shouts Mr. Lim.

All the nights in Chiang Mai are dreamlike, a rush of scents and neon, soft black mountains, low walls tipped with broken glass, children on bicycles, men selling pinwheels of colored lights, a blur of marionettes on a sidewalk, streetlights, fragments Jill recognizes but can never fit together. Traffic slows. They're near the Night Bazaar, in the center of town. They idle behind a truck full of pigs. Heidi yips at the driver in an electrifying torrent of Thai, then, digging at Maizie and Jill with her pointy shoes and tugging the men's ties, she forces them all out.

Jill follows the group into a tiny bar whirling with colored light. She feels Maizie stumbling behind her, gripping the back of her T-shirt so they won't be separated. The light pulses, strobing and uneven, and the air pulses, too, with the smell of alcohol, cigarettes, air freshener, and perfume. A bank of televisions plays karaoke, a white ball bouncing from word to word, a miked voice wails Cyndi Lauper's "Time After Time," off-key. Jill's hip bumps a table and upsets a woman's drink, and the woman squawks. Kyung bows and grins and flings baht. He steadies Jill's elbow and then strokes the small of her back with his palm. It makes her legs weak and she stumbles again. Yoo and Lim push them forward to a table near the stage. Maizie sits down and puts her hands over her ears.

Heidi sits in Mr. Yoo's lap. The gibbon clings to her neck and grabs with its back feet for Mr. Yoo's hands, which are trawling in Heidi's dress front.

"You like drink?" asks Mr. Lim.

"Thai iced tea," says Maizie.

"Me too, please," says Jill.

"No Thai iced tea here for American girl," says Mr. Lim. "Long Island iced tea. You try. You like."

The tea arrives in schooners spinning with ice. Jill takes a sip.

"It's okay, Maiz. Tastes like Snapple." Funny aftertaste, though. But then, Thai drinks are all kind of weird. She should have asked for a Sprite, if only to hear the waitress repeat it, "sa-plite," which makes her smile.

"I like Thai iced tea better," says Maizie ungraciously, but she drinks anyway.

"Thirsty!" Mr. Lim says. "Good, you drink."

Maizie bends forward and sips. Lim orders her another.

"You how old?" asks Kyung.

"Sixteen," lies Jill.

"I twenty-three," he says. "You, boyfriend?"

Jill blushes. "No." She twirls the ice in her tea with the straw.

"Very beautiful, you," says Kyung.

He puts a hand on her knee, moving his fingers delicately, just under the ruffle of her skirt. His fingers feel cool, deliberate, and mindless. Jill jiggles her leg, tries to scoot closer to Maizie. His fingers lift, return, then settle higher under the skirt.

Mr. Lim mounts the stage. The white ball bounces on the monitors.

"'Like a Prayer'! I love this song!" Jill says.

Maizie leans in and whispers, "Jill, I want to go."

"Go, then."

"I don't have any money!"

"That's not my fault. I didn't ask you to come."

"Please, Jill. Can we just go? I feel sick, and I'm really sleepy."

"Oh, boo-hoo."

"Nico keeps touching my hair, Jill. I'm scared."

"She's grooming you. It's because you're blond. You and Nico. Two dumb blondes. I'm staying."

Kyung's fingers lift, then settle higher up under Jill's skirt. She doesn't know if she wants him to stop or continue. She can't move. She can feel her heart, and every inch of skin. She gulps her drink and glares at Maizie.

"I'm going to find a phone and call Dad," says Maizie.

Jill glances at Kyung to see if he understands this. He nods to the music, smiling.

"Okay," Jill says. "We can go, I swear. Just finish your tea, okay? Please? We never have fun."

"This isn't fun! They're *old*, Jill. And Heidi's a prostitute. What if she has AIDS?"

"Shut up, she'll hear!"

"Do you promise we can go?"

"I promise! I swear."

Maizie gulps her tea and hoovers the straw around the remaining ice cubes. "There," she says. "All done." She stands up, staggers, and crumples back into her chair. "Jill?" Her eyes are squinty and confused.

"Serves you right," Jill says.

Maizie lays her head on the table.

"Sleepy!" laughs Mr. Yoo. He hauls Maizie upright and pins her with his arms. He shakes her back and forth in time to the music. Heidi straddles her and paints Maizie's eyes with a glittering green wand. The gibbon eats lychees. Onstage, Mr. Lim is singing surprisingly well. Maizie, Jill sees, is crying. She knows she should go to her, but Kyung's arm hangs around Jill's neck and his pale hand inches down toward her breast. One finger traces the little curve by her armpit. Adrenaline detonates her heart. Heidi paints Maizie's lips and Nico picks through her hair. Maizie struggles. Nico crouches over her and mumbles at the crown of Maizie's head. Kyung is stroking Jill's breast now, grazing the nipple with his fingertips, tickling around the sides. Onstage, Mr. Lim brings his song home.

Kyung slides his hand up past the elastic of her underpants and plunges a finger into her. Jill gasps. She is all slippery but it hurts. His finger works deeper. She tries to pull away but Kyung's other hand squeezes her breast and she can't move. Inside her is a wave she suspected when touching herself all alone, but this is different because it hurts and she can't get away. Then Kyung leans in to kiss her, and his tongue, thick with liquor and cold, wraps her tongue and she can't breathe. She doesn't know how to kiss back, and she can't breathe, so she, too panicked to care that they're in public, she bites him.

Kyung pulls back with a bleeding lip. He swears in Korean and pushes the table, hard. Glasses rattle, ice spills. Heidi dismounts Maizie's chair and slinks over to Kyung, cooing. She fishes ice up from the table, wraps it in a napkin, and presses it to Kyung's mouth. She strokes his hair with a free hand, presses her breasts against his arm, which steals out and encircles her. They glare at Jill. Jill stands up. Her legs are shaking and her stomach feels confused and her thighs are damp. Her chair clatters backwards because her legs don't want to hold her up. She shakes Maizie, who blinks, her eyes gummed green, her lips swollen.

"Let's go," Jill says.

Maizie groans.

"What's wrong with you, Maizie?"

Jill feels dizzy, the lights popping on and off and the karaoke ball bouncing.

Kyung is kissing Heidi, and the gibbon climbs onto Maizie's

shoulders. Mr. Lim gives it a cigarette, which it smokes. The lit end of the cigarette singes Maizie's hair, and Jill douses it with tea. The gibbon shrieks and shows its teeth.

"Jill," says Maizie, "get it off me."

Jill pulls on the gibbon, but it's much stronger than it looks and she recalls that a monkey is strong enough to break a person's arm if it wants, so she hauls Maizie to her feet and makes her jump up and down, but the gibbon won't let go. It hooks its fingers under Maizie's chin and raises its eyebrows, flashing its eyelids in warning.

Yoo and Lim are on stage together sharing a microphone, and Kyung has buried his face in Heidi's cleavage.

"Let's just run," Jill says. "If we run, it'll let go."

Jill pulls Maizie through the crowd, pushing aside chairs and butting against sweaty-backed Australian men who hoot at them, past twinkling women with glittering eyes—so many tiny women in scanty dresses, all of them laughing, the bar roaring with laughter, and dimly, as Jill pushes and burrows into the crowd, hauling her tottering sister, she hears Heidi screaming for Nico, who won't let go. They stagger out onto the street.

Jill hesitates in the blur of traffic and flashing lights, pedestrians stumbling, tourists laughing, ragged boys, and little girls with babies strapped to their backs approaching with outstretched hands, and why hasn't it rained? Rain would make everything clear again. Jill tries to flag a tuk-tuk, but none of them stop for her. The crowd drags the sisters down the pavement and into the dark beyond the Night Bazaar.

They're near the klang, one of the city's canals, along the old temple wall. It looks familiar, like a place she's seen through the smoked panes of the consulate car. Maybe they're closer to home than she thought.

"Jill," says Maizie, "Nico won't let go. I can't breathe."

The little hands are bruising Maizie's throat.

"Spin around really fast," says Jill.

Maizie spins.

"Maybe if you jump in the water?"

"I can't jump in there! It's dark. Dad says it's sewage."

"No, it isn't. We see kids swimming in there."

"It's dark."

"You can swim."

"Jill, don't make me. It smells like poop."

"There are water lilies, look."

There are, a drift of them, spinning in a path of light.

"Just stay in the light. Duck the monkey under. It'll let go."

"No!" Maizie sways. The monkey grins.

Jill hears a splash and a cry, and then nothing.

"Maizie?"

Jill leans out over the bank. Lights gleam on the water, on the lilies with their pale blades closed up for the night.

Maizie cries, "She won't let go!" She scrabbles at the bank. The water's shallow but the banks are high. The gibbon pulls at Maizie's shirt. She shivers, with the golden monkey riding her shoulders.

Jill lies on her stomach and holds out her arms. But she isn't strong enough to pull Maizie up over the bank. The gibbon makes her heavy.

"Why won't it let go?" Maizie wails.

"I don't know! Oh my god. I'm sorry. I'll go find a phone. I'll call Dad. I'm sorry, Maizie."

"Don't leave me by myself!"

From the shadow of a tree a figure detaches itself. It's some white tourist guy, punked out with spiky hair and wearing skinny black jeans and a Ramones T-shirt.

She hails him. "Please, do you speak English?"

He wades into the water, Doc Martens and all, and picks up Maizie and hoists her onto the bank. Then he hops it himself and walks off, back to his tree. Wait, Jill wants to say, don't go, but the man comes back carrying a candy box. He opens it to reveal a nest of white balloons, at least a dozen, uninflated but bulging. He works a finger into the neck of one and his finger emerges dusted with white powder. "What's her name?" he asks Jill.

"Maizie," Jill says.

Smoothly, he strokes the gibbon with his undusted hand, murmuring in a high and childlike voice, "Who's a little baby? Who's a good little Maizie girl?"

"No, Maizie is my sister. The monkey's name is Nico."

He pets Nico. "Actually, gibbons are small apes," he says. "They're going extinct. Golden ones are supposed to be protected. But nothing ever is." He says this without blame, just stating it. "Nico. That's a perfect name."

He scratches the gibbon around the neck and shoulders. The gibbon tips its head and smiles, and the man rubs white powder on Nico's shining black gums. The monkey rolls her eyes, sucks her teeth. The man strokes her.

"That's it," he says. "Who's my good little ape?"

Nico sighs, gurgles, and falls to the ground.

Jill crouches by the fallen gibbon. Her eyes are closed. Her chest rises in little pants, and her lips and eyelids tremble. Nico moans like a baby, then twitches and goes still.

"Is it dying?"

"I think maybe," says the man.

"This is all my fault."

Next to them, Maizie curls herself into a ball, shivering. Jill aches all over. Her throat burns. She is so ashamed. There's no taking Nico back to Heidi, no way to find the bar again in all that dark, bright tangle. But maybe Nico will wake up, climb the flame tree, and spend the rest of its life eating jackfruit and throwing flowers into the klang.

"Poor monkey," she whispers.

The man gathers Nico in his arms. He squeezes her feet. When she doesn't respond, he kisses her on the lips. No, not kisses. He's giving her mouth-to-mouth. Jill wants to giggle, but she can't. Mouth-to-mouth on a monkey. But Nico doesn't breathe. He unpins her diaper then, and flings it away. He lays her naked in the grass at the foot of the flame tree.

"There," he says, "at least you don't have to be a person anymore."

"I'm sorry," Jill says.

"Hey, don't cry," the man says. "Come on. You can help me. I need someone with me tonight. I don't want to be alone. You guys can help me now."

"No more," Jill says. "I want to go home."

"You're drunk. You'll never get home like that," he says. "Come with me. I promise to get you home."

Maizie is moaning among the tree roots, and at least he understands English, so Jill nods. They braid themselves around Maizie to help her walk.

"Come on," he says to Jill. "I've got a hotel room. We can clean up there. Hold this."

He gives her the candy box. He doesn't ask any questions and he speaks English and Jill feels relieved to be rescued by someone who speaks English, in spite of knowing what's in the box. It has nothing to do with her life, none of it.

"What's your name?" she asks.

"It used to be Peter Pandemonium. Sometimes Peter Panic. I don't know what it will be when I get back home."

"I'm Jill."

"Hi," he says, with that strange child's voice again.

In the hotel lobby he presses the elevator button, and the doors open and they lean together in the lifting mirrored space, all three of them, a skeleton man holding up a little girl covered in mud and a third, a girl, standing a little apart, and reasonably clean. She's holding a candy box and staring at herself as if to reassure herself that she's real.

They put Maizie under the shower and wash the klang mud from her clothes and the makeup from her face, and while she pukes Peter stirs the puddles so they dissolve down the drain. He gives her a hotel toothbrush and helps her brush her teeth, and then he discreetly shuts the door while Jill undresses Maizie and washes her again, and dries her. He passes clean clothes through the door, skinny black jeans Maizie barely fits into, his Ramones T-shirt, which hangs on her like a dress, and socks with skeletons on them. He tucks Maizie into the big hotel bed and puts the wastebasket next to her in case she pukes again.

Without his shirt he is the thinnest person Jill's ever seen. There are track marks on his arms.

He asks Jill if she wants to order some food.

"You're the skinny one," she says. "You're the one who's starving."

"I can't eat anything," he says. "It makes me puke. But I'll have a beer with you."

"You should eat ice cream," she says. "Ice cream is good if you haven't eaten in a long time."

"I can't afford to throw up," he says. "I have this thing to do."

White balloons in a pink candy box.

"I have to smuggle them back. Hide them away in this old skin bag," he says, looking down at himself. This man is someone her father would arrest, if he could, and hand over, if he knew. He's one of the bad guys. He's doing what she has only heard about and never really believed.

He tells her he's doing it because what's in the balloons creates a bliss so perfect that ordinary life ceases to matter; even sickness, even dying, can't hold out against the bliss. Weeks ago, back in the States, he faced a mirror and saw he was close to death, but health and the body seemed just an illusion compared to bliss. So he lay down in perfect bliss and died. Then an EMT ungraciously brought him back, and everything was different. He was different, because the bliss was an illusion. The bliss would kill you. The bliss killed bliss.

So he came here to swallow the balloons, to carry the bliss to people who still believe in it, because that's all he can do, if he wants to start again, if he wants to quit. To start a new life you need money. So he'll do it just this once. He'll get fifteen thousand dollars for it, which sounds like a lot to Jill. But she knows the risk. Her father talks about Thai prison. Or capture stateside.

He'll take the money and hit Mexico, he says, where you can buy opium-based cough syrup to get through the worst of withdrawal. Then he's going to Santa Fe. He's heard the vibe there is good. He'll drink his way through the rest. But you need money to quit. You need money to get by until you've quit.

The balloons look like shriveled eggs. Jill nudges one.

"I wish," he says, "I'd had a chance to see an opium flower before I did this."

"Are you scared?" Jill asks. "What if they catch you?"

He draws water into a glass.

"You shouldn't drink local water," says Jill. "It will make you sick."

"Just sit with me and make sure I don't choke."

So she sits in the chair and watches over him. Maizie snores from the bed, and Jill sits as tense as a stick, willing him ease and peace. The balloon is on his tongue. He tips his head back, and the balloon sticks in his throat. He gulps from the glass and closes his eyes. The balloon moves down his throat and Jill imagines it landing in his stomach. She wonders about the strength of the knot. He swallows a second, and a third. His eyes are watering. His lips are cracked and chapped and he needs a shave.

She jumps up and refills his glass. He drinks and swallows, and drinks again. He jiggles a balloon, testing the knot. He drinks. Finally the box is empty. The balloons are all inside him. But he drank the water. If he got a bad case of the Thailand trots, would the balloons simply slither out of him—in the toilet of the plane, maybe, or in the airport bathroom? And even if he makes it back into the States—then what? He has no gated walls; no one will salute or scold him. He is free.

Jill can't stand the pity of it. She reaches for him. She holds him tightly in her arms, pressing her cheeks painfully into his spiked hair. I am so selfish, she thinks. And then he kisses her. His mouth is awkward and hungry. It tastes bad, and his lips are so chapped, they scratch and catch on hers. Jill is afraid of all the things she, a virgin, and a good girl, never quite believed in—AIDS, prison, death—but she doesn't pull away. She kisses him back. More out of shame than anything. And she understands this about herself—that her shame will endanger her again and again. That curiosity and shame will bring her lip to lip with all of it, all the germs and uncertainties and suffering and terror from which nothing, certainly not her nationality, certainly not her virginity, will protect her. And part of her rejoices. But mostly she feels horror, and then a settled dread. She pulls away from him and runs to the bathroom, where she gives in to the urge to rinse her mouth.

Peter is not bad. But he is, she realizes, contagious. He carries the accident of his life and spreads it. And so does she. She buries her head in her hands. And, not for the last time, she prays. Let it be okay. I get it, I understand, you don't have to punish me; I see it, please, let us be okay. Let us all be okay.

He knocks on the door. Jill opens it.

"You should go home now," he says. "I'll be okay."

He gives Jill a fistful of baht and rouses Maizie, who is groggy and who, in spite of her shower, reeks. Jill wants to stay here, in his clean, cold room with its generic Western lines, its purple orchid bedspread and photograph of the king and queen. It's safe here. She's no one. She wants to be no one always, in a cold room where no one would ever dream she'd be, where her life won't touch anything or hurt anyone or make things spoiled. She doesn't want to want anything. It no longer seems worth the risk.

"I thought it would be beautiful," she says. "I thought it would be different from this."

He paces. She watches his bare feet on the carpet.

"It should add up to more than this. It's supposed to mean more than this. Isn't it?"

"I don't know," he tells her, "but you have to get yourself home."

He paces the room, rubbing his stomach; he cracks a beer and pours it past cracked lips, and she imagines the balloons in his gut rising to float on the golden foam.

Maizie lists hot and damp against her, and Jill holds her hard because the tuk-tuk bounces and swerves and they could spill out into the traffic. It would be so easy—the seat is slick and gummy and Jill is so tired. Maizie is coming awake now, leaning out of the tuk-tuk to vomit. Remember this, Jill tells herself, remember all of it, don't let it become a dream, remember it, hold on.

The tuk-tuk slows. The driver gestures at Maizie, looking at the two of them in disgust. He pulls over. *Mai di,* he says, *mai ow.* Jill gives their address again, insists. The driver shakes his head. But it's all right. Jill recognizes the road, the great field of sunflowers beside the AIDS billboard with its skeletons and needles.

The driver stops beside the ditch, and Jill pays him and pulls on Maizie, who wakes up without surprise. They step out beside the field of sunflowers, holding hands. Rows of sunflowers radiate back and back, a thousand bright mandalas wheeling against the line of mountains, where the sun is rising. On the mountains, racing clouds are blue-heavy, and a breeze kicks up and stirs the girls' hair. Jill hears thunder and smells ozone.

The girls stagger through the bright green grasses in the ditch, following the line of barbed wire that leads back to their compound, where, no doubt, there will be explanations, and punishment, and soda cans in the fridge. Sunflower petals come flying on the wind, damp and torn. They stick to Maizie's face, cling to Jill's neck, so the two of them are pasted all over with yellow petals, every inch of their drenched skin.

THE BALCONY

In the lull before morning recess, Danny looked up to see his mother's head framed in the window of his fourth grade classroom door. She grimaced, peered in, pressed the mesh with her vivid painted mouth. Danny sat in the back row, but even from his distance, he could see that her cheeks were flushed. She caught Danny's eye, pointed frantically down at something out of sight, and waved. Her knotted red kerchief sat askew on her hair. Generally she tied her head up jauntily, with the bandana knot centered over the part in her hair, the knot-ends as pert and symmetrical as cat ears, her Rosie the Riveter look, she called it. The bandana's knot, clumsy and loose, had slipped sideways and was in the process of undoing itself over her left ear.

Danny, heart pounding, bowed his head and wrote his name and the date on a fresh sheet of paper.

DANNY BOWMAN MARSH. September 19, 1967.

Maybe if he acted like he didn't notice her, she'd go away.

Danny erased a problem in long division, concentrating on the pink rubber shavings, the pencil smear. He blew them away, erased again. He erased so hard, he bore a hole in the paper. He liked long division, liked imagining the numbers entering a little house, fitting in neatly, with the remainders confined to the roof. The door squeaked, and his mother came in, slipping a little in her high heels. She weaved between the desks. Her perfume was like a blow from a fist.

Danny hunched further down in his chair, hoping that it was still early enough in the day that she hadn't let herself go wild. He dropped his pencil, bent to retrieve it, and came nose to nose with his basset hound, Orla, who gave his face a tentative lick, like she knew she was in the wrong place and needed to make an apology. He sniffed her tortilla scent and wished he could stay down there on the floor with her and never come back up.

Children scraped chairs and clustered around her, patting the dog's head, scratching between her shoulder blades. The boys crouched and grabbed her paws, said, "Shake, shake!" and the girls bent over her, fondled her long ears, and kissed the furrows on her forehead, cooing. "Aww, she's cute!"

"Class!" Mrs. Michaels, his fourth grade teacher, rapped her desk with a ruler.

His mother teetered beside him, and the leash swayed and tautened. Orla sat like an anchor. Danny held his breath.

"May I help you, Mrs. Marsh?"

"Oh, shoot," his mother laughed breathlessly. "It's Bowman now! Danny's daddy and I are D-I-V-O-R-C-E-D."

Danny kept his eyes down. He had not told Mrs. Michaels or anyone in the class about his daddy leaving. His Gigi said to hush on it. And to hush on his momma's friend Nestor Roche. *Ain't neither of them any good,* his Gigi said.

His mother popped the clasp on her pocketbook and fished out a box of Benson and Hedges. She shook one out and held it, unlit, between her long fingers. Her bangles clattered. She considered Mrs. Michaels, with a grin and a squint.

"Danny sure does talk about you," his mother said. "He's always going around quoting you and trying to get me to sing those rounds you teach him. I hate rounds. They get stuck in your head. It's not like you can sing them on your own. Rounds don't work if you're alone. It's dishonest, don't you think? Teaching kids songs that never end? Everything ends, doesn't it, and everyone ends up alone."

Danny saw with horror that tears were forming at the corners of her eyes. They thickened her voice when she quavered: "*My dame has a lame tame crane. My dame has a crane that is lame. Pray every day that my dame's lame tame crane feeds and comes home again.*" Her voice rose from guttural to high-pitched, a crescendo like the laughter of the Wicked Witch.

Around him, his classmates stared at his mother, or kept their eyes firmly on their desks.

His mother rubbed the back of Danny's neck in the way that he hated. Mrs. Michaels glanced at Orla, who was licking her privates with utter concentration. She looked at Danny's scarlet neck. She met his eyes. Danny looked away.

"Let's step outside, Mrs. Marsh," said Mrs. Michaels. She fingered her little cross.

"No reason for a tête-à-tête, teacher. I'm taking my son out of school. There's been a situation. Family. Not your concern. Danny, dig through my pocketbook and find me some matches."

Mrs. Michaels looked at Danny. He shrank in his chair. His mother was close, he could tell, to flying off the handle—*right off the handle of my broomstick, baby.*

"Danny, get me a light."

She threw her pocketbook on his desk. Lipsticks clacked, loose change jangled. A squiff of tissues poked out from the hinge. Gingerly, Danny fished for a pack of matches. If he took long enough maybe she would give up.

Digging through his mother's purse usually excited him. The smooth metal curve of lipsticks, the scent of perfume, the slippery silk lining with the tear where bobby pins or pennies fetched up, the ring of keys, the little hairbrush and compact, the crisp money she flung, loose, into the bottom of the bag, sprinkled sometimes with face powder. She liked him to go through her purse for her in the evenings before she went out, and he felt furtive and grown up. But here in the classroom, the open purse seemed to him as naked and shameful as a drawer full of her panties. He bent his head over it, pretending to search.

"Mrs. Marsh—"

"Bowman."

"Is it possible you just returned from a festive lunch? Perhaps you need some time to think over this decision. There is coffee in the teachers' lounge. Our school nurse could show you in."

"I can't find any matches," Danny lied.

"Give me that. I have to do everything myself." His mother grabbed her purse and dropped the cigarette. It rolled on the floor between Danny's feet. He brought his shoe down on the cigarette, and looked over at his teacher. Mrs. Michaels did not allow candy or chewing gum. Certainly not a cigarette. Why did his mother get to break all the rules?

Because she was a witch.

He ground the cigarette under his shoe.

His mother smacked him.

A girl in the back began to cry.

Shock and anger darted across his teacher's face. She strode over to Danny's mother. Danny, still at his desk, cowered between them. Orla weighted his feet. He couldn't move for shame.

"Mrs. Marsh," said Mrs. Michaels in a low tone, "the principal and I have asked you, on numerous occasions, not to interrupt my class."

His mother stood for a moment, cocky and squinting.

"You can't keep me from my child."

"And you can't keep taking him out of school. Mrs. Marsh, unless you want to be escorted from here by the police, I suggest you leave."

Danny's mother blinked. She looked down at Orla, who rolled sanpaku eyes and listed against Danny's ankle. She looked at Mitzi Tomkins, crying, and at Ben Henshaw, who had his hands over his ears, at Carly Swift, who was gulping down laughter, and at Mrs. Michaels, who stood beside Danny's desk with a hand planted firmly on Danny's shoulder.

Danny's mother put her palm over her mouth in dismay.

"My baby," she said, "I'm so sorry." She kissed Danny's cheek. Her mouth felt sloppy, and also greasy, as though she'd been eating butter.

Mrs. Michaels didn't seem particularly moved by his mother's tears. She just frowned and fingered her cross.

"Mrs. Michaels," said Danny's mother, suddenly crisp, "there has been a family emergency. I cannot spare you or this piddly little school another second of my time, so we will be going. Say goodbye, Danny."

Danny threw Mrs. Michaels a pleading look. She returned it, and for one moment he thought she might take him in her arms. Wouldn't she keep him here, in the classroom, where he could finish his math?

"Lipstick, Danny," said his teacher. She indicated her own cheek.

His mother laughed and thumbed his cheek clean, her tears forgotten. She snaked a tissue from her bag and blotted his face. She reapplied her lipstick, gaily. When she was done, she tugged Danny's arm. She tugged Orla's leash.

"Goodbye," said his teacher. Her face was very red and perplexed.

The door slammed. Danny waited outside it for a moment, hoping to hear what, if anything, Mrs. Michaels would say. But the classroom was silent.

"God Almighty, Danny," said his mother, "I never knew you were such an apple-polisher!"

She handed him Orla's leash, lit a cigarette, and strode down the hall, her skirt swinging jauntily. Her smoke cut through the school smell of bleach and floor polish.

"Come on, baby," she said in the laughing voice he loved.

She flicked a dead match into the path of the janitor and did a Gene Kelly move, scuffing her shoes through the janitor's cleaning foam. All at once the sound of his mother's high heels on the linoleum filled him with excitement, like the clatter of a train, and he ran to catch up with her. Orla's nails chittered and her stomach swung as she struggled to keep up. He looked down at her fondly.

"Come on, girl!"

The school corridor felt like an unfamiliar, enchanted tunnel. The light turned the hallway sepia, and Danny remembered the moment in *The Wizard of Oz*, the best moment, when Dorothy creeps through the shadowy umbers of her fallen house, opens the door, and to a swell of music emerges into Technicolor.

His mother reached up, straightened her red scarf, and turned the corner. Danny ran to catch up with her, Orla at his heels. They burst out the doors all three of them together, running to the curb, where her red Mustang waited, blazing in a world of light and color.

Danny had just about fallen asleep in the back when his mother said in a sharp voice: "Get up here, baby, and take the wheel. I'm driving blind."

Danny scooted forward over his spill of school papers and elbowed Orla to one side. He rubbed his eyes. They were still speeding through the hill country. Heat pools shimmered. The sun was hot and the light jab-jab-jabbed against the punching bag clouds.

"What do you mean, Momma?"

"I can't see the road!"

Her voice, normally lazy Texas with an upper-crust lilt, angled sharply. Danny glanced around the car's interior, looking for bottles. Had she stopped while he was asleep? He knew her flask was empty; he'd seen her finish it in the school parking lot. And there weren't any bottles, as far as he could see.

"Take the wheel, goddammit!"

She was going ninety. The road seared at that speed. She let go of the wheel and clutched her head. The speedometer crept to one hundred. Danny, terrified, leaned across the gap between the bucket seats and steered. They started to weave.

"Momma, you've got to slow down."

She kept her hands pressed hard against her eyes, her foot flooring the accelerator as if she was trying to speed herself back into sight. Danny held the wheel in both hands, struggling to keep the car straight. The road began to curve.

"Momma!"

He let go of the wheel with one hand and struck her as hard as he could on the knee. Her foot didn't budge. The car veered into the opposite lane. He yanked them back. Up ahead in their lane he could see a blue Chevy, traveling much more slowly. The Mustang gained speed.

"Momma, take your foot off the gas!"

He leaned over and grabbed her by the shin, pulling her foot. She just pressed the gas harder.

They were right on top of the Chevy. Danny hit the horn. The Chevy swerved. Danny swerved. They clipped its side mirror and kept going. Behind them, a horn blared, and he heard a man shouting. Danny was screaming. His mother was screaming. The wheel fought his grip. The car kept skidding. Danny focused on the dotted lines in the road, casting worried glances at his mother, who sank in a half crouch, holding her eyes, and at Orla, who pressed herself forward to get close to them, terrified, one paw scraping his wrist, the other slipping on the gearshift. The road rushed under them, a grainy blur of asphalt and heat, and the terrible whipping in his ears distracted him, and he felt battered by wind and speed. Please, God, just don't let them crash.

Orla leapt onto his mother's lap and then burrowed down into the footwell, between her feet. Her mother kicked the dog, screaming, and Orla scrambled back up, this time onto Danny, but his mother's foot came off the accelerator, and the car slowed down.

"Don't touch the pedals, Momma," said Danny. "I'm going to steer us off to the side."

They rolled onto the shoulder, and when the car was nearly stopped, Danny pulled the hand brake.

"Jesus," said his mother, "Jesus Christ." Then she leaned her head on the steering wheel and he pressed his face into Orla's neck and they both cried.

"Danny," she said when they were quiet, "here's what we're going to do. I want you to tie my kerchief around my eyes. Tie it tight. First we're going to pray hard. Then we're going to turn on the radio. And we're going to find us a song by Patsy Cline. And when the song is over, I'll be all right," she said.

She pulled the red bandana from her hair and waved it vaguely in his direction. She pushed the lighter in the dash.

"Pass me a cigarette, too," she said.

She tilted her head back, chin raised to the sky. Danny knelt beside her and bound the kerchief tight. She raised her face, wearing the blindfold, lips wrapped in a scowl around the unlit cigarette.

"I must look like I'm about to be shot," she said.

The lighter popped from the dash.

He reached over and lit the cigarette. She bent her head to pray.

If God was watching her, what would he see? White fingers, red nails, blue veins, no ring. The scarf a red slash across her face, above her mouth, where most of the lipstick had worn away, and long black mascara tracks creeping down her cheeks, sunlight through the fuzzy hair on her jaw, her tongue moving softly against her teeth.

When she finished praying, she said, "Turn on the radio, baby."

Danny did. Buck Owen came on, singing "Together Again."

His mother sighed. "That's a real good sign," she said. "You know, it was Gigi that ran him off, your father. Gigi. Not me. You understand? But I'm glad, hear me? I never loved your father like I love Nestor Roche. You're a smart boy, you're practically a grownup. I know you understand."

"Yes, Momma."

"Where are we, now?"

"I don't know, Momma."

"What do you see?"

"Lots of sky."

"Go on."

"Big clouds."

She smiled. "You ever notice, baby, how Texas clouds are usually shaped like Texas?"

"They look like anvils. Like in a Roadrunner cartoon."

"Acme Novelty clouds."

Danny watched her bring a forefinger to her mouth, bite her cuticle, and peel the skin to a bright red thread.

"There's an overpass up ahead," said Danny. "Maybe if we see a car I can wave it to stop. Somebody could help us."

"No," his mother said.

"But, Momma."

"No. You wave at anybody out there and I swear to God I will kill you."

She turned the red gash of the blindfold in his direction. Her mouth was wrinkled and mean.

"I mean it," she said. "Nobody gets in our business."

Danny nodded his head.

"You better be nodding."

She sank back. "Then that's that." Her mouth sagged. She looked confused. Her hand faltered as it brought the cigarette to her mouth.

"Baby? I just don't know what's wrong with me."

Up ahead, under the overpass, swallows flew in and out of their spitball houses stuck up under the elevated road. His mother collapsed forward, hugging the steering wheel, burrowing her blind face into her crossed arms. Her shoulder blades poked up like a grasshopper's knees. Cars passed. No one stopped.

"Nestor Roche is a devil, you know. And I'm a witch." She raised her head and turned her blindfolded gaze to him.

"You're not a witch, Momma."

"I am. No one loves me."

"I love you! I love you!" he cried in a passion, terrified to see her like this, blindfolded and white-faced, with too much skin hanging off of her little skull, and her shoulders crooked with despair. The rush of hot feeling was so intense in his chest, he thought he might die. He grabbed her around the waist, buried his face in her stomach, and felt his heart boom against her, hoping she would turn over, cough to life.

"No one," she said, listless. "Nobody." She unhooked Danny's hands. "No one but Roachie. You understand now, Danny? We've got to get to him. I need him. I need him," she repeated. "You understand."

She propped her head against the steering wheel with her right hand, bringing the cigarette up in graceful little sips. Even in pain her gestures were as elegant as a dancer's.

Telephone poles slipped past. Signs moved toward them, fell back. Mile marker, *flick*, speed limit, *flick*, grackles on wires, *slip slip slip*, the dotted lines on the road riffling along like pages in his composition book, *swoop swish*, another car, live oaks twinkling with sunlight, the bright blink of Indian paintbrush, and above them the monstrous clouds, pregnant with lightning. His mother steered, shifted, smoked. The afternoon deepened. Danny was hungry. He rummaged in the glove compartment. He ate her last Tic-Tac.

"Oh, Danny, Danny, Danny," his mother cried into the wind. "Look at that sky! Tornado weather!"

She threw her arms wide and floored the accelerator.

"I remember once the sky turned grass green and the wind threw road signs like a cardsharper and it was solid thunder and spouts of rain and whiplash electrical lines and no one wanted to go out into but me—cars might've floated, and I walked clear across town in it, with rainwater up to my knees. I never felt so happy. When you dance with a storm, Danny, you have to be nimble and strong and full of your own lightning. Three people died in that storm. But I walked all through the middle of it because nothing can carry me away."

He peed into an empty bottle as they drove. He crawled into the back seat and emptied it out over the side, watching it stream back along the road. At ninety miles per hour his pee flew in a banner and atomized to rainbows. If they got lost again, if she left him off on the side, he could find his way back following the blazes of urine striping the road.

His mother cracked the brake and tore out of the car so fast, she lost a shoe. "Home free!" she said.

Home was three motel buildings, set in a horseshoe around a motel swimming pool and fronted by a motel parking lot. His mother ran to the motel office without bothering to turn off the engine. Danny, still carsick and blurry from too much wind and haze, crawled over and switched off the ignition. In the parking spot to his left, a yellow VW Beetle, parked face-out, smiled at him. Someone had painted daisies on the hubcaps, purple ones, and flicked streamers of paint around the headlights to look like eyelashes. It looked so shining and friendly that Danny wanted to pet it.

He could see his mother behind the plate-glass of the office window, lighting a cigarette and scrawling on some papers. Her pictured her bare foot tapping the carpet. The clerk, a fat woman with a grey bouffant, pushed a key over to his mother.

Danny opened the driver's side door and leaned out to retrieve his mama's shoe, and as he straightened up he saw a woman's rump in a white gauze skirt bending over the Bug's trunk. Long brown hair slithered down the woman's back. She was barefoot. The soles of her feet were the same color as the asphalt. She had hair on her legs! She swung a knapsack out and shrugged back her sheet of waist-length hair. Her breasts swayed, free under the gauzy cotton. Big ones. Danny stared at her, open-mouthed, holding his mother's shoe. The woman smiled at him.

"I like your dog," she said. Then she padded away. Danny watched the sway of her hips.

"Franklin! Get your raggedy ass down here and grab the rest of our shit!"

She sang the sting out of the words.

A man, more hair than face, dungaree-thin, sloped out from under the motel awning.

"I feel like the road's still moving," he said.

"Poor baby." She scatted one hand over his thin chest and they headed toward the stairs.

Danny's mother flew out to the car.

"Come on, baby. Quit gawking at that draft-dodger peace-nik crapwagon and get on upstairs."

She grabbed a bottle from the trunk.

"Building on the right, second floor. I'll leave the door open," she called over her shoulder as she headed for the stairs.

"What about our suitcases?"

"We'll get them later."

"Should we put the top up?" The wind blew leaves in skirling spirals, and the clouds had massed. Not anvils. Ziggurats.

"Later!"

His mother paced inside their motel room, already on the phone, scattering ash as she poured herself some bourbon in a cloudy motel glass.

"I'm here!" she cried. "Honeybunch, I made it!" She slurped her drink. "I did ninety the whole way and I made it! No, Gigi doesn't suspect a thing."

She motioned for Danny to come in. The room was dark and cool, already filling with her smoke and perfume. His mother shut the door, bolted it, and slipped the chain. She lifted her hair off the back of her neck.

"What, honey?" she said into the phone. Her voice pitched low, murmured, then cracked. "Well, no. No, of course I brought him. I had to."

She paced, eyebrows and mouth quirked tight like she was trying to pull the conversation up with the muscles in her face. She rubbed the bridge of her nose.

"I wasn't lying, I just. I couldn't leave him this time. You said you were serious. We're going to be a family."

Danny snuck an ice cube from her glass and sucked on it. The bourbon burned and the ice did too. He watched his mother try to force the curl out of the phone cord.

"I do love you. I do."

Danny turned the air conditioner up higher. A thin stream of air, cold as a sharpened pencil on the tongue, blew out, smelling like dust. He wanted to ask for the room key so he could go out to the car and get his comic books, but he was afraid to interrupt her. He knew this mood. If he left the room without the key, she wouldn't answer his knocks until she hung up the phone, which wouldn't be for a long time. It was hot outside. So Danny waited.

"Come on, honey, I'm here. Where are you?"

She slapped Danny's hand away from her glass.

"Nothing matters but us."

She covered the mouthpiece and hissed, "Danny, patio, get!"

Danny didn't move. He still felt sweaty, and the room was cool. Orla huffed in the corner next to the air conditioner. Her eyeballs were red. Danny lay down next to the dog. The carpet made his eyes ache.

"Orla, you sure do smell," he said to her. "What? To a dog that's a compliment. You are *sooo* stinky," he crooned, fondling her ears, "stinky as a pile of poop." She licked her chops and rolled to one side, showing her belly.

"Danny, get!" his mother goosed him in the backside with her big toe. She had on her fierce face; she'd reapplied her lipstick and was looking in the mirror, scrubbing a forefinger along her front tooth.

"Patio, now!"

If he didn't move now, she would kick. Barefoot or not, she could land a good one.

He got up on all fours and crawled toward the sliding glass doors to the balcony, panting like a dog.

"He won't be a problem. I promise. He won't make a peep, you won't even see him, honeybunch, I swear. I swear. Danny, patio, now!"

"Can I at least go swim in the pool?"

"Not while there's lightning."

"It's not even raining yet."

"Get!"

She shoved him onto the patio and heaved the sliding door. A moment later she opened it again and scooted Orla out. The drapes hitched. He heard the latch click.

The patio had one plastic-slatted chair beside a pebbled-glass-topped table. An ashtray containing a single bent Marlboro butt and dusted with the impatient streaks of ground-out cigarettes sat on it. The slats of the chair gave slightly when Danny sat on it. The smell of the ashtray in the moist air made him angry. The pool lay directly below in a little courtyard, and he could see the balconies of the rooms opposite. Off to the left in the parking lot, their car was a red and open pit. The yellow Beetle flirted its cute round eyes, and the empty parking spaces waited for Nestor Roche.

"Jesus, that is one saggy-titted cur," said Nestor Roche, hours later. Danny, stiff and sleepy, blinked down feebly, his heart thudding. Roche stepped out of his car and stretched his arms up to the night. Danny knew better than to reply, so he played with the Marlboro butt, drawing evil swastikas in the dead ash. He never could remember which way the arms on the crosses went.

"Got a puss on her like LBJ," said Roche, grinning up at the balcony.

Danny felt such hatred, he wanted to bite the railing, taste the hot metal, break his teeth against it.

Roche closed the door to his truck with a gentleness that was almost like regret. Roche was not a violent man, Danny's mother insisted when Danny showed her the marks. Look how he closes doors. You can tell a lot about a man by how he closes a door. He never slams. And she was right. Roche struck soundlessly, like a knife. He spoke in soft, cultivated tones—crude words in tender modulations. He never banged furniture around like Danny's dad used to, he never punched a wall or peeled out of a driveway. He could lay his hand on you so steadily and so quietly that no one would ever, ever guess how you came by that deep starfish bruise.

Roche turned to haul a clinking paper sack from the bed of his truck. Just get closer, thought Danny, come a little closer to the pool and I'll land one on you. He let the spit gather in his mouth. Roche sent Danny a sharp, gloating grin, like he could slit Danny's throat with it.

Danny heard him take the stairs on the outside edge of the motel, tried to guess how long before he'd turn onto the landing. Now he'd be passing the soda pop machines and the ice-maker. Finally Roche's knock on the outside door of their room: "Open up, it's the police!" and his mother throwing back the chain and crying "Honeybunch!" and then the blare of the TV.

Out on the balcony the air was heavy and still. Darkness painted over the heat. The night clouds were a dull, waiting color, not purple, not green, aching with unshed rain. Orla panted and drooled against his ankle. His shirt stuck to his back, clammy under the arms. Voices from the television inside the room sounded so certain of themselves, so pleased, they made the studio audience erupt in laughter, and he hated them. Roche's boots thumped one after another onto the carpet.

"Jesus Christ, Loretta, you brought the dog, too?"

His mother laughed. She laughed. Danny hated her.

Danny woke from a doze. He was tired and thirsty and bored. He scratched Orla absently. She shook her head in irritation, too hot to be petted. Danny decided he needed to pee. They had to let him in for that. He knocked on the glass. The curtains parted with a snap and a swish. Roche's face flashed in the gap:

livid eyes and a glare of teeth. He held up one finger, shook his head and racked the curtains shut.

Orla rolled to her side. Below him, the unlit pool was a small, dingy rectangle, but the water looked cool. He was so thirsty. He watched the spit drip from Orla's tongue. He thought longingly of his comic books, of the bottles of Coke in the car, likely warm now from hours in the open. He leaned out over the railing and yes, he could see his pile of comics in the bright, open Mustang, *Scrooge McDuck* and *Mighty Mouse* slipping out from underneath his backpack. He had never wanted anything so much as he wanted a swig of Coke and to fold back the slick cover of one of those comic books. But it was too dark to read.

The wind picked up. The air before the rain pressed him like palms on each side of his head, and he wanted to cry but couldn't. He tried the sliding door again. He sat on the plastic chair. He put his feet up on the railing. He got down and knelt by Orla. He wrapped his hands in her floppy ears and they felt good, warm and alive.

"Orla," he said, "shake, girl."

She sighed.

"Shake!"

The dog growled in a complaining way.

My mother is selfish. The thought, detached and clear, floated forward.

My mother is selfish. The thought was very quiet, and its authority was absolute.

He sat up and shoved Orla's head from his leg. The loneliness, like the heat, pressed down on him, crept inside him and stuck his tongue to the roof of his mouth. He wanted a drink of water. He wanted to be in an icy room on a cheap bedspread beside his mother, glugging down a glass of tap water, even if it tasted rusty, even if it wasn't cold, and watching anything on the motel television, even the news. The grimy glass was locked against him and it was too far to jump from the balcony into the pool. Orla grunted and resettled herself dinosaur-like, her neck stretched long on the grimy patio.

The squeak of the pool gate startled Danny. He looked down to see the hippie man and woman padding barefoot to the pool. The man flicked on the underwater lights and the pool glowed like a mysterious heart. Danny smelled warm chlorine, and something indefinable, a thundery smell that came from the sky.

The woman wore her white dress but she jumped straight in. The pool lights turned her magnesium blue, a dazzle of floating dress and limbs. The dress stuck to her when she came up and showed dark brown nipples and a black triangle between her legs. Danny looked at her dark navel and rounded belly, the wet curves of her, how her breasts sprang when she burst up out of the water, shaking back her hair. She moved through the water by bounding, sinking under in a blur of floating dress and then shooting straight up out of the water with the dress clinging and wet and see-through, stuck in the crack of her behind, winding around her thighs, molded to her back. She popped and spun and brought her arms down flat, sending sheets of water up like wings on either side. She bounded over to the man, who dangled his legs over the ladder, and grabbed him by the waistband of his pants and dragged him into the water.

"Dammit, Libby!" he laughed, and dunked her, and she leaped onto his back and whispered in his ear. He flung her backwards and as she fell Danny caught a flash of wet black curls between white legs. She even had hair under her arms. She wound herself around the man and they kissed, barely keeping their footing in the center of the pool. Lightning pulsed in the clouds, and she bit him on the neck beneath his ear and wrapped her legs around his waist. Thunder. Raindrops pecked the surface of the water. The sky opened and a sudden burst of rain fell as hard and fast as split bag of rice. They pulled themselves out of the pool and ran, goosing and giggling, for the stairs.

The rain swept sideways onto the balcony. It was warm and felt good at first, but it rained harder and Orla's fur turned dark with wet and the wind blew grit into his teeth and soaked his sneakers and puddled in the pits of the unevenly poured cement. Goose bumps twinkled on Danny's skin. Lightning boomed so close he could smell it. Orla whined and backed under the table. Down in the parking lot their open car became a bucket, and he knew his comic books were ruined, everything was ruined and he was chilled and wet and still, in spite of all the rain, so thirsty. He tried to crawl under the table next to Orla but he didn't fit.

Inside the room behind him he heard his mother weeping, and the sound of a terrible knocking over and over. The rain sounded like a John Wayne movie. Mounted cavalry storming a hill. Gunfire. Indian whoops. Danny tried the sliding door. He banged it. He kicked the door but the flapping rubber sole of his sneaker only smeared the glass. He pressed his face against the door. Something flew toward his eyes and struck. He fell back, startled, staring at the crack that zigzagged down the door like captured lightning. His mother's shoe, the heel broken, lay on carpet between the curtain and the glass. The knocking inside the room continued.

Rain jeered in the gutters. Hailstones pelted the pool, rattled on the plastic deck chairs, and opened fire on the pavement. Little balls of ice rolled along the balcony. He put one in his mouth.

Then, just as suddenly, truce. The hail slowed and turned back to rain; the rain softened to a drizzle and stopped.

Across the way, Danny watched the woman emerge onto her balcony, peel off her wet dress, and drape it over the railing. She picked up a handful of hailstones and rubbed them on her neck. Her plate-glass balcony door was slid back so Danny could see inside her room. The man lay on her bed with his belt undone. The woman padded back inside the room. She leaned deliberately over the man so her breasts brushed his face as she switched on the light. The whole room lit up like a slide on a pull-down classroom screen. The man sat up and reached for her. She dropped the ice onto his stomach, and he pulled her onto him.

Outside above the motel pool the sky turned deep indigo between chinks of cloud. Lightning wavered in the moving thunderheads. The couple kissed. Danny leaned forward, pressing his chest against the railing. He licked fat drops of rain from the iron railing. It tasted dirty and made him thirstier. He watched everything they did across the way, with their balcony door wide open and the murky light shuttered with thunder and the rain slowing to hesitant drops and then crescendoing again in gusts of drenching wind. The rain thickened and he no longer knew what he was seeing and what he simply guessed at. His chest felt strange, fluttery and tight, and his whole belly down between his legs and into the soles of his feet melted aching and hot. His heart hurt him and his throat was dry and now he was crying. He didn't understand how something so secret and exciting could make him feel so terrible. It rained and stopped, and rained, and stopped again.

The woman came back out onto her balcony wrapped in a towel. She leaned over the railing and lit a cigarette.

"You been out there the whole time?" she called.

Danny nodded.

"You little dickens."

Wind blew water off the trees in a spattering gust.

Danny gave a big theatrical shrug. He suddenly felt very happy.

"You should go inside," she shouted. "Didn't anyone teach you not to stare?"

He shook his head wildly.

"I like your dog," she called. "What's her name?"

"Orla!"

The woman smiled again and dragged on her cigarette. She looked so beautiful in her white towel, with her glowing cigarette. Danny bent over and grabbed Orla. He lifted her onto his lap for the woman to see. He spread her ears out into a sort of curtsey, grabbed one of her paws to make her wave. Orla didn't like this. She slithered down onto the floor of the balcony and retreated under the table. Danny hauled her out by the tail. He felt hectic with his need to show off, to show the woman something special, to make her laugh and shake her head and readjust the towel around her breasts and wave at him.

He grabbed Orla around her fat middle and hoisted her high

over his head. She slipped in his grip, but he held her under the armpits and hefted her so that her paws finally balanced on the balcony railing.

"Tightrope walker!" he yelled.

Orla scrabbled desperately, clawing at his chest. The woman leaned forward in alarm. She waved, a wave that meant no, but Danny, completely carried away, grabbed Orla's front paw and waved with it again. Orla struggled backwards, digging her claws into him. She was surprisingly heavy and strong.

"Come on girl, wave!"

Orla blocked his view of the lady; he could only hope she was charmed and waving back wildly. Orla twisted and kicked. Her torpedo body twisted in his grip. He squeezed her harder and she yelped sharply and then jackknifed out of his grip over the balcony rail.

The woman screamed.

Orla fell.

Danny watched the slash of her tail, the sweet sail of ears as her stubby legs rowed empty space.

Then she smashed into the pool and sank.

"Jesus Christ!" shouted the woman.

Danny squeezed the railing, looking down, watching Orla spiral against the pool lights in the deep end. His chest was covered in dog hair. Orla shed furiously when she was scared. The scratches on his arms hurt.

"Jesus Christ! Franklin!" the woman called into her room. "That kid just threw his dog into the pool!"

The man came out to look. Orla surfaced. She paddled frantically, snorting and choking on the water.

"Go get your dog, kid!"

Danny couldn't do anything but grip the railing and look down into the pool where Orla was drowning. Her nose slipped under and her rattling barks when she coughed up water filled him with shame. Orla panted, spun in circles, looking for a way out. She paddled the water with stumpy legs. Her ears floated wide.

"Do something, you little shit," cried the woman. "Oh, for fuck's sake."

Moments later, damp-haired and still wearing the towel, she knelt at the pool's edge.

"Come here, baby," she called, and clapped her hands. "Here, baby girl!"

Orla struggled toward the woman. Her nose went under. Her forepaws diddled the water.

"Oh, for fuck's sake," said the woman. She let the towel fall and dove into the pool and deposited Orla at the edge. She hoisted herself out and wrapped the dog in her towel, rubbing and cooing.

The woman glared up at him from the pool deck, Orla shivering in her arms. Danny sidled back into the shadow of his balcony until his head hit the plate glass. The girl hoisted the swaddled dog, let herself out by the gate.

He watched her put Orla on the big bed where she had straddled the man. From far back on his balcony, Danny looked. The way her breasts moved. The slit of her backside, her belly, her breasts again. Livid scratches scored her stomach and chest.

She was talking to the man, rubbing Orla with the towel, gesturing out the balcony toward Danny.

The man came out.

"Jesus, kid, what's wrong with you?"

The man went back inside. The woman poked her head out, looked Danny dead in the eye, shook her head once, and then slammed her balcony door. She drew the drapes.

At dawn he watched Nestor Roche cross the pool deck and let himself out by the gate. When Danny's voice came, it was a croak.

"Mr. Roche," he said.

The morning was so still, he knew the man heard him. But Roche did not pause or look up.

"My dog fell in the pool," Danny said. "Those people took her to their room." He pointed to their balcony.

"Let me out," said Danny. "Momma doesn't hear me knocking."

The hippie couple crept across the parking lot, trying to move as noiselessly as possible. The girl had tied a bright purple belt to Orla's collar.

Roche nodded to them. He hunkered down and patted Orla.

"Nice dog you folks have," he said. "Got a puss on her like LBJ."

"No!" shouted Danny. "That's Orla! Tell them!"

Roche slid into his truck and started it. His headlights flooded the balcony. Danny threw an arm against his eyes and missed the moment when Libby hoisted Orla into the back of the Bug. But he heard the car door slam. He heard them drive away.

Five hours later Libby sat up groggily in the back seat of the Bug, rubbed the drool from her cheek and said, "Jesus, Franklin, that kid."

Frank reached over and scratched the basset hound behind the ears. The dog licked his hand.

"I know," he said. "Dude was unglued. But the dog seems okay."

"He was still out there. On the balcony."

Frank looked at Libby in the rearview mirror, and their eyes met.

"Frank," she said, "oh, God, Frank. I think we really fucked up."

On the road to El Paso, Danny's mother spotted a Mexican man at a roadside stand. He was trying to sell a monkey. She bought it for Danny, along with a supply of disposable diapers and half a bunch of bananas. Then they turned west.

ENDANGERED CREATURES

Jill and Maizie were in disgrace, and their father wasn't speaking to them. Instead, he left tiny, detailed messages on Post-it notes. For ten days he had papered the house with the wan yellow slips. They fluttered from the girls' bathroom mirror, frilled the surface of the fridge and television, and appeared bound with hair ties around the handles of the hairbrushes on their nightstands. That particular shade of Post-it yellow made them feel ashamed and sick.

Jill collected their father's correctional notes in a fat wad and read them to Maizie out loud.

> We are out of Raid. Have tenants been using it to conduct cockroach races? Do tenants realize that the compound commissary does not always sell Raid, and that local measures against roaches are highly toxic, not to

mention ineffective? Future canisters will be deducted from tenants' allowance.

Signed, The Management

Miss Manners says there is nothing more disagreeable than the smell of formic acid. Responsible tenants replace the ant bait and don't neglect to clean up the ants. Remember, here in Thailand, those ants might have been your grandmother. Give them a decent funeral.

Signed, The Management

"Tenants? He can't even admit that we're his!" said Jill.

Sunday morning, Jill and Maizie sat on the porch, swatting flies and feeding them to Maizie's turtle. Jill peeled their father's latest note off of the turtle tank. She read it to herself, but waved it out of reach when Maizie snatched.

"What?" asked Maizie.

Jill ignored her and shoved the note deep into her purse.

"Go get ready for church," she said.

It was ridiculous to dress up for church in Chiang Mai, thought Maizie, buttoning her shirt with sweaty fingertips, especially when you had to wear respectful sleeves. Even though they filled their sandals with baby powder and flung it into their armpits, making confectionary spills down the sides of their blouses, they sweated, as Jill liked to say, worse than Jesus in Gethsemane. The morning's heat pushed even harder against the screens when Maizie came back out on the porch. Maizie let flies crawl on her forearm, a cooling tickle. *Phwap!* Jill brought their fly swatter down, and a fly fell dead on the table.

"Dad's sending us to an orphanage," Jill said.

Maizie's turtle stretched his scraggy neck upward and beaked the dead fly from Jill's index finger.

"You're lying."

"See for yourself."

Maizie unfolded the paper.

"He's sending us to an orphanage? Why? What about Mom?" Maizie said.

Thwap! Another fly crumpled on the table.

"A million miles away."

The injustice of it burned Maizie's nose. Jill's swatter blurred and its freckles of dead fly looked smeary and strange. I only went along with you to make sure you were okay, Maizie thought. I am always going along with you. Sometimes she didn't know where she began and Jill left off.

"Do you think I'm in your thrall?" she asked Jill. She used the Post-it to flip a dead fly onto the floor.

"What does that even mean?"

"I overheard Dad yelling at you."

If something hurt, it had to be true.

"Do I really do everything you tell me to?"

"If you did everything I told you to do, I'd be an only child," said Jill, smacking at nothing in particular.

They heard their father start the car. He honked the horn twice, so they knew they had exactly two minutes to get in.

"Even an orphanage has to be better than living like this. At least it will be an experience," said Jill.

Jill thought everything was an experience. Then she complained about it.

"He can't be sending us for real," said Maizie. "He's our dad."

"He doesn't love us."

Jill sounded so certain. When she sounded that way, nothing Maizie could say changed Jill's mind. Maybe their dad did hate them. How would she know? If it weren't for the Post-its that flourished like fungi throughout the house, Maizie would have thought their father saw them as a pair of stray cats he put out food for, and nothing more. They weren't exactly being punished. Just erased.

"I packed us underwear and T-shirts and all my allowance money. We can escape back to the consulate. He can't just send us to be orphans. We have rights."

Jill let Maizie peep in her purse at the tight cylinders of panties and T-shirts, rolled up the way their father taught them.

"I've got forty dollars. Do you have any money?"

"I spent it all at the night market."

"Never mind. You can bring toilet paper."

At church Maizie sat cross-legged on the sticky matting, tugging her skirt over her knees. It was puddle-butt hot. The chapel was cooled by a single limp fan with a frayed electric cord, and all it did was flutter the hem of Father O'Bannion's cassock. All through the garbled hymns picked out clumsily on Sigrid Aldren's guitar and the rising and the kneeling and the wafer on the tongue, Maizie's fear sleeted down her back and ribs. An orphanage? Who would want them, if their father didn't? She and Jill didn't even speak Thai. Maizie could say the numbers, tens and hundreds, she could say thank you and hello, but that was it. Jill was even worse. She had to ask Maizie to bargain in the markets, even though Maizie was only eleven and a half and Jill was two years older.

Maizie prayed as hard as she could, and flicked the Post-it covertly against her leg. She'd folded and refolded it, and the penciled words were vanishing in the fuzzy creases. Would Father O'Bannion help her if she showed him? But he was so luminously good that Maizie always felt she had to hide from him some terrible secret knowledge, some sinfulness in herself that she couldn't name. Father O'Bannion's transparent-heeled socks and stained uppers, his wrinkles from years and years of smiling in the sun, made Maizie feel—as she supposed they were supposed to—insufficient, made her not exactly want to be good, but conscious that she wasn't better. She and Jill agreed on the imposture of this churchaday goodness—no one could work that hard, care that much about people they didn't know. There must be something wrong with Father O'Bannion. Their father's classified job was doing good for the United States of America, he claimed. And, as Jill said, God knows there was plenty wrong with *him*.

"Our business is awe," said Father O'Bannion. "We should fall to our knees before creation. Creation is awful, dear ones. Cherish it."

After the sign of peace and the dismissal, Maizie and Jill sat with their father in the rectory, trying to sweat unobtrusively while he talked to the priest. Maizie memorized her father's familiar profile, the tangly eyebrows shelved over his big nose, the small violet squiggles of vein on his cheeks. She could smell his dad smell, camphor-sharp and comforting. As tiny girls she and Jill used his white cotton undershirts as nightgowns, and his smell wafted through the fabric and embraced them.

Mrs. Aldren, the consul general's wife, quietly washed the liturgical vessels at the sink. Mrs. Aldren's enormous daughter

Sigrid (who was in Jill's class at school but acted like she was forty) had already folded the altar linens with her usual fearful efficiency, stowed them, and sat serenely tuning her guitar. Father O'Bannion served the girls dry toast from a plastic packet, clotted it with unspeakable jam, and poured them mugs of stewed tea the color of his teeth. Maizie sipped politely and tried to catch Jill's eye. Jill watched the clock and jiggled a foot. Her father's foot danced just that way. Jill's ears were shaped the same as their father's, as if they were coming unrolled at the top.

The clock hands sheared the hour. Novices brought Maizie and Jill lychees still on the branch. The girls peeled the pebbled skins and sucked the white flesh to take off the taint of the priest's tea. They made a tower of lychee hulls; whoever placed the last one without toppling the stack won. Maizie was adjusting the pile when Sigrid stood over them, blocking the light. Lychee hulls fell and scattered.

"Pick those up. We use them for mulch in the church garden," Sigrid said, swinging her long red braid over one shoulder. "And then get ready. We're leaving as soon as we load the vehicle."

Jill made a face at Maizie. They agreed that Sigrid was loathsome. They agreed that they hated Sigrid's mother, too. Perfect Mrs. Aldren, as tiny as Sigrid was tall, a smiling perfume bottle of a woman who never seemed to sweat and who shoved a relentless velvet headband over her strawberry flip.

"Everything about her tilts up in a smile," Jill had once said in disgust. "She actually turns up the ends of her hair so it's smiling on either shoulder, and that stupid headband is shaped like an upside-down smile."

"You mean a frown?" said Maizie.

"I bet her head is so empty that it she has to wear those stupid pearls to keep it on. She is so pastel," Jill said, "definitely a Summer." The girls had spent hours committing their mother's old copy of *Color Me Beautiful* to memory, and Jill defined people by their seasons—Summers were washed-out wimps, Autumns like Sigrid were rusty bores. Springs were rarest—Marilyn Monroe was a Spring. After wrapping herself and Maizie in a series of colored beach towels, Jill declared that they were Winters, crisp and jewel-like, the vividest of seasons, although secretly Maizie suspected that she herself was a Spring.

"Sigrid and her mom, all they do is shop and do good."

"We like to shop," Maizie pointed out.

"It's not the same. Jesus, Maizie. If we ever turn out like either of them we have to kill ourselves. Promise?"

Maizie promised. Being united in opinion with Jill made her feel less alone.

Sigrid and her mother loaded blankets, towels, untwinned sheets, dingy, matted-furred, and missing-eyed stuffed animals, diapers, and scarred plastic bottles for the orphans into the back of the consulate vehicle. The driver drove them up the mountains, past the temple of Doi Suthep, along a rutted dirt road parting the jungle. Maizie, carsick, kept her mouth shut and concentrated on the valleys in their haze of smoke, the charred fields with sad banana trees sticking out like sore thumbs.

In spite of the sealed windows, the scratchy scent of car exhaust and burned fields and a jungley odor like the bottom of a garbage can filled the car. Mrs. Aldren adjusted the ends of her hair so they smiled harder than ever against her shoulders, settled her headband more firmly, and fished in her shot-silk satchel to bring out an air freshener in a squat orange canister. She stuck it on the dash, below the little jasmine garland that hung from the rearview mirror, and turned up the a/c, blowing the confusing chemical aroma of orange blossom back over the girls. Maizie covered her nose and mouth and counted the links in Sigrid's long red braid to distract herself from the cold air freshener headache tightening her temples.

The car was turning and crackling over fallen branches, and the driver shifted into four-wheel drive. They rumbled past a man and a young boy excavating an enormous hole by the side of the road. Rubble from the hole clogged the road; clods of dirt and heaps of roots and stone blocked the car's path.

Mrs. Aldren and the driver stepped out of the van.

"Sigrid, stay with the girls. I don't want them running off."

Bored, Maizie lowered her window. The man was dragging a dog-size, dark brown armor-plated animal with a long tail like an alligator's, and it was digging fiercely, trying to get back in the hole. Maizie thought it might be a snapping turtle—she had never seen one. The man hauled on the tail and hoisted the animal into the air.

It rolled and twisted feebly, trying to curl into a protective ball. The man dropped it in the dirt, took the shovel from the boy, and clubbed the animal until it stopped struggling. A tiny scrap of something pink and moving clung to the base of the animal's spine. The boy plucked it off and tucked it under his shirt.

The man started down the road with the animal draped around his neck. Mrs. Aldren trotted beside him, speaking Thai rapidly and gesturing furiously. The man broke into a calm jog and veered off into the jungle.

The boy bobbed up in Maizie's window and knocked on the tinted glass with a rock.

"Don't," said Sigrid.

Maizie hit the window button. The glass slid down and heat and light whooshed over her. The boy thrust something at Maizie, and, blinded, she took it. Her hands registered warm scaliness, a snout nosing at and moistening her palm. The little animal curled around her wrist, gripped her forearm with long, curved claws. Maizie's eyes adjusted. In the square of sun, the creature's scales glowed with the same soft lights as Mrs. Aldren's rosy-grey pearls. Maizie turned it on its back, balanced in her palm, and stroked the tender pink belly. The animal flicked out a loopy chewing gum tongue.

"It's like a dragon and a sloth had a kitten," said Jill.

Sigrid craned her head around to see it.

"That's its baby," she said flatly. "They're pangolins."

Sigrid knew the right word for everything.

Maizie drew her forefinger along the artichoke plates on its back. His scales felt new, and tender, like a baby's fingernails. She felt a terrible happiness, just to be touching something so alive and new.

"It's a newborn," said Sigrid. "Look how small it is."

When Jill reached for the pangolin it rolled up into a tight ball by clamping its tail around itself. Maizie and Jill pried and pulled, but it stayed as tightly sealed as a green pinecone.

"The boy wants money," said Sigrid. "Give it back."

Maizie hugged the pangolin to her chest. "I'll buy it."

"They're endangered," said Sigrid. "You'll just encourage them to hunt more."

She wrenched the pangolin away from Maizie and handed it back through the window.

The boy flung the pangolin casually in the air and played catch with it as he walked away.

Jill gave Maizie her Felix the Cat purse. Maizie ran after the boy and thrust Jill's forty dollars at him, took the animal, and settled herself back in the car, wrapping the pangolin protectively in the tail of her blouse.

"When Mom gets back she'll make you let it go. I've never seen her this mad. Listen to her!"

Mrs. Aldren turned her fluent burst on the boy, who backed away making conciliatory gestures. Mrs. Aldren reached up to adjust her headband, swept if off in disgust, and snapped it in two.

"What's happening?" Maizie asked Sigrid.

Sigrid spoke fluent Thai but she would rarely translate. Now she waved an impatient hand, saying, "It's too complicated."

Mrs. Aldren slid into the front seat.

"I'm keeping it," said Maizie.

"It's too young to live without its mother," Mrs. Aldren said.

"Baby animals always die," added Sigrid, so smugly that Maizie wanted to smack her.

"Not necessarily," said Jill, "not if we take care of it."

"You can't," said Sigrid. "You guys are leaving Chiang Mai."

"Who says?"

"Your dad told my mom."

"He can't make us be orphans when we have a mother. It's illegal," said Jill.

"What are you, dehydrated?" said Sigrid. "Nobody thinks you're orphans. He's sending you back to your mom. We fired our best gate guards thanks to you guys. And you almost got your dad sacked."

"Sigrid!" said Mrs. Aldren.

"Even if you made it through customs. It would die."

"What do they eat, anyway?" asked Maizie.

Not even Sigrid knew.

The car crept up the road. Mrs. Aldren wiped her ruined mascara with a Handiwipe, and combed her hair in the visor mirror. She polished her pearls with a tiny scrap of chamois.

"You have to let it go, girls," said Mrs. Aldren, stuffing the wipe and comb back into her tote. "You can watch it starve in a shoebox or you can give it back to the jungle."

"You're horrible," said Jill.

"Nevertheless," said Mrs. Aldren as the car pulled onto the patchy gravel in front of the orphanage.

They walked into a sacred grove in front of the orphanage. All the trees wore monks' robes. One tree stood off to the side, festooned with rags and beads, its branches thick with paper flags. Up close, the flags turned out to be photographs, some black-and-white, some faded in the lurid umbers of old color film, others Polaroids, the people in them ghosting from exposure, but most were glossy thick squares the size of postcards. A different woman appeared in each photo. Some smiled and others squinted, whether at sunlight or from pain, Maizie couldn't tell. Many, the majority, looked solemn. Their durian-sized bellies asserted themselves. Maizie turned over the nearest photograph as it swung on its string. Someone had covered the back with closely written curly characters. A name? A prayer?

"Leave it here, girls," said Mrs. Aldren.

"Maizie," said Jill. "Let me."

The play of the pangolin's tongue flicked Maizie's inner wrist, a sweeter touch than the feet of flies. The dark eyes, bright as beetles, blinked. Trusting little scrap. What business did they have with it?

"You girls are doing the right thing," said Mrs. Aldren.

Jill hoisted herself into the tree and set the baby pangolin carefully in a crook between branch and trunk. The baby nosed at the bark, his tongue darting out. Jill stroked his head and left him curled among the offerings, the sun-bleached smiling women, the faded flags. She marked the spot with a strand of silver beads and scrambled down. She smiled at Maizie, and flashed her two crossed fingers behind her back.

A thin cat, pale as water, slipped out from under their vehicle and trotted across the gravel toward the grove. More cats watched from the orphanage walls. One by one they slipped down from their perches between the glass shards tipping the cinderblock and slunk over to the tree. The pale cat stood on its hind legs and sniffed the base of the trunk. High in the branches, the pangolin squirmed and hissed. Maizie nudged the cat back with her toe. It sank its claws into her ankle.

The cats circled the base of the tree, lithe and blue, switching their kinked tails and rubbing their cheeks against the trunk. They slipped over the grass in a ring, padding around the tree, sniffing at the roots, arching backs and scratching the bark. A teenage girl who had been praying under one of the monk-trees watched them. She unfolded herself, revealing the beginnings of a belly, picked up a cat, and walked away. The rest of the cats followed her. She led them into the forest until only the tips of their tails could be seen, lifted above the bracken like periscopes.

"Jill, you're being very mature. I'm proud of you," said Sigrid.

Jill looked at the Aldrens, thrust out her chin, and wound herself around the tree, locking her arms and ankles and pressing her cheek to its bark.

"I'm protesting."

"I take it back," said Sigrid.

"You're being very dramatic, Jill," said Mrs. Aldren. "And you're not doing anyone any good. Come inside when you're ready. Maizie?"

Maizie, torn, followed Sigrid and Mrs. Aldren.

"Traitor!" yelled Jill.

Maizie did feel like a traitor. But she didn't know what else to do. She didn't want to be in Jill's thrall. Maizie would have preferred to sit in the grove, beneath all those fluttering mothers, holding the pangolin and complaining with Jill, but she couldn't stand up to people like Jill could. She followed whoever was strongest.

"Never mind her, Maizie," Mrs. Aldren said to her in an undertone as they passed under the trees, "I'm glad to have a chance to speak to you privately. Sigrid misspoke. You won't be leaving Chiang Mai."

She smoothed a wayward strand of Maizie's hair back from her temple and tucked it behind Maizie's ear.

"Only Jill is leaving. You'll stay."

Maizie craned her neck and studied Jill, still wrapped around the tree and singing the "The Times They Are A-Changin'" in her high, pure soprano. Jill was so brave, far braver than Maizie. The sight made Maizie sad. Jill's protests meant nothing. If she sat-in, their father could haul Jill to her feet. If she planted herself, he'd uproot her.

"Your father thought it was better I told you. He knows I'm fond of you. We all are."

"What about Jill?"

"We all feel she has an unwholesome influence on you. All this was confirmed after Jill induced you to run away from home."

"She didn't induce me," said Maizie. "We didn't run away,"

"The point is, no eleven-year-old girl should be wandering the streets at two o'clock in the morning intoxicated to the point of illness. Your parents think it might be better for each of you if you lived apart. You don't get along, your father says. You bicker constantly, I can attest to that."

"We get along," Maizie protested. "We only pretend-fight. It's not real. We get along, I swear."

"You're a good girl. Your father and your mother have decided that you will remain here, with him, and that your sister will live with your grandparents in Iowa. Chiang Mai international school only goes up to eighth grade, so there would be no place for her after this year anyway. It's for the best."

Adults always said that. As if they had any idea. Grownups merely said what was convenient, and what was convenient always denied a child's desire or anguish. Sometimes they insisted brightly, in response to your fear or despair, that "life isn't fair"; at others, "it will all work out." They would say, "I'm not a mind reader" and then tell you "I know you better than you know yourself." Above all adults loved to proclaim, with implacable certainty, that your worst, most shattering disappointments were always "for the best."

Separating her and Jill would not be for the best. How could it be? Without Jill she would be alone. And without Maizie, Jill would have no one to protect her from the things that hurt her. Maizie knew her better than anyone.

"I'm her best friend," said Maizie.

"Sisters should not be so dependent on one another. It's unhealthy. She'll make other friends," said Mrs. Aldren. "You both will."

Adults always said that, too. But sometimes you didn't. And even if you did, friends didn't count. Well, they counted, but they moved away, or you did. If Jill left Maizie now, she would finish high school and then go to college and then when would they see each other again? At the door Jill caught up to them, out of breath and tearful.

"I hate you," she said to Maizie. But when Maizie took her hand, Jill let her.

If Maizie pictured an orphanage, she thought of a narrow row house covered in ivy, looming in a pea soup fog in turn-of-the-century London. But the orphaned babies of Chiang Mai lived in a single low room, dim and hot. Why did heat make everything feel dirty? In Thailand, the more important you were, the colder you kept your rooms. Malls were cold; markets, hot. The fanciest places froze your breath: hotel lobbies, or the rose bower mausoleum of Nina Pub, where rich Thai people and diplomats ate. Charles Aldren, the American consul general, and his family kept their car and house bright and icy, chilled to polar perfection. But poor people, missionaries, Peace Corps, and many locals lived in sweltering boxes with cracks between the boards in the walls, through which insects and light wandered into rooms where sluggish fans refolded the heat. The orphanage was hot because the orphans were nobodies.

Maizie tried not to breathe the incense of too many babies crowded together: their evaporated sweat, pee, and tears. Two nuns with shaved heads and white robes smiled and beckoned her to follow them down the rows of cribs. Maizie had never seen so many babies all at once, a barracks of babies in rows of barred metal, three to a crib, all holding out their arms and howling.

Mrs. Aldren settled in a plastic chair, and a nun plumped a baby onto her lap. The baby reached up and grabbed Mrs. Aldren's Hong Kong pearls. She unfastened the strand and gave it to the baby to suck. Maizie liked her a little bit then. Sigrid bent and offered her braid to a baby lying flat on his back. The baby gripped it in its fist, gummed it. The baby next to him held herself and rocked.

Farther into the room, the smell intensified; a slick, putrid smell that Maizie could taste: unwashed bodies, overdue diapers, sickness, hunger, unchecked tears. Diarrhea, urine, vomit, sweat, and breath. The babies' straining muscles gave off a smell; their need gave off a smell, and her own anguish—that, too, produced a bitter odor. Loneliness had a smell. Neglect had a smell. All the baby powder in the world could not mask it.

"Why don't they take better care of them?" asked Jill.

"You're a bright girl. Do the math," said Mrs. Aldren.

Many of the children in the farthest cribs rocked themselves and turned their heads away when Maizie made eye contact. Their cribs shook. The ones who could stand pressed themselves against their crib rails and held out their arms, open-mouthed, their gazes following Maizie as she passed from one to the next, too appalled to pick them up. The ones who couldn't stand waved their fists and cried out for her. Their sweet black hair had been rubbed away in patches, and raw sores, which the flies would not leave alone, flocked the babies' scalps and backs.

The first nun unpacked the boxes the Americans had brought from the compound, bestowing a toy here, a sheet there. The air blurred with sound and movement. The babies' cries were not loud, and all the sadder for being so muffled, but the room felt thick with sound and hunger. Sigrid snuggled a baby, inhaled its neck. She kissed it in spite of its sores. Around her, the unheld babies squalled harder. Down the rows she and her mother went, cuddling, replacing, lifting, unpicking hands that gripped and would not let go, calmly kissing palms that rose from the bracken of arms and tucking them back, while the second nun plugged the chorus of red mouths with bottles filled with watery formula.

Jill and Maizie hesitated in the center aisle, stunned and helpless.

Sigrid exchanged a swollen diaper for a skinny one, tented the baby's wavering little penis as an arc of pee shot toward her. The babies reached out, so many, a thicket of arms and dimpled fists. Mrs. Aldren replaced the first baby. It struggled and cried when she set it down. She stroked its wet cheeks and plucked up its crib-mate. The baby struck at her neck like a hawk, sucking, tugging at her earlobes.

"They're so—" Jill began.

"Pick one. Then pick it up," Mrs. Aldren said. "They don't get picked up enough. Lying there flattens their skulls. They get

bedsores, too." She creamed a baby with a huge glob of ointment, swabbed its eyes with a Q-tip, put it down, moved on.

Maizie fished into Jill's bag for something to wipe the closest baby's nose. Maizie brought out a white men's undershirt,
ragged at the neck. She sniffed it. The T-shirts Jill had packed
were their father's. Maizie dabbed the baby's face. To her surprise, he laughed and swatted at the fabric. Breathing through
her mouth, Maizie hauled the baby up out of the crib. The other
babies wailed harder, reached harder. She hoisted the baby to
her shoulder and closed her eyes to shut out the weight of all
that wanting, but it pulled at her, tugged her off-balance. Maizie planted her feet and steadied the baby, swayed but didn't
fall. The baby clasped Maizie's hand with cool and sticky palms.
His mouth tugged powerfully at her pinkie.

"He's strong," she said to the nun. The nun smiled without
comprehension.

"Come here, Jill," said Mrs. Aldren. "Maizie, too. I want you
to meet someone."

Down the corridor of cots, at the back of the room, a door
stood ajar. From behind it came a heavy mechanical wheezing,
rhythmic and labored. Mrs. Aldren opened the door wider. "Go
in," she said.

Jill hung in the doorway. Maizie, too. The baby wiggled in
Maizie's arms. She held him against her shoulder, breathed the
slight buttery scent of his neck, and peered over his head into
the room. A tiny girl lay in a large box with tubes running out of
her mouth and nose. The baby's head bobbed against Maizie and
she peeked through his hair, taking in as little as she could of the
mangled child among the tubes. A huge, heavy machine grunted
in the corner. It puffed and wheezed, and drove the girl's lungs.

"Come in here, girls," said Mrs. Aldren, and Maizie sagged into a chair beside the girl in the box and adjusted the baby on her lap. Mrs. Aldren sat on the other side, combing the girl's thin hair. The child's fingers crabbed against her palms; her legs looked twisted, like her feet were put on wrong. Her naked chest was skin and ribs. Her eyes rolled back in her head, showing the whites, and her two little front teeth looked rabbity and dry. Looking at her made Maizie's lungs ache.

Behind her, Jill swore softly.

"We come here every week," said Mrs. Aldren. "Otherwise, she doesn't get touched."

"Why are you doing this to us?" Jill asked Mrs. Aldren. "Why did our dad make you do this?"

This time Maizie followed Jill outside. The baby rode against Maizie's shoulder, blinking and grimacing at the sudden sun. As Maizie waded into the shade of the grove he relaxed against her and stared up at the shifting light and leaves. When a series of farts rippled out of his backside, he squawked in surprise. Jill lay splayed out under the offering tree, winding strands of her hair into truculent braids.

"It's horrible in there. The smell."

Maizie agreed.

"How come no one cares?"

Maizie jiggled the baby and said nothing.

"We're not leaving the pangolin here."

Jill wanted things so much, but she never had any idea what to do. How would she manage without Maizie? Maizie wanted to tell her the news, but Jill rarely gave Maizie a chance to speak. Now she scrambled up the tree, and all the photographs danced. She had marked the pangolin's branch so carefully with silver beads, but when she reached the spot, the beads came away in her fist and nothing else was there.

Shade passed into shadow and a rising wind shook Jill in her perch. Rain hit the tree in a gust, sweeping down ornaments and photographs. It knuckled Maizie's skull and left wet blisters on the baby's face.

"Come down, Jill," said Maizie.

Rain pummeled the grove, plastered the robes to the trees, flung flowers and leaves and sticks.

"Jill!"

Up in the tree, Jill shouted and stormed above the wind and reports of branches breaking.

"Why can't we ever be like other people? Things *work* for other people."

Maizie felt herself uncouple from Jill and float free. Jill had so much energy. Maizie should be back inside with Sigrid and Mrs. Aldren; she should take the baby in out of the storm. Maizie bent her neck over the baby, hunched into the rain, and waded through the grass. The rain fell into the baby's red wailing mouth, jeweled his hair. She left Jill there in the grove, still searching.

Inside, the smell assaulted her and she wanted to run back out into the rain, but she handed off the baby to be dried, then barreled through to the girl who lay crooked-limbed and hooked to the hulking respirator. The machine pushed air into the girl, breathing for her. Maizie forced herself to sit still, to lean in, to pick up the girl's skeletal hand.

Jill stormed in, sopping. Maizie could see that Jill had rolled the pangolin in her sleeve as she'd seen men do with cigarette packs and then pulled her wet hair over her shoulder in an attempt to camouflage the bulge. The nuns swarmed Jill with sweetly alarmed coos. They dried her hair and wound it in a limp yellow towel, and draped another towel patterned with Minnie Mouse across her shoulders. Jill glowered at Maizie from under her turban.

Sigrid handed Jill a clean diaper and pointed to the nearest crib.

"I can't," said Jill. "I hate it here. So does Maizie."

Maizie didn't hate it the way Jill did. Thailand was like a game that Maizie was learning to play and Jill wasn't. It made her feel queasy and proud to know she was better at it. Not as good as Mrs. Aldren and Sigrid, but better than Jill, who hid in the grove and had to act like she knew everything because she didn't really know what to do about anything.

Rain pounded the windows and roof, and the orphanage went dark. Babies wailed. Sigrid came over with headlamps on elastic bands dangling from her hands.

"Put these on," she said. "Hurry."

"What happened?" asked Maizie.

"Brownout. But the backup generator isn't working. Probably someone stole the diesel and sold it. Mother is going out to siphon the truck."

Jill stamped her foot, shook her head like a dog so the towel unwound and fell to the floor.

"I. Can't. Stand. This."

"Jill, you can feel things or you can do things. If you're going to have hysterics, come with me and sit in the car," said Mrs. Aldren.

Jill shoved the headlamp over her hair and shut up.

"Maizie, Jill, we need your hands."

A nun lit a candle next to Maizie's face. Its light wavered over the girl, who was no longer breathing. The nuns unhooked her respirator with the swiftness of long practice. They prayed while one clamped the bag valve mask over the child's face and the other squeezed the oxygen bulb, demonstrating how to accordion air into the tiny lungs. The girl's chest rose and fell, frail in the trembling of the candle flame. A nun placed Maizie's hands around the mask, showing her how to cup the child's jaw with her fingers, to keep the seal tight with the heels of her hands and her thumbs. The other showed Jill how count the breaths while pumping the bulb. They hurried off to attend to the other orphans.

Maizie and Jill shined their lamps into each other's eyes other across the body of the girl.

"I found him. No thanks to you," Jill said.

Maizie bent her head to cut the glare. She saw the pangolin shifting against Jill's shoulder, struggling against the fabric that wound it in place.

Jill's hands squeezed, pumped.

"It's scratching me," said Jill.

Crawl away, Maizie willed it. Disappear.

"I think it's slipping," said Jill. She lifted a hand to adjust it.

Could you love someone and still be horribly, absolutely separate from her?

The girl wheezed. Her wasted legs twitched, and her chest labored.

"Why didn't you help me?" Jill asked.

Maizie could not explain. Her hands ached from clamping the mask over the child's lax and sweaty face.

"It was gone," she said.

"It wasn't," cried Jill. "I found it."

"You're not counting the pauses right," said Maizie.

"She's never going to wake up."

"Pay attention," said Maizie.

"There are too many babies. No one cares."

Jill was wrong. Mrs. Aldren, and the nuns, and Sigrid, and even she, Maizie, cared. Because here they were. And Jill. Jill cared so much that she thought she had to fight to the death or else give up. Jill would say anything less was nothing, worse than nothing. Not enough was the same as nothing, so why bother? Even if they came every week, like Sigrid, like Mrs. Aldren, there were too many and too few. And the things they did were nothing because they weren't enough.

The girl beneath their hands didn't wake, wouldn't wake, but as long as Maizie held the mask in place and Jill squashed the air bulb, at least she would breathe.

"God," said Jill, "what does it matter?"

"It matters," said Maizie.

"It doesn't mean anything."

"It doesn't have to mean anything to matter."

"Yes it does! Otherwise, what's the point?"

Maizie's palms were growing slick. A charley horse seized her biceps, and the mask slipped from the girl's face. Maizie slid it back, biting her lip in pain. Jill pumped, squeezed, pumped, squeezed. It was so hot.

The pangolin worked its way free of Jill's shirtsleeve and tipped out onto the bed. Mrs. Aldren's headlamp loomed over them, lit the struggling girl and the rosy face of the baby pangolin blinking in the sudden glare. She replaced Jill's hands on the respirator with her own, and gave both sisters a look of terrible, absolute disgust. Jill scooped the pangolin up and gathered it to her. The sprung elastic of her headlamp had come loose and it dangled over one ear, lighting her jaw, which she'd set to keep from crying. Jill's face was flushed, and little curly tendrils of hair sprang into her damp and furious eyes.

Maizie felt very protective of her. Jill always shouted, at the height of her frustration with Maizie, with their father, or their mother, that she wished she were an only child. And now she would be. They both would be.

Jill cuddled the tiny pangolin and refused to look at Mrs. Aldren or at Maizie. How could anyone think Jill was bad, when she was simply angry? Her anger and her goodness were the same. When her anger flared it only lit her goodness more brightly. She was good and she was right to be angry. No one bothered to ask Jill why she was angry, or what about. They didn't see that her rage was a futile demand for love.

"I love you, Jill," said Maizie.

The lights dawdled on. The nuns hooked the little girl back onto her electric respirator, and only Maizie's sore arms and drenched church clothes told her anything had happened at all. Jill carried the pangolin, in open defiance, back to the consulate vehicle. Mrs. Aldren let her.

They piloted the car in neutral down the mountain with the windows down to save what was left of their gas. When they reached the switchback where the pangolin's burrow had been, the boy surfaced from a ditch and flagged the car. He shouted in rapid Thai, frantic and out of breath, pounding the windshield. Dust and tears muddled his face, and red streaked the windshield where his raw palms beat.

"What?" Maizie asked Sigrid. "What's he saying?"

"She woke up," said Sigrid, horrified.

The boy pounded harder. Mrs. Aldren and the driver scrambled out, both speaking to the boy at once. The tones and syllables pattered over Maizie and Jill like a cloudburst.

"Who woke up?"

Maizie was still thinking of the little girl. Confused, she craned her head out the window. A few yards ahead, the boy's father lay absolutely still on the road, with the enormous pangolin locked around his throat.

"He was carrying it draped around his neck. They thought the adult pangolin was dead," said Sigrid, "but she woke up. You saw how they curl into balls when they're frightened."

Jill slid open her door.

"Stay there!" Mrs. Aldren booted the door back.

"Don't look," Sigrid said, and pressed the master button that slid the windows up. As the tinted glass rose they glimpsed Mrs. Aldren and the driver crouched over the motionless man. Head and tail, they tugged on the pangolin. The man's head lolled back and forth, but the pangolin had clamped herself and did not budge.

"This is all Dad's fault," said Jill.

Mrs. Aldren returned with the driver. The driver spoke into the dispatch radio, more Thai rumpled by static, the answering voices spiky and surprised. Though everyone speaking Thai sounded surprised to Maizie.

"Our driver will take you girls to the bottom of the mountain," said Mrs. Aldren. "There will be a car waiting to take you home. Another car will come for Sigrid and me."

"Is that man dead?"

Mrs. Aldren didn't answer. Instead, she leaned in and took

the baby pangolin away. Mrs. Aldren carried the baby over to its mother, who stirred, feebly. Blood oozed from a wound in the pangolin's head, and she listed as she unwound herself from the supine man. The driver put a hand on the boy's shoulder and drew him away, and Mrs. Aldren set the baby on the base of its mother's tail. The pangolin's tail rose to curl over her infant.

Neither girl spoke for the rest of the drive. When they reached their compound gates, Jill turned to Maizie.

"I'm glad we're leaving. Aren't you?"

"No," said Maizie, sounding surprised.

BEASTS AND CHILDREN

L ate one July afternoon, two weeks after Gerald Ferrell Jr. turned six, his mother sat him on the steps of their porch, popped the dents out of the buckled screen door with the toe of her Sunday shoe, turned her key in the lock, hitched up her purse, and left him for good.

When she leaned over him to kiss the top of his head he smelled her broken mixture of new-spritzed perfume, breath mints, and the sharp brown pine needle scent that enveloped her after she'd been crying. She balanced a stack of baloney and an orange on the step below his feet. Then she stuck an envelope in the top pocket of his overhauls *my little mailbox* and he barked at her *now puppy, don't bite the mailman* and then she petted the crown of his head where his cow-lick stood up like a red Indian feather. *Jerry, I want you to sit right here and count up to six hundred and back down again. Can you do that for me? I know how well you count. By the time you get done, your father will be home.*

She slid into a shiny car he didn't recognize with a brand-new Reagan/Bush sticker pasted to the bumper, and the car drove her away. But his father planned to vote for Mondale.

A mosquito lit on his finger, took shivering little sips.

Mississippi one

Mississippi two

Wind in the fields fletched with corn. Sound of the blood in his ears.

Missisippi three

Jerry stared at the deep ruts the car had left on the empty gravel track. The click of the car door as it closed on her repeated itself in the stillness. He felt the long white envelope tick against his chin when he turned his head.

Mississippi seventy-two

He tired of counting and he didn't know what else to do, so he picked a few specks of dirt off the naked pink surface of the baloney and unstuck the first slice from its cushion. His favorite part was unpeeling the red string from around the edges. The baloney was mushy and comforting in his mouth.

A few minutes later Jerry sat tinseled over with red string, sucking thin grease from his fingers. His mouth felt raw and buttered. The orange glowed like a little planet by his feet. He dug at the peel with his fingers, but since he bit his nails down to nubbins *aw let him Linda it's cheaper than candy* they couldn't break through the waxed skin. The orange popped away from him and rolled in the dirt. He chased it, buffed it on his britches, and turned it over in his fingers. His mouth felt salty and slick. He burped and blew out the thick meaty aftertaste.

Jerry set an eyetooth against the skin and gnawed, but his teeth grated the surface feebly and the peel coated his tongue

with a poison taste. He needed to split that orange, to pop a segment between his teeth so the juice squirted over his tongue. He
rubbed his eyes. The zest off the peel stung and his eyes teared
up but it wasn't really crying. It wasn't crying but why hadn't
she fixed his orange like always? She always cut a starter slit in
every orange she gave him, cut a little flap with her green paring knife. How could she leave him an orange he couldn't peel?

The orange was heavy and round. The blue date stamp was
smeared and he couldn't read the numbers, and he realized he
shouldn't have stopped counting. The car that drove her off
was gone. His orange wouldn't peel and he'd lost track of his
counting and now he wouldn't know when his father would
come.

What if he didn't come?

This scared Jerry so much, he couldn't breathe. He would
be left here forever on the steps with a bad taste in his mouth
and a useless orange.

His crying bounced off the gravel and the trees drank it up.
He sobbed down at the tips of his shoes, at his laces in half-
bows. His feet didn't look right. His voice didn't sound real
when he was the only one who heard it crying. He could cry
forever and no one would come.

His father came up the walk. Jerry's relief was sharp and
total, and almost immediately replaced with indignation. He
cried harder, although by this time he was forcing it. It felt good
to force it. His father would be sorry.

His father was smiling because it was Friday. His mom always said that smile looked like a fistful of loose change. That
made his dad laugh and she'd say, "Jackpot!" Sometimes they
would kiss.

His father carried a Styrofoam spit cup and pecked tobacco into it. The late-afternoon sun flamed on his cartoon-colored hair.

"What's all this, boy?"

Gerald Ferrell Sr. cut his eyes over to the locked door, then to the thick green line of snot on his son's upper lip. Except for the occasional spatter of chew in his cup, he was quiet for a long time.

Finally he said, "Wipe your nose."

Jerry snotted across the back of his wrist.

"Now tell me what's going on."

Jerry held out the orange.

His father looked at the house again, set down his spit cup, and hunkered. He took the orange from Jerry and considered it.

"Time I showed you how a *man* peels an orange."

He twanged the "man" to make Jerry laugh, but Jerry only twitched his mouth, a muscle-smile his father didn't notice was fake. His daddy wrapped his fist around the orange (he bit his nails too; there was grime in the quicks) and set it on the step just below. He leaned over. Jerry leaned too, looking sideways at his father, at the yellow pouches under his eyes, the grain of burn and stubble on his neck.

"Watch, now."

His father pressed the orange and rolled it back and forth, round and round, all over the top of the step.

"Now here's the secret, son. You loosen the skin, see? You try. Push down real good and let her roll."

"That's it. Use both hands if you have to."

Jerry leaned on the orange and rolled it.

His father hooked a finger deep into the orange and worked the first bit of peel free.

"Now try her."

The skin came away in easy chunks.

His father slid the envelope out from Jerry's top pocket and slit the flap with his key. Jerry broke the orange carefully down the seam.

Jerry stayed put when his father stumped up the steps, paused at the screen door to push in a loose tack, and unlocked the house.

Well, where'd she go?

She say anything to you?

I had no idea. Not one goddamned idea.

You don't know or won't say? You're her best friend, Karen. Was it that fucking real estate guy? Am I right?

Yeah, no. Jerry seems fine. Look, just forget it. No. Yeah. Forget it, I said! Jesus!

He came back with a can of beer and sat on the step beside his son. His knees popped. Then the beer tab. His throat made a series of thick, satisfied glugs. He wiped his mouth by shrugging a shoulder against his lips, and set the can between his shoes. And then he started to cry.

Frightened, Jerry looked at the mess he had made on the porch—jagged triangles of peel, and red scribbles of plastic baloney string. He cupped the orange segments in his lap and carefully, so as not to disturb his father, scooped bits of peel and stacked them inside one another. He squared them into a nice neat tower, then picked baloney string from the cracks in the step, from the legs of his pants, from the gravel, wadded them into a nest, and tucked them into the uppermost bit of peel.

The paper crackled. His father's fingers caught the edges of the sheet and crumpled it into a ball, one-handed. Jerry snuck an orange segment and held it between his teeth without breaking the skin. His lips stretched tight around it. His father took Jerry's chin and tipped his head up to make Jerry look at him. His father's eyes were red and his whole face looked itchy. The lines around his eyes were wet, and a tobacco flake, suspended in a little drop, hung at the side of his mouth. Jerry's eyes bugged a little from holding his mouth around the orange.

His father rubbed his nose with one hand, cleared his throat.

"Your mother's gone off."

Jerry bit down. Juice burned the back of his throat, and he started to choke.

"Chew," said his father.

Jerry chewed mightily; the orange turned to pulp, bitter and stringy. He spat it into one hand, coughing.

"Give it here."

His father smoothed out the note and held it toward Jerry. Jerry tipped the mess, which clung briefly, like snot, to the underside of his palm, and onto the letter. His father crammed it into his spit cup. He took the parted halves of the orange out of Jerry's lap and threw them down the gravel track as far as he could.

They watched TV until the flag came on and the anthem played, and then they watched the colored test pattern until his daddy said he couldn't stand the whining and who picked those colors anyway and he shut off the set. The color winked down to a dot and then the living room was solid dark and so quiet that Jerry shivered.

"You can sleep with me tonight. If you want."

"Okay."

They lay in his parents' waterbed. The pillow smelled like

his mother, her crying smell, which was a little sugary—like when he used to wet the bed, but nicer—and he buried his face in the pillow and tried not to throw up, because every time his father shifted in the bed big billows tossed Jerry and made his stomach lurch. He used to love the waterbed, loved to bounce in the middle and get that flying feeling until his father told him to quit unless he wanted what-for, which he would get if he popped the damn bed. Now his father turned over so often that the bed rippled like a gluey earthquake and there was nothing to hold on to but the pillow that smelled like his mother. The room was too dark and he felt like he was falling with nothing to catch him and then he couldn't help it, he threw up. Pink foamy curds all over the pillow so it smelled sour like baloney and oranges and he started to cry and rolled to the floor with the pillow clutched to his chest covered in throw-up and he crawled with it into the bathroom and was sick some more.

His father's hand cupped the back of his neck, set a Dixie cup of water to his lips. The smell of beer and chew made Jerry sick again. He drank some water after, swished miserably, spat, and watched the bubbles spiral on the bright blue surface of the toilet water.

"My turn," his father said, and peed.

"Gimme that."

He took the pillow, stripped the case, threw it in the bathtub, ran the faucet, hard, to dissolve the chunks. He left it there in a puddle. Then he rammed the pillow into the tiny trash can under the sink, but it refused to be contained; even when he stamped it down it rose back up, smeared and shadowy.

• • •

The next morning his father switched off the cartoons, poured Jerry some Grape-Nuts and told him to eat them quick because they were going out on the route.

"But it's Saturday."

"So?"

"How come you're working on a Saturday?"

"Who wants to wants sit around the house all day?"

"I can't eat Grape-Nuts fast. They hurt my mouth."

"Add more milk."

"It tastes like kitty litter."

"Add sugar."

Jerry glanced up at his father, who unscrewed a fresh can of Skoal and sat there looking at the tobacco like he couldn't remember what to do next.

"You're not eating."

"I'm grown."

Jerry scraped the contents of the sugar bowl onto his cereal. His father didn't seem to mind. He stirred slowly, still watching his father, and then dug a crater in the cereal and plunged his spoon to the bottom of the bowl. He brought up a spoonful of silvery grains of wet sugar without a single speck of cereal, and he put it in his mouth.

His father took Jerry around to the paddy wagon and had him sit up front with the seatbelt cutting into his neck. He had never spent this much time alone with his father. He thought he should feel happy.

Jerry's dad got a call and so they went driving through the green summer blur out to a field with big spotted cows that looked stupid and friendly. Jerry loved animals and cars just like his dad. Jerry's dad told him to unbuckle and hop out and follow him. His dad walked over to the bobwire fence and paced along it until he came to a soggy cardboard box sitting on a patch of clovers. Jerry started looking for a four leaf but his father pointed to the box and told him to look inside.

Jerry reached in cautiously and the puppy wriggled and licked his hand. Its tongue felt like a smart wet feather and licked him all over every finger. The puppy bit him, which tickled. Jerry laughed.

"Quit that," said his father, and Jerry knew he meant it.

"Give it here. We keep them in the back."

His father took the cardboard box and Jerry followed him to the van. His father flung the doors open. Inside it was dark and empty. The cages jingled.

Jerry's father took the puppy and locked it in the racketing back. When the doors slammed, the puppy howled like it wanted to die. Jerry's father told him to buckle up and never mind. He threw the van into gear. Still the puppy cried *ai ai ai* and then drew out into long sobbing *ooooo*s. Jerry held his ears but even then he felt it in his chest, in his head, behind his eyes. He caught a view of himself in the side mirror and his face looked small and sad.

His seat belt was too tight. He fussed with the button but he was too little to get it to work right. He struggled to get free and he tried not to cry. But the harder he struggled against the seat belt, the more certain he was that he was going to cry. And he did.

"Goddammit." His father stopped the van.

"You leave that belt alone this minute. You can't come with me if you're going to cry. This is life I'm showing you. Only dogs cry. Not men. And we're men. Right? Am I right?"

Jerry took a big shuddering breath and said that he was.

When his father dealt with the big dog, Jerry stayed locked in the van. He watched everything through the windshield, his father wielding the wire loop and snagging the dog around the neck, pulling it tight, the dog's tongue snapping between its teeth, legs buckling, and his dad dragging it into a cage. In the back, the dog went wild. It snarled. It scratched the wire. It barked big mean barks like it wanted to chew right through all the metal, and Jerry heard thuds that meant it was throwing itself against the cage doors trying to get at his father, to get at him, to get out.

They drove for a while, way out along a road that threaded through big white trees, and pulled up alongside a brown and black dog tied to a mailbox.

His father hopped down out of the truck's cab and with his wire loop slung over one shoulder went over to the dog. The dog looked directly up into his father's face and moved its tail up and down a little. His father set the loop in the grass and scratched the dog behind the ears. The dog sighed so hard even Jerry could see it through the windshield, and its tail moved faster. His father patted it again, brought a cage out of the back, and untied the dog. It bowed and stretched and came quietly into the cage.

Jerry listened but no new bark or howls joined the outcries that rose when his father slammed the back doors.

"Son of a bitch," his father said. He didn't start the van right away. He just sat looking at the empty collar and leash dangling from the mailbox.

"Somebody called that dog in. Said it was vicious and needed to be destroyed. It's just old. And they set him by the side of the road, like trash. Lied to cover their own ass."

He started the car.

"People," he said, "are no-good goddamn cowards. Am I right?"

Jerry said that he was.

On the last run of the morning, his father shot a dog.

It had been hit by a car and thrown onto the gravel at the shoulder of the highway.

It was a white dog but parts of it were pink and parts of it were— He knew about road kill but his mom always told him not to look and sped up so he never could see much. But this was a dog and his father stopped the car. He could see it. It was still alive. Jerry looked. His father shot it and Jerry looked.

"You all right?"

His father stuck his head in through Jerry's window. He leaned across Jerry to rummage in the glove compartment. He snapped on a pair of latex gloves.

Jerry nodded.

"Good boy."

His father went back over and picked up the dog. The animals in the cages were absolutely quiet when he slung it in the back.

Back at the shelter, Jerry's father showed him the little fridge that held his mayonnaise sandwiches. They nestled in a crumpled brown bag next to some cans of store-brand cola and a rack of mysterious glow-green cylinders.

"Have a sandwich if you get hungry. You're allowed half a Coke. *Half.* But don't touch anything else. That green stuff's called FatalPlus. It's not Gatorade."

"C'mon, I'll give you the tour. This here's Reception."

Jerry stopped to look at a colored poster of a dog's big heart oozing like a colander full of spaghetti.

"Heartworms," said his father.

Heartworms, Jerry whispered. He felt a thrill of disgust imagining his own heart threaded through with flat, eyeless worms.

Jerry's father led him down one short hall banked with cages of cats. Some curled up in unhappy knots in their litter boxes and glared. A few opened their mouths and cried tiny noiseless cries.

"Don't touch them, son. C'mon. Hustle it up."

At the end of the hall stood three doors.

"Never open these doors unless I'm with you and I say. The last one's locked anyway. And this first one goes out to the dog pens. You don't want to go near there. Am I right?"

Jerry said he was. The dogs scared him, with their open mouths, their ruffled inner jowls the color of raw meat, the pebbles of spit hanging on their tongues, their big teeth.

His father opened to the second door quick and then shut it again. It didn't latch right and Jerry watched it steal open behind his father, who didn't notice.

"Supply closet. Nothing in there for you."

His father didn't say anything about what was behind the locked door. It was a big metal door, heavy and thick, with a coat of paint the color of canned peas, all scratched over with big silver grins. Jerry spotted two light bulbs, a red one and a green one, up above the top of the door, and his father let him play with the switch. STOP, GO. But he didn't offer to unlock the door. Jerry pressed his ear against it but heard nothing. Any animals in there kept silent.

"Don't touch the animals unless I say. And don't go giving them names. I catch you naming animals and you'll know why. Here." He unlocked a wire cage and drew out a small kitten. "You can play with this one while I deal with the dogs out in back. Pet her like I showed you last time. Soft. Don't squeeze her. And don't give her a name."

Jerry went out to the waiting room and sat on the vinyl couch with the kitten in his lap.

She was shy, a tailless tortoiseshell. His mom called them "torties" and they were her favorites. She said they were magical because torties were always girls, never boys, not ever and wasn't that magic?

You could never be a tortie, pup.

But you're glad I'm a boy?

You're glad I'm a boy, am I right?

She said she was.

The tortie had one folded ear. She blinked at Jerry and butted his hand.

"Magic Kitten," he said. "You're a Magic Kitten."

He didn't mean it as a name so he wasn't really going against his father. Except when he looked at the kitten again, it *was* Magic Kitten. Maybe giving it a name was okay if he hadn't meant to?

Magic Kitten scaled down his leg like a squirrel and sniffed at his shoelaces. She batted the frayed ends, jumped up high, attacked again. Jerry picked her up and held her to his chest.

She climbed his shirt, bit an earlobe, purred under his chin. The tortie tickled his throat with her purrs. It made him feel good—strong, and big. She was knitted and fragile, and he could take care of her. When his mom came back he would give her Magic as a present.

Jerry heard the squall of the big cages as his father hauled them out of the van. The dogs made a ruckus. Magic Kitten hissed, puffed up like a dandelion, jumped sideways, and streaked down the hall. Jerry ran after her. Jerry saw her squeeze into the supply closet.

"Magic Kitten?" he whispered and edged the door wider. The closet was dark. His eyes adjusted, and Jerry glimpsed skulls and crossbones on giant white bottles. Something on the top shelf snagged his vision, a gleam, like cat's eyes.

"Magic?"

Jerry eased himself all the way in. His hand grazed, then steadied, a broom and he saw a clutter of cages, old towels and stiff sponges. And the high-up gleam again.

"Don't be scared."

He boosted himself to the first shelf. He climbed good if he didn't look down. He felt along the edge of the top shelf, trying to grab her by the neck if he could.

Something stung his hand, a quick hot flick along his palm. He pulled it back and it was all bloody, a long line of blood from pinky to thumb. He cried out and fell. The broom crashed into a bucket. His father came and yanked him out of the heap of towels and brushes and the cracked plastic bottle of bleach that had broken his fall.

His father caught his palm and looked at the wound and carried him out to the waiting room and painted it purple. He blew on it and closed it with three butterfly bandaids and Jerry didn't cry.

"All right. Wanna see what bit you?"

He took Jerry back to the supply closet and boosted his son so he could peer down at the uppermost shelf.

"Get a good look."

Not Magic Kitten, but stainless-steel saws.

"They're for cutting off heads."

"Like Granddad's deer?" Jerry thought of the brown buck's head that kept a lookout over his grandfather's TV.

"A potentially rabid animal is not a hunting trophy, son. No. They're for the dogs. Or raccoons, sometimes. Anything that might have a case of rabies. I pick up the carcass and saw off her head, send her head to the vet for tests."

Behind the first door, the dogs broke into a chorus of yelps. Jerry imagined their angry sawed-off heads, bounding on barking jaws, all red bloody tongues and bright teeth.

His father pointed out the smallest saw.

"That's the one that bit ya. Better to be bit by the saws then the dogs they're meant for. Remember what I told you about rabies?"

Jerry did.

"You know how bad one shot hurts, am I right? Just in the arm. Well, twenty-two shots in the stomach'll make that feel like your mother's kisses."

Jerry squirmed. His hand burned and he wanted down. The saws smiled at him.

The rest of the afternoon they sat and played Chinese checkers and waited for people to come in. Jerry lost the first game because he was afraid someone would arrive and adopt Magic Kitten. He fretted about it until his father told him, "Quit yapping. No one wants that kitten, I promise you."

The entrance bell jingled. His Aunt Karen.

Aunt Karen was his dad's sister and his mom's best friend. She sometimes came to their house and sat with Jerry's parents and drank beer. She was a nurse and she rescued animals. She didn't have a husband of her own or kids, which was probably why she had the energy to be such a good person, Jerry's mom said.

"Hey, brother, hey, Jerry Junior. What's new?" Aunt Karen caught herself, because his father turned red and even Jerry could tell she wished she'd said something different. To help her out he volunteered,

"I cut my hand on a rabies saw. And daddy shot a dog."

She turned to look at him. Her face was yellow, like a dried rose.

"Shot a dog?"

"It was hurt bad. He put it out of its misery."

"I see." Karen pushed the faded red hair out of her eyes and tried to look bright. She boosted a cardboard carton onto the counter.

"Jesus, Karen, more?"

Jerry stood on tiptoe to see.

More puppies. He was getting used to them.

Aunt Karen ran a hand over a pup's head.

"Bet you the farm they've got worms," said Jerry's dad.

"Hear from Linda?" Karen asked.

"I might ask you the same thing," his dad said.

Aunt Karen kind of stood there and started to pet a puppy but remembered about the worms. She drew back and put her hand in her pocket, and Jerry felt sorry for her. His dad must have too, because he picked up the box and headed out to the back. Aunt Karen followed him.

Once the dog door shut behind them Jerry snuck down the hall to see Magic Kitten. He peeked through the grid that held her water bowl and asked her to come to the front of the cage.

You shot a dog right in front of him?

Magic Kitten came up right away and rubbed her cheeks against the wire. He tickled Magic Kitten under her chin with his pinky and she purred.

He's got to learn.

Magic Kitten's purring was very loud in the hall. Jerry tried to make her hush, but she only purred louder. He swatted her on the nose. She recoiled.

"I'm sorry, Kitten! I'm sorry. Shhh, shhh, come on back."

The kitten turned her back on him and washed her shoulder.

She's not coming back.

And then a twanging metal sound and a high yelp and probably his father kicked a cage door or slammed his fist against it. The door flung back and his aunt came out with a hand in front of her face. She walked past Jerry with quick tight steps. The front bell jingled. Jerry heard Aunt Karen start her truck. Magic Kitten purred.

"Didn't I tell you to stay away from the animals?"

He grabbed Jerry's elbow and spun him down the hall. His grip hurt; Jerry felt fury buzz out of his father's fingers and into Jerry's crazy bone. His father's face was a strange red twist.

At reception, his father ducked behind the counter and ripped open a drawer so the contents rattled. He pawed through it, scattering tubes and boxes and packets wrapped in crackling cellophane.

"Some people think a lie is better just 'cause it makes you feel better. It's not. Hear me? It's not. Lies are worse than pain."

Jerry stood very still. He was too scared to even rub his elbow. It still hurt. His hand hurt. But he stood still and he did not cry. He stood still and watched his father tear the drawer apart.

His father found what he wanted, a sealed needle like a doctor's for giving shots.

"See this? It's a syringe. With a twenty-five-gauge needle."

Cellophane flashed on the counter. He held up the syringe. The needle grinned.

"One time I swallowed a quilting needle—nearly this big. I was your age. I went in crying to my mama and told her what I did. First she fed me mayonnaise sandwiches to cushion the needle and then took me out to my daddy and he whipped me for being dumber than a bag of hammers. I was so dumb, I thought that nothing, not even a big steel needle, could mess with my insides. I won't ever let you be that dumb. Hear? So take this."

He handed Jerry the syringe. It was lighter than it looked. Jerry's father reached into the fridge and brought out the sack of green cylinders.

"I'll teach you about needles."

He walked down the hall.

Jerry stood still. He still couldn't move. The syringe fascinated him. He tested the tip. He heard his father unfasten a cage, then his clipped steps, a key turning in a lock, and the squeal of a heavy steel door.

"Get in here!" called his father. "Turn on the red light and shut the door."

Jerry walked down the hall, hypnotized by the needle. He held it gently in both hands, like he was lighting his way with a candle. The door closed with a sigh and a click.

The room was empty except for a high, filthy window that showed a patch of sky. The dirt turned the summer dismal, and a grimy light fell on the wide steel counter in the center of the room. A torn corduroy cushion, the color of clay and dented with a deep groove, lay in the center of the counter. Orange, white, and yellow hairs wound in a snarl around the covered buttons. The rack of vials sat in front of the cushion. His father dragged a milk crate up to the counter.

"Step up on that and set the needle down," said his father. "And take her."

Jerry took the kitten and at once she began to purr and he knew she still loved him and wasn't mad that he swatted her.

"Set her on the cushion, son, make her stay still, and keep her calm."

Jerry looked into the tortie's eyes and begged her silently to hold still for his father. The tortie kneaded the cushion, sniffed a button, and tried to nurse. Jerry petted her.

"Keep petting, but watch me."

His father popped the big needle into a vial and drew the plunger. The syringe glowed in the dirty light.

"You're doing a real good job, son."

Jerry stroked the kitten's coat, gold spots on black.

"Now take this," said his father. He held out the needle.

Jerry drew back, although the tips of his fingers kept smoothing the kitten's fur. His father set a hand on the kitten's chest. The needle pointed up from his other fist like a poisoned spindle.

"Do what I tell you. Take it."

Jerry took it.

"Now, take a deep breath, and when you're ready, stick it in her, between my fingers and at the bottom of her belly."

Jerry looked at his father over the needle. Maybe this wasn't his real father. Maybe that's where his mom was. With his real dad. This man had a straight line for a mouth and red eyeballs. Jerry's father had blue eyes, and his teeth stuck out when he smiled. This man's teeth didn't show at all.

"You ready to make her sleep, son?"

This was a test. If he passed, his real father would come. His real father would rumple his hair so it turned to feathers and take him out driving to see his mom. But he didn't know what he was supposed to do. The kitten purred.

"Is she sick?" he asked the man. "She got rabies?"

"No. Just no one wants her."

What about me? Jerry wondered. I want her.

Maybe if he passed this test his real father would take him home and they would watch TV and eat cereal. His mom would come out of the kitchen with her hands wet from washing dishes and she would tickle them both and take their empty bowls.

"Go on, son. Send her."

But it was his dad. It really was.

And because it was, Jerry slipped the needle between the V of his father's fingers and pressed it to the spot on the kitten's belly.

"All the way in. Don't look at me. Do it."

Jerry pushed on the needle until it sank into the kitten.

"Little more. Now press down on the plunger. That's the top part."

The liquid eased down, out of the syringe and into Magic Kitten.

"Now she'll sleep."

Jerry withdrew the needle without being told and petted the kitten slowly. Magic Kitten breathed rapidly, twitched once, and then expanded her ribs with a big intake of breath, so long and slow it was like she was trying to take all the air out of the room and keep it inside her. He hoped to hear her purring but she let it out without any sound at all and then he knew she was dead.

"Pick her up."

"No."

"Do it."

Jerry bit his tongue and reached for the thing that was no longer Magic Kitten. He swung the limp body by the scruff, holding it as far from himself as he could.

"Follow me, and don't forget the needle."

The man led Jerry out into the hot blue day. (But it was his father. It was.) The air was full of flies. They walked through a back lot full of weeds and broken glass. (Maybe they were going to bury her. But his father didn't carry a shovel.) They stopped by a big metal box with a long word printed on it. He could only make out the first two letters, I-N, and it gave off smoke and a bad stink. A row of plastic barrels stood by. They also had long words printed on them that he couldn't sound out but they must be garbage because when his father pried off the lid Jerry smelled a sweet, sick smell, a shrimp cocktail smell, and the buzz of flies intensified.

"Toss her in."

Jerry looked down into the barrel.

"No!"

He dropped the dead kitten on the gravel and tightened his fingers around the needle. He shook his head over and over until he felt dizzy and his vision blurred and still he could see what was in that barrel, and beyond that, his father, standing unshakeable and so tall he took up the whole world.

"You gonna toss her, or do I have to make you?"

"I want my mother."

"You can't have her."

"I want her!"

"She doesn't want you."

Jerry swung the syringe back and stabbed his father in the thigh.

"I hate you!"

He rammed the needle straight down with all his force, sawing past the heavy denim to fight it into the muscle. Jerry heard his father howl, and with savage joy he pressed the plunger.

The needle quivered in his father's leg.

Jerry had never seen his dad look so surprised. The flies buzzed and a single tree moved in the wind. His father staggered, looked Jerry full in the face, and shook his head. He took in one big breath and held it, and Jerry knew he was about to die.

"I'm sorry, Daddy!"

He sprang at his father, yanked on the needle, but it was

wedged too deep in the leg. His father batted him away, hollered LEAVE IT, but Jerry, sobbing, snatched at it, caught hold, and wouldn't let go.

"Please don't die!"

His father clipped him across the ear. Jerry crumpled and fell on the gravel next to the dead cat. His father pulled the syringe from his leg, gave one sharp bark, and threw it in the barrel. He reached down, and caught Jerry by the scruff. He hauled him up and held him high above the barrel. Jerry kicked and his shoelaces whipped the barrel's rim. He squeezed his eyes tight so he wouldn't have to look down—no matter what his father did to him he would never look at the soft and stiffening heap, the dry tongues caught in dull teeth, at the eyes, all the eyes blank and astonished and staring at nothing, at nothing like sleep.

"I'm trying," his father cried, "to make you smart. Nobody taught me. Nobody showed me what things are like. I just want you to be smarter than me."

His father gathered Jerry to him and held him tight.

"That's all I want. Just be smarter than me."

He set Jerry on his feet. Jerry buried his face in his father's thigh. He opened his eye a crack and looked at the puncture in the denim where a little red bead was welling up. He closed his eyes again and moved his cheek to cover the hole.

"Jerry. Gerald. You're hurting my leg."

Jerry kept his eyes squeezed shut. When he felt his father move away from him he expected to be scared, but the ground held him up. Still, he couldn't open his eyes. As long as he kept them closed there were no barrels, no kitten, just the ground holding him up and the sound of the flies and the softer brush of the wind and his father close by. He stood in a warm darkness and felt the light move against his lids. It was a different dark than at night. He wasn't scared, and he wasn't waiting for the morning. Any time he wanted he could let in the light.

CATASTROPHIC MOLT

The year Mother died, Carline and I were barely out of adolescence, and we took her entirely for granted. We had no idea she had terminal cancer, or that she'd just lost a lover. She had been hiding her inner life from us for so long still that we assumed she didn't have one. She worked hard, she indulged a serious perfume hobby, she mentioned a pen pal with whom she corresponded about perfume, a man in Maryland, but we thought this was mere quaintness on her part and not a sign of any serious attachment.

We did not know that late in her life our mother discovered a great and secret gift, a talent so rare that had she trained it, she could have tripped down paths that were strewn with roses. She was that rare olfactory savant, a supersmeller. The same lover who apprised her of this gift, a U.S. Navy linguist and perfume hobbyist named Laurence, a lover she kept secret from us and from everyone, a very short time later discovered a mole with irregular margins on her right shoulder blade, just under the graze of his lips. But he noticed it during their leave-taking lovemaking, and the sadness of parting blotted everything else out—all other alarm, all pleasure—so though she promised to get it checked, she had more pressing irregularities to attend. She waited until it was too late; the mole was malignant so the melanoma metastasized, and the radiation treatments took her sense of smell away almost entirely. Later the cancer eventually and then rapidly took her life.

Carline and I had to piece all this together from fragments long after Mother died, and time and experience have proved that most of my understanding of those closest to me is fictitious. This grieves me. It also grieves me that our mother skidded from us before we had a chance to grow up enough to know her. All our lives Carline and I would sit around and analyze her to death and feel so wise and solid in our tale-telling. But she always contradicted us while she was alive. That moment of shock when you realize how separate you and the other person really are? Its temperature never deviates, the chill.

Carline is terrible with money. I should know; I do her taxes. Carline is always calling me to brainstorm "alternate income streams." Sonny needs orthodontia, she phoned today and told me, so she was finally going to unlock Mother's osmothèque.

Mother's osmothèque was deeply private and Carline had always been after it. Mother haunted estate sales and duty-free shops and amassed dozens of bottles of pure *parfum*. It was just a standard five-drawer filing cabinet named for the famous scent library near Paris. In it Mother filed perfume tester strips in small plastic bags, and it was where she stashed her sample vials, perfume nips, her pipettes and funnels. The thing was a sneeze detonator—it reeked of oak moss. I don't know how Mother kept all the scents straight. From time to time she urged a sample on one of us, telling me that with my skin chemistry I should steer clear of Chanel because on me it turned fecalic, but try anything by Caron—a little old fashioned but those old formulas were masterpieces. And Carline should always wear Guerlains because whatever her skin did to the Guerlainade accord was beyond divine.

When we were children she took her keen nose for granted—eyes in the back of her head was how she explained it, though really she could sniff out absolutely anything.

"Cissy, dear, you're getting sick," she would say, although I felt perfectly fine. "You're sending off cinnamon and carnation. Stay home and drink orange juice today."

Lo and behold, by the middle of the morning I'd be sweating into blankets in fulfillment of her curse, blighting blossoms of Kleenex with caterpillars of snot. Carline tried to fool her—rubbed cinnamon and vanilla all over her chest—but Mother simply called her Snickerdoodle and sent her to school.

"Cissy, dear, is something bothering you?" Mother could smell anxiety, *wet pennies and decaying flowers,* and sadness, *below the level of comparison, but it's a raw umber smell, if that makes sense.* It didn't.

"Her olfactive detection skills aside, her supernose turned us kids into paranoid clean freaks," says Carline. "With Mother sniffing my bra straps every few seconds and saying *Maybe you should shower, dear* and slipping me some Kotex on the sly—and forget about sneaking cigarettes or a nip or stealing a kiss—she couldn't just smell *if* we'd been kissed. She could smell *who*."

"That's whom, dear," I said.

Mother's nose could only be defeated by the massive *sillage* of cheap perfume. In high school I wore scent as a mask and an annunciation. My moving veil of molecules cussed a blue streak in the air. If it came in a novelty flask shaped like an owl or a mouse-bride bearing an orange flower bouquet, if it were packaged under a plastic five-and-dime dome of any stripe, it blew out her sense of smell.

"Cissy, you're no better than a vindictive tomcat," Mother said, in the throes of an aldehyde migraine. "At least use decent juice."

The cheap perfume gave me headaches too, but at least I knew I was there. If I couldn't look like Carline and Mother, I could at least trail fumes. It was my olfactory graffiti—Kilroy was here—I, Cissy, passed through your territory, you beautiful ones, and you did not catch me.

At her death, Mother willed the osmothèque to Carline (the marginally less philistine daughter), its key sealed in a big square envelope. The tiny key weighted the corner of the envelope, which was cream-yellow and big enough to sleeve an Easter card. Over the years, Carline had lifted it to the light many times; she had memorized the stubby shape of the key, the precise angles of its little teeth, but the paper stock was so thick that she couldn't be sure the envelope held any other message, any note. The osmothèque banged her hip each time she took a load of laundry down to the basement, and it smelled, on rainy afternoons, like our mother—the lining of her leather trench coat, the inside of her makeup bag.

Carline found this disturbing and she hated the squat metal cabinet quietly for many years. She covered it with a polyester afghan, she piled boxes on top of it—Christmas ornaments and appliance cartons—and eventually the afghan grew manky and the smell of years of laundry and damp mingled with the faint perfume signatures. But it was heavy to move, so Carline bore the barked shins and unsettling whiffs that wriggled and ghosted from the cabinet. On some level she felt she owed Mother the queasiness and the bruises.

An idle afternoon's drifting in the bayous of eBay had taught her much about the value of perfume.

"It's a gold mine," she said to me.

"Seriously? A cabinet of turned perfume?"

"That's a myth. Perfume doesn't go bad; it just evaporates. But if it's kept in the right conditions—storage, for example—it's still good! You know what a bottle of Hermès Doblis fetches on eBay? Neither do I, because they don't exist anymore! That's how rare it is. But Mother wore it. I remember her telling me that it was suede in a bottle. And L'Heure Bleue—the caramelly sad one that she wore for evenings out when we were kids? A sealed Baccarat bottle of extrait fetches up to a grand. Who knows what-all else she has in there! And with partial bottles—I can auction them off or sell decants! Seriously, there are collectors out there who pay drug-addict prices for the vintage stuff. Sonny's overbite's going to be corrected by the House of Guerlain."

• • •

We crouched side by side before the osmothèque like middle-aged Bobbsey Twins at a pagan altar, the overhead chain still swinging from a hastily yanked light. Carline slit the envelope and cast it on top of the heap of cartons she'd swept to one side. She fitted and turned the key. The top drawer rustled open.

It was empty except for a composition notebook, a few pages penciled hastily. The second drawer revealed Mother's decanting paraphernalia, tester strips, and a sheaf of index cards hai-kued with the trippy purple prose Carline claims is par for the perfumista (*flaming june! Seared roses and the sweat of siesta-slumber; chypre in sari silks, trailing clouds of glory*). Flipping through them I wanted to cry—here is where our mother had stored her secret sweetness, an enthusiasm she hid from us—her normal reserve reversed into bursts of poetry so different from the notes in her Fannie Farmer cookbook (which she left to me) that drily amended the level of rosemary or suggested where butter could be halved or dispensed with entirely.

Carline opened the third drawer, pawed back the tissue paper, and drew out sealed packages of Vol de Nuit, Après L'Ondée, Mitsouko.

"I knew it," she said. "Gold mine. Now, Doblis, Doblis, come on Doblis."

"Maybe she used it all up. Anyway, she switched perfumes when we moved to California. Remember? Here."

I pulled out a tiny round flask with a black Bakelite narcissus stopper; dried perfume residue darkened the crystal.

"Narcisse Noir."

"Shoot! That stuff's worth a fortune. Are there any full bottles?"

"I always thought it smelled like grape bubblegum and communion wine."

"You have no nose, Cissy. It's black narcissus"—she read the note card—"*a white flower dipped in oblivion—it's a swoon.*"

"Mother never swooned in her life."

"Never mind, I can get fifty bucks for the empty bottle."

Carline dug out a jade-green cylinder covered in marbled leather with a long pale sage silk tassel drifting off the end.

She shuffled through Mother's note cards. "*Nuit de Noel. Original shagreen box. Shagreen is leather made from a shark's or ray's skin, and it has a pebbled, orbicular quality to the grain. Shagreen: the word derives from 'chagrin.'*"

"That's mine!"

"*Nuit de Noel. A coil of dark roses wreathed in myrrh. Melancholy. Awe. Pine needles woven into chilled fox pelts. Undertones of blood and birth, stabled in the cold, fragrant night. Lantern grease, frankincense, colostrum, and stars.*"

"Jesus, Mother."

Carline slid the box apart, shook one end gently, and the familiar black crystal bottle slipped into her palm.

"She *begged* me to wear that," I told Carline.

It was a purply-black bottle, one that suggested poison, or an elixir to heal a wounded heart. I never even opened it. I'd toyed with the Baccarat many times, twiddled the ground-glass stopper, traced the flapper's headband of silver ribbon around its neck.

Carline held the box out of reach while she consulted the price list she'd written on the back of her hand.

"Hundred bucks and it's yours again."

"Fine."

"What the hell is this?"

Carline peeked into the box, dug a finger deep into the bottom, and fished out a plastic bag containing a shriveled hank of what looked like a palm-size flake of nori.

I snatched it from her. I rolled up the trophy of catastrophic molt and replaced it inside the shagreen perfume box. Witty of Mother to hide her sealskin inside my sharkskin. And to indicate, using shagreen, her chagrin.

Our mother's inexplicable venom toward the elephant seal colony at Piedras Blancas was the first sign that something in her life might be amiss. I cannot deny that, as a species, elephant seals are boobyish creatures, natural butts. Their lives are entirely pointless. They're so large that they don't fear anything, and a human can walk right up to one and club it on the head, or shoot it point-blank. Their docility practically did them in, a century ago. At sea, they're solitary; on land, they form a lumpen mass, they pile on top of each other in heaps yet remain completely oblivious to one another. At sea, they eat constantly. On land, they starve, living off their fat reserves while lurking, mating, birthing, and nursing. The females don't rear their young like most mammals. They slip back into the surf at the earliest opportunity, already pregnant again. They head out for the open sea, where they will feed alone in the deep cold water. They make terrible parents.

Mother, elegant and frail-boned, was about as far from an elephant seal as you could get. Looking back, I suppose we should have been grateful that she vented her spleen and terror on a herd of foul-smelling pinnipeds, that she hurled her disappointments at seals rather than at her nearest relations. But at the time I took her jeremiads personally.

"If anyone identified with an elephant seal, it would be you, Cissy. But Jesus, give yourself a little credit," says Carline. "You're not *that* fat."

I'm not sure how long Mother had been hiding her pilgrimages to Piedras Blancas from us. Her long drives up the coast, which she claimed were to San Simeon to sketch the furniture, didn't really register with us. Little about her did. Carline and I were barely in our twenties at the time and inflated with the helium of self-regard. We bucked against the strings that tethered us to her. We must have seemed to her swollen with oblivious youth. In our defense, our mother concealed what was happening to her with all the power of the various cosmetics, spiritual and actual, in her considerable arsenal.

Mother's neat little instep trod the gumdrop path of sugar and spice. This path, Carline informs me, looks delicate but requires a ferrous backbone and a martyr's devotion to mortification of the flesh. Whatever ugliness Mother couldn't transcend she shrouded in emotional candy-floss. She marzipanned all her hatreds and smothered her disappointments in fluffy social nougat. Carline and I never questioned what these confectionaries might have cost her.

She had to learn to hustle after Daddy's death. In the ten years after our family's relocation to Pasadena she insinuated herself among the rich; she made her presence ubiquitous but welcome; she pushed. She'd had Danny to keep in boarding school, and then that last year, college. She "did" one or two minor celebrity houses. And she charmed her way onto showroom floors and enchanted buyers into carrying her line of furniture.

But it must have stung, that her own daughters could be so easily misled by superficial charm. Did she feel betrayed by our willingness to accept the surfaces she offered? By our lazy lack of perception? What can I say in our defense except that by that point Mother had become terminally chic.

She must have grown tired of waiting for us to notice either her failing body or her broken heart, because finally she shanghaied us on a Sunday when I had no classes and Carline could be persuaded to rise by noon. Mother drove us to Piedras Blancas to see the elephant seals. She insisted it was the safest way to indulge in schadenfreude.

"All of us need a little pepping up," she said. "Carline and her cattle calls. Cissy grinding away at her accounting. When you see the seals, you can't help but feel superior. As a metaphysical exercise it bucks me right up. Tones the system, like sea air. I ask myself, what kind of God would make an animal with a face that screams PENIS?"

Mother's frank use of the words "fart" and "penis" shocked us. Her genius for euphemism had been ascendant all our lives, and now her language appeared to be undergoing a violent eclipse.

"Seriously, it gives one pause. Ask yourselves, girls, what kind of God would fashion such sloppy, ill-considered creatures? Any way you look at them, metaphorically or literally, they are grotesque. There have size without majesty, power without grace. Their hideousness is unmitigated by the pacific, bovine appeal of, say, a manatee—they're brutal, they're stupid, they're smelly, they're freakishly docile and yet notoriously belligerent. They are always pregnant. They are nature's bowel movement, stunning only in their total and absolute lack of attraction. Pay attention, girls. They beg Blake's question, what immortal hand or eye could frame thy turdlike symmetry?"

In December pregnant females hide in the safety of the willows.

Mother read the signboard, then turned and gazed into the withy tangle along the dunes, searching for gravid seals. Although it was almost June and the sign assured us that the elephant seals birthed in March, Mother's look was so intent, I was half convinced that she could see the liquid shine of a cow's eyes peeping back at her. She knotted her fingers, the knuckles ochre-colored and gnarled, in an unconscious imitation of the willow scrub.

"I like that," said my mother. "You're so vulnerable in pregnancy. Animals know it. Women feel it. I bet that's why so many women love wicker."

I was never able to follow the leaps of my mother's mind.

The boardwalk through the dunes curved off and away, but we three huddled out of the wind by the glassed-off information board, reading pointlessly about plovers, red-legged frogs, and the elephant seal breeding season.

"The pups, Jesus, they have to teach themselves everything! What other mammal does that? Abandons her pups? They don't have anyone to show them how to swim, how to survive—they're just stranded. It's unforgiveable."

The wind picked up and carried to us the cries of the seal colony and the marshy smell of molting seals and sun-fermented seaweed. Carline retched and bound a little silk neck square over her nose. My eyes watered and I felt dizzy, but Mother leaned into the reek and took deep whiffs. She opened her mouth wide to let the stink gather on her tongue. She rolled it around her palate, chewed the air as a dog will chew it when you let it ride with its head out the car window. I noticed, with a shock, that she had sores on the inside of her mouth, terrible and raw.

The wind tore back her headscarf and crazed her flippy blond wig. Of course I knew she was wearing a wig—but Mother often wore wigs, many women did in those days. She had a whole collection, real human hair, every length and hue. When the wind skirled off with the wig I saw that underneath it she hadn't bothered with a wig cap. She was completely bald.

I chased the wig. She brushed me off when I tried to resettle it onto her head. She just jammed it on, and tilted her face back to take the wind into her throat.

"I can smell them!"

Why this should have pleased her I couldn't begin to guess. There was no avoiding the smell. But she jumped up and down on the spot and clapped with glee, capering in circles, her thinness not chic but shocking in her flamingo-colored pantsuit, every fingernail a shining coral, her lipstick coral, and the rippled, raw skin over her sternum a Pucci swirl of violet.

Did Carline see what I saw? Or was the stench of the seals too much for her? She fled to the car, flapping a hand at us to go on without her, a wedge of lemon crushed between her teeth. Mother insisted that lemon was the best cure for nausea, and since she was so nauseated herself lately (from change of life, she claimed), she carried small plastic bags of wedges with her everywhere. Mother begged lemon wedges shamelessly from bartenders whenever we went out to lunch, as if she couldn't just cadge them from neighborhood trees. She pierced them with swizzle sticks, the more mermaid-shaped the better. Said it made the nausea more festive.

"Get back here, Carline!" I shouted. I did not want to be alone with our mother and her strange new bruises. Everything about the beach was too piercing—the water reflected light too brightly, the sky was too clear. I could see every line and wrinkle on my mother's face.

"Oh, let your sister be, Cissy. You mustn't clutch at people so."

I could see her settling it with herself that I was crying from the rank wind and not for any other reason. In Mother's opinion I cried too much.

"Lemon wedge?"

She tripped down the path on her 6B talons, shoving a mask of sunglasses over her eyes as she went. From the back, she looked slender and springy, like a water bird picking its way lightly across the beach.

It was haul-out season. The flat water beyond the breakers shivered, its transparent skin goose-fleshed by the heads of incoming animals. Their bodies rippled and thrashed, now bellying forward, now yawing side to side, hummocking and divoting the sand, crowding one another, a billowing, thrashing body made up of hundreds of seals that lolled fatly against the horizon. The seals continually flipped sand over themselves, sending up tawny clouds of dust. The expanse of beach was punctuated by these small explosions.

When we drew closer we could see the pattern of their molt—the old bark flaked from their bodies in palm-size patches. It curled up, vulcanized around the edges of new summer fur. The bulls' heads looked especially grotesque, like rubber monster masks left too long in the sun. Where the skin peeled away from their faces they had a Lon Chaney look—Phantoms of the Opera. Some animals showed threads of red infection on their hulls, where the flayed skin had been stripped and edges of the new coat scratched and scored with grit. The oozing cracks attracted flies in clouds.

"These benighted animals haul out and then just literally fall to pieces."

Mother turned her blank Onassis gaze to me, to check what I made of their tormented skins. I wanted to take her by the shoulder, draw the sunglasses away, fold them up, meet her eyes square, and tell her I saw her now. But diffidence strait-jacketed me.

"Why do these conservation freaks make such effort to keep them around? Water retention and cartilage, that's all they are. They're like nylon socks filled with suet. The bulls are hopeless. Falstaffs by way of Bosch. Why isn't there some local legend or myth about how these dumb fatsos got cursed with inflatable dong faces? What kind of God would make them? The same God who makes cellulite and cancer."

We picked our way among the seaweed and the scraps of shredded sealskin. The animals used their hind flukes to cast sand over their wounds, and, burrowing and rolling, sanded away their heavy mantles of used-up winter skin. They shifted to reveal bellies crazed by molt, a parquetry of new skin emerging. One subadult male turned his full gaze at us. He had a cast over one eye, pink as a carbuncle.

"They look sick," I muttered.

"Gigantic coprolites."

"That one looks diseased."

"Jesus among the lepers, Cissy," said Mother. "Everyone here looks diseased."

"We should help him," I said.

"Mother Nature hates a busybody," she said.

"It must hurt," I ventured.

"Nonsense," she said. "You there," she called over a park ranger, who detached himself from a team of UCSB eggheads who were stowing scraps of fur in plastic bags.

"My daughter thinks these animals are diseased," she said. "She believes that one may have gangrene."

"It's just dead skin. Looks worse than it is," he said to me. "This is the way it's supposed to be."

He looked at me expectantly, as if anticipating some further query, but after a moment's uncomfortable blinking, he retreated down the beach.

The bull with the cast turned his blind eye toward Mother again. He reared and displayed his chest shield.

"Look, he's showing off for us. You're nauseating! You turgid chancre!"

The bull slumped suddenly, as if overcome by ennui, shut up his pink eye, and collapsed back into sleep. She tiptoed over to him, her hands folded under her chin, watching him breathe. The pumping of his heart was tangible, as if a fist were pummeling up under the thick skin of the breast shield; the skin surged and subsided rhythmically.

"Aren't you simply *vile?* And you get to be alive."

She removed her suit jacket and flung it on the sand. I rushed, courtier-like, to pick it up. Bruises mottled her arms, and when she leaned forward the gaping armhole of her blouse revealed a map of melanoma laying claim to the territory of her flesh.

She laid her palm flat over the seal's huge, beating heart.

The pulse set little ripples playing in the loose flesh of her upper arm.

The bull snored on. His proboscis drooped over a hummock of the sand like a cast-off stocking.

"He doesn't even know I'm here," she said.

Her gaze went vague and cunning as she circled her palm. Her hand paused to stroke a velvety patch of mouse-colored new fur and then moved on, seeking the rough dying skin. She worked a finger into the cracked hide and tugged.

"Wake up, Goddamn you," she said flatly. My mother, who never cursed.

I heard a sharp, vicious rip. She flapped the flag of skin, cawing in triumph. Seagulls circled. The nares on the animal's face flew open and the monster reared upright, his proboscis engorged and trumpeting, his eye a weeping red flame. He knocked Mother into me, so both of us staggered back. He roared, revealing the raw pink of his open mouth, and tusks of a musty, evil yellow. Mother leaned out and smacked the bull on the nose with a fist, waved her prize pennon of skin, and took off in stilted zigzags for the parking lot. The bull rustled all his bulk into a charge, humping toward me over the sand with unbelievable speed, honking and expanding like a galloping concertina.

Another bull, larger, older, and offended by the rumpus, bellowed a challenge, and the half-blind beta, distracted from me, lapsed back onto the sand and went to sleep.

Back in the parking lot, Mother wrapped the torn piece of fur in her handkerchief and stowed it in her purse.

"You left me!"

"Cecilia, that bull was charging. Silver liners! Did you expect me to just stand there? But honestly, who knew either of you could move that fast?"

Still gasping, she collapsed against the car.

"I think I finally understand your father. It certainly makes you feel brisk, doesn't it, getting so close to wild beasts?"

Carline cranked down the car window and leaned out, her face puffy with sleep. She'd been sleeping a lot lately. The stress of auditions, she claimed. Late nights rehearsing sides.

"Why are your teeth chattering?" she asked me.

My fingers and lips felt numb.

"Tell her," I said to our mother.

I could not understand her bright false cheerfulness. She had lost a shoe in her flight and turned her ankle—already it was puffing into a fine black bruise—and her face was pale, her mouth trembling.

"You need the hospital," I said.

"What the heck happened out there?" asked Carline.

Mother slept, her fingers curled around the handkerchief with the stolen sealskin wrapped in it. I combed out her wig. Carline spritzed herself with some of Mother's Narcisse Noir. Monitors monitored, drips dripped.

"I knew something was wrong with her skin," said Carline. "I asked her about it. She told me it was *a touch of eczema.* Another time a *soupçon of poison oak.* I said, 'Mother, I don't see you scratching.' She said, 'Ladies do not scratch, Caroline, they exert self-control.' Why is she so artificial? She lives like she's in a set piece. Some Victorian game of charades where you need six or seven people and three costume changes just to spell out one cotton-picking word. Even here, in this pissant hospital, she's acting like she's not three tosses away from skipping off her hopscotch grid and Miss Mary Mack–ing her way into the black."

"I think she's brave," I lied.

"I think she's a bone liar and you've caught the disease. Jeez, Cissy, you used to snitch about everything. Did you know that Danny knows? *Danny.* I just called him and he knows already. He's been taking her to her appointments. She always liked him best."

"No," I soothed. "It's because of Aunt Loretta. Mother wouldn't want her diagnosis to come as a shock to him after what happened to his mama."

"But what about us, Cissy?"

"Shhh," I said. "She might not be asleep."

She wasn't.

Mother licked her dry lips and asked for her compact. As she drew the pink chamois over her nose to take the shine off, her hand shook. She snapped her fingers at me for her purse, for her lipstick in its gold filigree cover. She freshened her mouth, blotted on a Kleenex. Little shreds of white clung to the red on her lips. She picked them off.

"Caroline Louise, please try to be less vulgar," she said. "Now if you would hand me my scarf I can make myself fit to be seen."

Good grooming: the sure sign of an iron will. The mental lacquer that taming all that animal requires—never mind the physical fortitude—to carry off that level of ceremonial dress. The freshly honed nails in their stiff coats, how they weight the hands. The posture, the hair, the foundation garments, the precise, cruel little shoes, the strictures of neatness. What kind of soul puts those demands on the body?

Back in the basement, just beneath the little round bottle of Narcisse Noir, Carline found a black-and-white photograph. She examined the picture, flipped it over, and showed me a perfect Marilyn moue of lipstick pressed onto the back.

"When was our mother ever maudlin enough to buss a photograph?" she asked.

The photo was just an eight-by-ten, a military portrait of a handsome man in crisp service blues, unsmiling, but with warm eyes that looked right at you. A little mischief, a little wicked glint contradicting that stern chin.

"That must be Laurence," I said. "I always wondered what he looked like."

"Laurence who?"

"Her boyfriend. Her companion. Whatever. Mother called him her 'gentleman friend.' The perfume guy she was always going on about, you remember."

"That guy was her lover? And you *knew*?"

"She told me in the hospital. She would have told both of us, but you stopped coming to see her. Not that she blamed you."

"She really loved him," I added.

"I refuse to believe this," Carline said.

What shocked Carline about the photograph was not that Mother had dated someone after Daddy, but that she had dated—apparently loved—a man who was black. I didn't understand her chagrin. After all, it had been the seventies, and we weren't in Texas then. I felt proud of our mother, and sad, because what had become of him?

"There's no way. Don't you remember, Cissy? How when we were kids she swore up and down to Danny that Lisa in the book *Corduroy* wasn't a Negro, she was just really *suntanned?*"

"Mixed marriage was good enough for Peggy Lipton," I said. "And she used to be your idol. Carline, I thought you were more open-minded."

"It's not that," she said. "It's that I never knew her, Cissy. Our own mother. I knew nothing about her."

"At least we know who all her glamour was for at the end," I said to Carline, "the refusal to shed her formal skin. Not for us. Or even for herself. It was for him."

Before radiation treatments destroyed her sense of smell, before Laurence Strong left for Maryland, he inducted Mother into the language of perfumery, and she kept a scent diary as a devotion to him—as a love letter, I suppose. They would trade their diaries, they promised, in the meantime concocting scents that, they hoped, would link to memories of moods and states that could sustain their separation (he'd been certain it was temporary; they were mature—he pronounced it "matoor"—enough to be faithful, he just had to be there for his boy during the difficult teenage years, Mother understood, she'd been through it, just squeaked through, she understood, it was temporary, they could wait and they loved each other, they weren't kids, they knew what love meant, how rare it was and how worth the wait, and meanwhile they'd exchange perfume logs, and arrange visits). They were sensible people, continent, composed. She was only forty-two. He was slightly older. They had plenty of time.

Dear Laurence, does every thing that happens leave a
scent? Do all interactions produce smell—any friction?
If we were sensitive enough, and quick enough, could
we detect unseen losses, avert disagreements, catch
hold before what we love takes flight?

Going over the diaries that Carline found, the ones Mother
didn't send to Laurence but kept for herself, scents pyramided
and annotated in her careful lists, it appears that she was
searching for some fixative to stop time.

The scent of our babies: baby.

"See, Carline? She did think about us."

Our childhood starched many pages.

hot tar and ddt, and the children racing after the insec-
ticide trucks down the streets in summer putting down
fresh pressed cotton pillowslips ironed by Gigi's maid
when Danny peed the bed the sheets smelled like cinnamon sugar all those petticoats the girls wore their
toasty smell of starch so stiff they stood up by themselves on the floor of our cedar closets, and underneath
them the whiff of sweet licorice from Cissy's squirrel-
cache of Good n Plenties

In other notes, she looked for an accord that could draw our
father back, to recreate him, healed, restored.

Mark at 16, hay, engine oil, clove attar and clementine
his civet-armpits, leatheric kisses

She was trying to scrub out the ionones of her anger, his anger, and bring him back. She tried to concoct a scent trail that would help her understand his time away from us, the war time when he was utterly unreachable and alone.

> The rotting meat flower in Indonesia, amorphophal-
> lus titum aram, a corpse flower, "they grow preferen-
> tially on disturbed grounds" like others I could name
> the stink of the flower, the maw of predator sleeping
> off its kill

Those notes were also a confession.

> Semen is cut grass, every time I smell cut grass I re-
> member him pulling out the heat on my belly the shock
> and the green salt smell of crushed lawn. Crabapple
> blossoms. Delirium of love. Drunk as wasps. His smell.
> Laurence. The fenugreek of skin.

"Or a fantasy," says Carline. "Olfactory fictions. That's all perfume is—fantasy. And fantasy's just an attempt to invent a better memory. She felt guilty."

Carline set all the truly valuable bottles—the fulls and partials—carefully to one side. She swept the small fry, little glass nips and half-ounce sample vials with too little juice in them to sell, into a Tupperware bowl and rattled it thoughtfully.

"Carline, you have to forgive her."

She picked up a tiny flacon of Fidji, uncorked it, and poured it down the drain in the laundry room floor. Tuberose burped up from the trough.

"She forgave you. She did."

Carline emptied another vial. Joy. Strangling tendrils of jasmine. She tipped out an ounce of Mon Péché, an atomizer of Arpège. She snapped the glass nips in half and shook the drops from her drenched hands. Femme. Madame. Ma Griffe. She poured out the testers until a Greek chorus of fumes rose wailing from the drain, Bellodgia, Bal à Versailles, an army of insinuating shades tainted by the rich sulfur stench of the drain, Magie Noire, Ivoire, Vent Vert rising, crowded and confused, supplicant—the glandular funk of civet and beaver castorum, the pungent musk of tiny Chinese deer, the waxy sweet sickness spouted from whales, the pale beckoning sweats of flowers bedded in fat, the cool sex of white blossoms and the churlish green of crushed leaves, the bright golden squeal of citrus rinds, the sharp cinnabar spools of cinnamon peel, the purplish dust of orris root, the pith of fruits, the dry and smoky woods, the honeys and vanillas and the pulverized pods and gums and resins, all the precious aromatics, Carline poured them out, unmoved. Shalimar Shocking Chamade Cabochard Calèche Chanel Chanel—she released the cloying ghost-personae our mother had sampled, rejected, kept coffered, reserved for some future self who would warm them to life with her particular skin. Fracas Bandit Coup de Fouet—who knows what they meant to her? L'Interdit. Je Reviens. Mystère.

Once Mother went into hospice, Carline bullied her like a Cold War interrogator, waking her from a morphine doze and assaulting her with crude questions. *When did you lose your virginity? Why did you marry Daddy? What's the worst thing you ever did? Never did?*

Carline couldn't leave Mother alone. As if inheriting Mother's fine bones and rapturous little face weren't enough, or her voiceprint, or her prejudices, her grammar and her hunger for color. Carline couldn't see how she'd already gotten the best of Mother.

Granted, Carline at that time was rarely sober, and she was going off the rails in her own farouche way. Later I found out that she had been pregnant at the time. She didn't know if she was going to let it continue, so she never told Mother, or anyone else. I think Carline was trying to figure out what a mother was, how to be a mother, how to be a daughter, with that little seed ticking away inside her. I think about that niece or nephew that never was. Sonny's sweet, but I wonder who that first child would have been. If she'd have been one of us, a Bowman girl, fierce and sappy. Would she have carried our germ of self-defeat and let it explode in her like a dandelion clock?

To all of Carline's questions, Mother assumed her Shangri-La face (not too difficult, given how much morphine she was veining, at the end) and deigned not to reply.

"That's not how you find things out," I said.

"I should suck up, I suppose. Fiddlesticks. Mother's a liar all the way down."

Carline, Mother's favorite, grew more and more distant. She stopped coming to the hospital, stopped calling.

"I'd rather tap dance on fondant," she said.

My sister and I played with our versions of Mother the way we used to play with our detested Barbies: grudgingly, and always pitting them in contests. Who was right? Who was better?

"It's self-loathing. She was never comfortable with herself, with her beauty," said Carline.

"Or she was its docent."

"Either way, pathetic. She and Daddy raised us to be completely unfit for life. You were fine, Cissy, you had enough time to get it together, but me! Can you believe her pushing me into that pageant stuff, those auditions? It was like she was possessed by Daddy. He was the one who believed in me. Mother knew better."

"You're why we left Texas!"

"She had no business. I'm a casualty of Daddy's delusions. You're lucky. You never had that pressure."

"She gambled on you. We all did."

"Mother just didn't want me to turn out like Aunt Loretta. That's why we left Texas. We were never real to her."

I dabbed some Nuit de Noel and held my nose to my wrist.

Cissy, don't sniff right away. You have to let the alcohol dissipate or it will exhaust your nose. Let the top notes settle. Not real to me? My God, you kids were so real to me, I felt like to die from it when you were babies. It was more than I can handle. And then before I got used to it I realized I'd missed it, because you started being false with me.

Carline and I have always had to tear her down and assemble her into someone comprehensible. If she had lived longer, would we ever have solved the puzzle of mothers and daughters? Probably not. But I tried. All those days in the hospital, I edged closer. Was it devotion to my mother, as I let Danny, and the nurses, and especially Carline, suppose? Possibly. Or possibly I just wanted to see if cancer would crack her open at last. I wanted to be there if it did.

"Mangosteens," Mother said once, toward the end. "I've never smelled mangosteens."

Danny hunted all the markets in San Francisco's China-town and found her one, and she clutched it, the thick purple rind inking her fingertips. She held the pearly segments to her nose, but got nothing. Frustrated, she ate it anyway, every sin-gle white lobe, and spat the smooth, fat pits into her handker-chief. The texture, without fragrance to redeem it, must have been unpleasant. Tears ran down her face but she thanked Danny effusively; he'd been to some trouble, she was sure. It was positively delicious.

"Pencil shavings," she said another time, when I thought she was sleeping. "Emptying the cedar fluff from the metal sharpener bolted to the wall in Miss Beaton's classroom. I can feel it, the precise sensation of twisting it off, shaking the pubic clump into the wastebasket—I can taste the gritty slate of the pointed pencil tip."

Which led her to the scent of chalk on wooly erasers, and classroom dust and the slight greenish stink of the turtle tank.

"Fountain pen ink," she said, "such a rainy smell, dark, like wet stone. If you ever doubt that the world is beautiful, Cissy, go sniff a bottle of black ink."

The black nori flake in the bag inside my Nuit de Noel was an-other message I couldn't read. Carline insists I am making it up about the young bull elephant seal, Mother's later trips to comb and brush him. She says there's no way a woman as sick as our mother could have hauled herself out there to the colony. Even if she had been the kind of person who would approach such unattractive, untamable quarry.

Our mother was a compulsive groomer, not just of herself but of others, one of those women deeply in touch with her inner chimp. Everyone knows one, a cornflake-picker, a Q-tip swooper, a zit-popping amateur blackhead squeezer who cannot keep from interfering with the clogged pore, the errant hair. When we were teenagers all our friends availed themselves of her strong stomach and steady hands. Carline and I were fortunate in our complexions, but she squeezed poor Danny's blackheads, extruding long ribbons of sebum from his pores like anchovy paste.

Her hands were restless. She wanted to give everyone and everything new skin. I think that's why she refinished antique furniture. Any work that involved stripping, sanding, buffing away at uneven surfaces, she loved. She was practically evangelical about it, as if peeling off the dead skin were a baptism. Shelling hard-cooked eggs gave her great joy. Shucking corn. Stripping peas from their hulls. Scraping off old varnish and paint. It didn't matter. I saw her peel a willow switch and skin a chicken with equal accuracy and pleasure. Nothing delighted her more than a second-degree sunburn. Pulling back the flakes to reveal the tender, raw place where the skin was new. I loved her, but the memory of that French manicure bearing down on all and sundry makes me wince. She was always beautifully groomed, herself.

"Well now, Cissy, it's a bonding activity, grooming. It's just being sociable. Not to mention helpful. Let me see those split ends."

But the grooming of the elephant seal elevated the obsession to radical heights. First, it was dangerous. Second, it was illegal. Third, what was the point?

"It's just so satisfying," she said. "And he lets me do it. I'm circling the drain, Cissy. Are you going to help me with this or not?"

Her splenetic hatred toward the animals had mellowed, turned maternal. That scrap of skin connected her to the young bull, and he behaved as if she had vanquished him. Though he was the size of a VW Beetle, and Mother barely five feet tall, he let her touch him. The seal loved being scratched under his itchy coat.

"We're just facilitating a natural process," she said. "That's all. Stand guard."

She unpacked Carline's old rubber currycomb and an alarmingly toothy metal collie brush.

"Didn't you say something about how Mother Nature hates a busybody?"

"Changed my mind," she said.

She drew the rubber comb down the seal's face, pulling gently at the skin around his maimed eye. She combed clots of fur from his body.

"If your face didn't look like the business end of a squid you'd be almost cute. Old swamp thing."

If I tried to touch him, he rushed me, but Mother stood by him stroking over his neck and he rolled in ecstasy at her feet. It made me jealous, though of which one of them I can't quite say.

"I think I can beat this, Cissy," she said to me, back in her hospital bed. "It's just skin."

She was only able to brush a quadrant over the seal's right shoulder before her arms tired and I had to help her back to the car.

"The pups. The ones that don't get squashed by their own fathers—they're just left behind by their mothers. Stars above. You poor girls."

She insisted I bring her back when she was rested, to finish the job. It took weeks. Every time, she managed a little less. The elephant seal shed its coat and mother shed weight. Eventually, she made me do it.

"He won't let me."

"Don't be such a goose. Cecilia, these are not bright animals."

Touching him was even more frightening than touching her. His aliveness. Wild things are filled with aliveness. Though he had been tamed, a little. His instincts turned, his reflexes governed. But in those last days of her life Mother took on that wild aliveness. In dying, she was finally returning to the wild. In spite of the lipstick, the posture. Every cell had run wild, and she fought at first. But she wasn't fighting now. She inhabited her body fully. Perhaps the seal accepted her because death was bringing her to his place of wildness. And he, in submitting to our caresses, allowed his wildness to die a little. Something was exchanged.

Mother drew the rubber comb across the elephant seal's back for the final stroke.

"There," she said, "plush as a Pullman seat."

The seal's tawny coat felt like velveteen.

"He's still patently hideous, but at least he doesn't look like the survivor of a nuclear winter. I was wrong, Cissy. They have every right to live. Even if they are as pointless as I think, they have the right."

Lolloping and beatific, the bull absolved her wrath. Clumsy, drab, he shrove her. In grooming him, she sloughed off her own coat of life-betraying skin; she was at peace.

"That's pure 'Last Leaf' O. Henry horseshit," Carline said to me. "Our mother was the kind of woman who spent her adult entire life wearing a girdle she didn't need. Remember that catchphrase? 'Silver liners, silver clouds'? That should be her epitaph, Cissy."

Maybe Carline is right. Maybe I invented this coda because the reality of Mother's death was too bleak to dwell on. There are no words for the implacable cruelty of her dissolution.

"Cissy, I know this is terribly silly, but please find Laurence and tell him what is happening to me," my mother begged. "I want to say goodbye."

I didn't even know how to find him. I would try Fort Meade. I would send a letter to that APO address. Surely he must come. Death brings love flying. Doesn't it?

I found Lieutenant Strong through Nestor Roche, of all people. After Father died, Roche, that family dybbuk, kept up with us, or perhaps kept tabs is a more accurate assessment—though he had been banned from contact by our mother and Danny swore that if he ever met him face to face he would kill him.

Roche resurfaced every couple years, poking his head up from the slime of the past and phoning me or Carline, generally me, generally in the small hours, and generally in the month of November. Maybe he had a circuit, kept a calendar. Perhaps every month he spoke with a different family, tested his teeth against the ragged flesh of any number of hearts. November air has a bite that still makes me think of Roche—that chill voice, exciting and wearying—a sugar skull voice if there ever was one.

"I still see myself as y'all's uncle," he said. Usually to me. I was particularly susceptible to him. God knows why. But everyone else had died—all the adults in my life. But Roche. He stayed in touch. And as long as he was alive—that sower of di-

saster, that old enemy—something of our family remained intact. I can't explain it any better than that. And he was useful.
His ability to discover and know things—especially in the years
before the Internet, spooked me. But it was handy. He never hit
me up for money, and he never flirted with me (though he did
both to Carline before she, too, finally refused to speak to him).
He just phoned me every few years for a few minutes of conversation.

Talking with him left me feeling like I'd lapped poison from
the surface of a puddle to quench some terrible thirst. But I
never refused his call. He had heard Mother died. How? DMV
records, he said. He didn't elaborate. (This was years before the
stalker laws were instituted in California.) I asked him, could
he find someone for me?

"For you, darlin', any little thing."

He sent me an address. I wrote.

A year later, I received a reply from Lieutenant Laurence
Strong. The usual platitudes. *Terribly sorry for your loss.* His heavy
dark handwriting had the typical backwards slant of a lefty. *She
was a lovely person.* A few words blanked over with Wite-Out. I
tried my hardest to interpolate his grief. If Mother loved anyone, naturally she would love a stoic. I sniffed the paper for
traces of his scent. I held it to the light to see if I could discern
what the correction fluid covered. But the Wite-Out remained
opaque and the paper only smelled of paper.

THE CORPSE DIVER

On Saturday, just before dawn, the sky broke. Jill sat on the bedroom floor with her chin on the sill and watched her daughter Piper's plastic sled boil with rain down in the backyard. The dog dish became a little cauldron. The silver maple flung sticks and leaves and the rain hammered the deck like gravel. Thunder cracked, loud and close, and the lightning that followed lit up two bare-breasted girls running out of the house across the alley. They rushed out into their yard, followed by a French bulldog, bodies flickering. Jill pressed her nose to the wet screen and watched them dancing and shrieking in the wet grass, the little dog running rockets between them.

The storm didn't wake Jerry, or Piper. Jill thought about calling her sister in California, just for some company, but she was too sleep-bewildered to calculate the time difference, and wasn't even sure she had a current number.

Jill padded downstairs to the living room, comforted her dog. He had once barked challenges at lightning, just as, not so long ago, she had danced her share of storms. Piper's arrival had vanquished them both.

Her phone rang. Five o'clock in the morning. Only one person it could be. She set her teeth and picked up.

"Did you hear sirens, Mrs. Guzman? No sirens, *no esta* tornado. *Solamenta una* rainstorm, Mrs. Guzman. Uh *lluvia? Piove?*"

Apparently both Jerry and her high school Spanish had forsaken her.

"No sirens, no tornado!"

Jill made a childish face worthy of Piper. She mimed throwing the phone for the benefit of the dog.

"You may not speak to Jerry. *No habla con* Jerry *ahora.* He was on a dive last night. *El (dormir? duerme?)* He's sleeping!"

"*Volver a su* bed, Mrs. Guzman. The storm is *finito.*"

A crack of lightning contradicted her, but Jill didn't care. She hung up.

Jerry shuffled out of the bathroom, knuckling sleep from his eyes.

"What was that about?"

"La Guzman."

"I wish you wouldn't call her that."

"It's her name."

"It's insulting and you know it."

"It's not like they don't have weather in Colombia," Jill said.

"They have things that are worse."

"What kind of person brings his pregnant wife and retarded child to America and then abandons them?"

"Honey," said Jerry, "She's worried sick. C'mere."

She allowed him to fold her into his arms.

"I don't understand why I hate her," Jill said. "I'm a brat."

"You wanted me to sleep in. It's sweet," said Jerry. "And you're worried that she's you. I won't let that happen."

"I worry about you down there."

"I should go check on them," he said, disengaging his arms and giving her a double pat on the shoulder blade.

Jill pushed in Piper's high chair and busied herself scratching last night's dried mashed potato off the table.

"You do too much for other people. And even when you're here, you're gone."

Jerry looked exhausted. He bent his head, firmed his jaw. She used to kiss the thinning spot on the crown of his head—his crop circle, she called it. Now the sight of it was as unappealing as a monk's tonsure. He slipped his feet into rubber boots and rummaged in the closet for his umbrella.

"Don't go, Jerry. You'll see her tomorrow at church."

He smiled. "Piper's asleep and your boobs are showing." He kissed her cheek. "Back in a few."

Jill looked down, then closed her robe and fumed.

When Piper was born, Jill got tired and Jerry got religion. He wanted their daughter to have a belief structure, he said. He wanted her to be prepared for life, because if you weren't prepared to deal with evil, or suffering, you'd lose yourself—mind, heart, soul. This alarmed Jill because since when did Jerry, matter-of-fact practical Jerry, talk about the soul? When Jill had agreed that yes, structure was good, Jerry went on to argue that his daughter would also need to experience grace.

But Piper was still too young for either, and with growing resentment Jill watched Jerry become more and more fervent in his faith. Sunday, his usual childcare day, became devoted instead to this new Mennonite church, where La Guzman was also a member. He took Piper to Sunday school for a measly hour and afterward dumped her with Jill and returned to the church, where he stayed all day because he insisted he needed to spend time with his faith family. When Jill protested, he became reasonable.

"You could come too," he pointed out. "You're always welcome."

Jill recalled the dreary churches of her overseas childhood. Congregations of upbeat, unblinking missionaries whose insistent smiles and boundless good cheer made her feel as though she'd been cornered by a gang of wholesome bullies; tireless priests and the bands of the faithful who swept the floor after service and stacked the sitting cushions and padded across the sticky linoleum in tiny rubber slippers, or, eager to practice their English on her, suffered her to eat waxy sweets in the little rectories that were too hot. During the service and sermon she hung on the moment when she could get up and devour the Eucharist—sometimes she tucked the papery wafer into a cheek and let the sip of wine dissolve it slowly, trying to make it last until the recessional, which meant freedom and an escape to air conditioning.

Still, Jill had no particular beef with religion as long as it stayed on the other side of the street. When she sighted paired-up Mormon kids in their starched shirts and ties walking along Riverside, she found them touching, from a distance. And her sister, Maizie, was, intermittently, a Buddhist. But Jerry's faith demanded so much of him, and as Jerry dove deeper he had less left over for their life together.

"Your doubt family," Jill said to him, "that's what we are."

Jill believed in community (if not holy) spirit. She did. She organized the community garden. She brought fruit salad to potlucks and she waved at other mothers, including Mrs. Guzman and her upsetting son and their other baby whose sex she never bothered to determine.

She knew she was selfish. She suspected that having Piper had turned her into a monster. She had nothing left for anyone else, and her own meagerness frightened her. But with a small child there was just always so much to do. Jill didn't know where her time went. She woke up at dawn and by sundown she could not tell you why she was so shattered. There were limits to what an unrelated person should ask you for, weren't there? Reasonable limits?

Jerry didn't think so. He pulled energy from an unlimited source. Since his honorable discharge from the army Jerry did rescue and retrieval diving. Mainly he salvaged wrecks. But they lived near a river that flooded, and people died in floods. Other people had to drag the bodies from the river. That was Jerry. Jerry was other people.

She hadn't known how hard it would be to live with someone who saved everybody. Except that he doesn't save anyone, the small voice in her head argued. He only comes in after the tragedy. It's not heroic. It's just kind of gross. That's not fair, she insisted. Sometimes all you can do is recover is the body.

In the upstairs bedroom Piper slept hard, bottom in the air, face burrowed into the body of her plush Canada goose, creatively named "Goose," which always made Jill think of *Top Gun* and its manufactured tragedies. She actually missed the clarity of the Cold War.

A rivery sunlight filled the bedroom. Through the open window, from the house across the way Jill heard a man shouting, his voice brutal with invective.

"This is fucking *bullshit. Fuck you.*"

Jill shivered and shut the window. How could such anger and those two free spirits spill out of the same house? She identified more with that invisible rage-filled voice than those carefree girls dancing in the rain.

Personally, Jill thought that Jerry's current church phase had more to do with his tours in Afghanistan than with their daughter. She hadn't known how hard it would be to live with someone who had decided he needed to save everyone.

Now they were broke, since Jerry, in renouncing violence and strife, had also renounced his VA benefits and pension. Her little job as a receptionist at the Gym Nest barely covered the mortgage. She was terrified they would lose the house.

God will provide, he said.

He never raised a hand to her or Piper, even during that spell of heavy drinking, when Piper was just tiny and nursing constantly and Jill barely coping and Jerry was self-medicating into blackouts so he could pass out rather than risk normal sleep. All through the worst of it he forced himself to stay upright and aboveground. Diving was his substitute for suicide.

She should be grateful. How could she tell anyone, my husband is too good, and I feel left out? She couldn't even confess it to Maizie, much as she wished to. Maizie approved of Jerry.

When Jill first got married Maizie was going through her anar-chist phase and tended to be vocally, passionately anti-govern-ment. Jerry, newly sworn in to the army, stood up in his dress uniform and Jill had been terrified that Maizie would pick a fight with him after the ceremony. Instead, Jerry and Maizie spent most of the reception comparing notes on their experi-ences working suicide hotlines.

Jill was struggling into a bra—two years since she'd had Piper and still her body didn't fit—when she heard them downstairs in the dining room: Jerry, La Guzman, Manny, and presumably the baby. La Guzman's shy laughter sounded delib-erately coy to Jill.

La Guzman sat in Jill's place at Jill's dining table, her long rayon skirt smoothed over her legs and her high-necked blouse buttoned crooked with a little baby spit on the collar. Her son Manny wore a knapsack disguised as an adorable stuffed mon-key—which on Manny's broad seven-year-old back looked tiny and out of place—with a leash attached to it: Manny was a bolter.

Jerry loved Manny. Loved his little wizened old man's face and his gappy grin, loved how he would never outgrow his in-nocent exuberance. Jill thought there was something sad and perverse about a seven-year-old boy who looked eighty and acted two. Not Jerry. Jerry thought he was angelic. He hun-kered next to the boy, spinning a coin.

La Guzman's long dark hair hung lank, and Jill noticed a large hank had been chopped raggedly off the front.

"You hair," Jill said, taken aback.

"Baby," said La Guzman. "No let go—"

She made a tugging motion, then scissored two fingers in the air.

La Guzman always looked prettier in person than she did in Jill's head, which Jill found annoying. Still, she felt a fleeting touch of sympathy for her. It went away as soon as she noted that Jerry had given the woman coffee in Jill's own pink mug. The rim of it bore La Guzman's smudgy maroon lip-burn. The baby's head was also covered in the woman's lip-prints.

Jerry poured Jill the dregs from the French press, gritty and tepid.

"Thanks," Jill said, trying not to mean it ironically. Jerry's coffee made her think of the slime that leaches out when flowers are left in a vase too long, rich and corrupt.

"Marisol," Jerry said, fishing in his pocket, "here's a key to the outside door of our basement. If you're ever worried about a tornado, just come over."

Marisol took the key matter-of-factly and put it in her purse. Like it was just something that people did.

"Jill, we have been talking about the diving, how Jerry he and Bano—he is Bano, your partner, yes?—will expand business to train other divers."

"It's Benno." She turned to Jerry. "You never mentioned this."

Jerry cut a glance at Marisol Guzman and shook his head imperceptibly at Jill. He hated scenes.

"Jerry, it doesn't make money. Bad things don't happen that often around here."

"Thank the Lord," said La Guzman. "Praise God."

"They happen enough," he said.

She followed Jerry into the kitchen. Manny sat on the floor surrounded by the ravaged contents of their bottom cabinet. He was stacking Tupperware and knocking it over.

"We need to talk about this."

Jerry cracked eggs into a yellow mixing bowl. He tossed the shells back into the egg carton, sliming it. Behind him, on the stove, the pan smoked. Jerry always buttered it too early.

"The heat's too high," Jill said. She edged him to one side, and turned the flame down. He poured batter directly from the bowl into the skillet. Some of it oozed over the rim and fell onto the stove. It would puff up, Jill knew, and harden, and she'd have to scrape it off the burner with a butter knife later.

"It's not just underwater criminal investigation. It's dive training. Recreational inland dives are getting more popular. Later, honey, I promise. When we don't have company."

"Don't use them as an excuse to avoid discussing this with me," said Jill.

"Who's ready for a pancake?" he called into the dining room. "Specialty de la casa!"

Marisol laughed. "Oh, very good Spanish, *muy bien.*"

Does she have to talk like a caricature? Jill thought. No, that's racist, she chastised herself. The woman can't help it if her English is bad. Jill had never bothered to learn any of the languages of the host countries of her childhood, so how could she judge Marisol Guzman? Besides, all her life Jill had parsed the accents of speakers who addressed her in halting English. She was good at it, took pride in her patience and quick comprehension. Why then, did Marisol Guzman's voice enrage her?

But it was exhausting, having to listen hard and pay attention when she just wanted a simple morning with her husband—God forbid that on the one morning Piper slept in she and Jerry would actually get a chance to talk. Why was this woman always dropping by? She always wanted something, help or company or conversation—it was unsettling.

Jill resigned herself to a pretense of kindness.

"So, where are you from again in Colombia?"

"Bucaramanga. You know my country?"

"Um, paramilitary groups, cocaine, civil war?"

Marisol Guzman looked down into her cup.

"Bucaramanga was very safe. There is a university. My husband studied—how do you say it—to be minister—"

"Divinity?"

The baby wanting to nurse, nuzzled at her mother's blouse, smearing the white fabric with traces of lipstick. La Guzman unbuttoned her shirt and put the child to her breast.

"Many terrible things happen in Colombia."

I just can't hear this right now, thought Jill. Most days I can barely keep track of my checking account. But this woman pressed her.

"By grace of God, Héctor and I found the church sponsor to Iowa. We have American children, Christian children. And here, there is school for Manny. But my father, he was taken by the FARC—they kidnap for money. The church will not help. They will not give money to fund the guerrilla, even if it saves my father. But God has a plan. And we must be waiting."

Mrs. Guzman looked down, stroked the baby's head.

"It must be difficult," said Jill, "I'm sorry."

"It is grace."

Why was it so hard for Jill listen to someone who frames everything with God? Why should it matter, or make La Guzman and her trouble less real?

"Do you believe in Jesus Christ, Mrs. Ferrell?"

"Um, I used to be Catholic. I don't really have anything against religion, but Jerry's the one who—

"I do not understand why God tests those who already believe, and gives so much to—others who do not. But His ways are a mystery."

Her English improved when she talked about God. Probably the only English she heard was God-talk. She must be very lonely. Well, so was Jill.

"My husband, he goes back to Colombia to help my mother raise money to ransom my father's return. Héctor tell me, stay with the church, God will look after you. Now I wait. I hear nothing. I pray. I hear nothing."

The baby curled a fist against La Guzman's exposed throat, playing with her necklace. Jill looked at the swirl of fuzzy black hair, listened to the audible sucking. She could smell the woman's milk, and scorched butter, and the golden steam of pancakes Jerry was heaping on a plate.

"I was never able to nurse Piper," she said. "It hurt, I could never get it right, and I gave up. Doesn't it hurt?"

La Guzman didn't meet her eyes. "Yes, it hurts sometimes."

She stroked the baby's ear with a fingertip.

Guiltily, Jill said, "We're heading to the farmer's market today. It's stopped raining."

"Manny, Graciela, and me, we will join you, yes? To buy tomatoes?"

"And you'll stay for pancakes, I hope," said Jerry.

Jill dragged herself upstairs to dress Piper.

"Hey," Jerry said, coming into their bedroom, "you're doing great down there, Jill."

She shrugged him off. Piper squirmed and tried to shin up Jerry's leg.

"God, Jerry—I was just being polite. Now we're saddled with them all day."

He hoisted their daughter. She played with his nose and he pretended to bite her fingers.

How could she explain?

"It's too much. It's just too much. I need you to save some of your time for us."

"I help people."

"No, you don't. You're just a glorified golden retriever."

He looked at her, stunned. Her own words shocked her. She backed away from him, holding his eyes with defiance and shame. She had run away with herself, stepped over her own invisible line.

"You can't keep punishing me for my work," he said.

"You could have done anything else. Anything! You must have known, you must have known it would wreck you."

"I'm not wrecked," he said.

"Well, us, then. It wrecked us."

"I know you don't mean that," he said, "and I have to forgive you. But right now, we have a guest. Come down when you're more collected."

Forgive 'em and forsake 'em, that was Jerry.

When they met freshman year in college, he was just a farm kid from Oxford, a corn-fed oaf, she'd thought, and she still playing the bitter outcast with her out-of-style tartan Docs and fake Aussie accent—an affectation she'd clung to since her parents dumped her in Iowa. But his decency exerted a powerful pull.

The day after 9/11 they'd shared a couch in the dorm's common room, watched the footage, unable to part from the television or from one another. His big frame shook with sorrow and she wanted to comfort and protect him, so she invited him up to her room. He had been too honorable (or chickenshit) to come in, had simply hovered in her doorway for hours, until he was swaying with exhaustion, just holding her hands in his big silky mitts and talking endlessly, not understanding that by this point she was trembling not with sorrow but with desire.

What on earth had he seen in her? She never gave him a moment's peace. When he joined the ROTC she blistered him with her scorn. She stole his combat boots and wore them all winter—he got a mess of demerits for losing them. God, Jerry. She'd hated ROTC. But Jerry never quit anything. And so it went. And here they were.

Jill huddled on the unmade bed, brushing stray eyelashes from the pillowcase. Something was very wrong with her. When did she get so mean? Only someone as decent as Jerry, God bless him, could turn PTSD into philanthropy. Jerry's diving jobs and his church—good things hurt her for no good reason. But he kept himself apart from her and Piper. Aloof. He punished himself physically. At the gym, in the cold river, or out barn raising or Habitating for Humanity or sorting piles and piles of castoffs at the Mennonite charity store, the Cluttered Closet. Didn't he know how she needed him? And needed him to need her? Jill tried smiling; Jerry said that smiling deliberately made you feel good. But it just made her conscious that she was starching up her face with wrinkles.

• • •

At the farmer's market, Jill was struck by the placid fecundity of the crowd—every third woman was six months pregnant and the rest pushed strollers or wore babies in slings or herded toddlers in bright hats between rows of cruciferous vegetables. Children chased dogs and fathers chased children. Couples held hands and selected lilies. The farmer who sold them their collards had just had a baby. Even the clouds were swollen and the maples heavy with keys.

Jill cruised the stalls, remembering her pregnancy, how she'd been charmed by her own fertility, how exciting it had seemed. Then Jerry accepted a deployment and she plunged into a state of terror and resentment. She delivered Piper by herself, among strangers. Back then Maizie lived in an ashram in Oregon and wasn't allowed to leave. Her father was posted in Pakistan, her mother in Japan. Jerry returned stateside when Piper was two months old and Jill was so sleep deprived, she had waking visions of throwing the baby down the flight of stairs that led to the basement, of cutting off her tiny, vulnerable fingers with kitchen shears, of gouging out her milky peepers, or simply leaving her asleep in the house and never returning. She couldn't tell Jerry, or anyone, about these visions, not when his night terrors were certainly more appalling. He never shared them.

Jill smiled ruefully at the other farmer's market mothers, trying to enjoy the bustle of people buying their summer produce, but as the coffee buzz wore off and Piper poked her in the ass repeatedly with a bamboo stick and Jerry went off to talk to Benno, she felt oppressed. Other families in their contentedness looked self-congratulatory: their bellies smug and the children creepy with their perfect pores and cornshock Mid-westerners' hair or too-big new grownup teeth. She felt little and lonely, left out, even though here she was with her daughter, whose damp curls and tomato cheeks caused passersby to stop and have what she thought of as the baby conversation. What would become of them all?

She must be catching a contact low from La Guzman, who hovered—why did she have to hover so much? Marisol stuck close to her, with the baby on her back and Manny on his leash. Couldn't she take those kids and wander off on her own for even a second?

On the park lawn just outside the farmer's market entrance, a young woman with a guitar began a folk song in Spanish.

> *Solo le pido a Dios*
> *Que el dolor no me sea indiferente*

Marisol's face lit up and she hurried toward the singer, pulling Manny after her. She looked . . . not exactly prettier, but more defined. As though she had just caught sight of an old friend on the street, a friend who loved her. The song had a haunting melody. It sounded fragile and strong, pleading and protesting at the same time. Tears popped into Jill's eyes and she brushed them off, feeling silly.

"This is beautiful," said Jill. "What is she singing?"

Marisol kept her eyes fixed on the singer.

"It is a famous song."

"Oh. Who sings it?"

"Mercedes Soza. You know Mercedes Soza?"

"No."

"She is like . . . Janis Joplin, but of Argentina. We called her La Negra."

"I'll have to Google her."

"She died. I never thought to hear her music here." Marisol wiped her eyes. "This is my favorite song."

"What does it say?"

"It says, 'All I ask of God is that He not let me be indifferent to suffering.' Please stop talking now. It has been so long for me. I must listen."

Try to make polite to some people and they bite your head off.

When the song ended, Marisol Guzman hurried up to the busker and addressed her in rapid Spanish. La Guzman's gestures were confident—flamboyant, even—not the tentative wringing motions she made when she spoke English. Marisol caught Jill staring. She beamed. Jill turned away.

On the walk home, Piper spotted the ducks. The Burlington bridge spillway was like a printer's drum, spilling ink onto endless sheets of rolling paper. Piper liked to watch the current twirl its wild lottery of objects: basketballs wheeling in wet orbit, two-by-fours popping to the surface and smacking and falling; Big Gulp cups whirling and garbage chuffing in zigzags along the hem of water.

All this flotsam huddled together as if for guidance, but it was just the indifferent movement of the water that held it in place. The bits and bobs bounced and drifted along the margin of the spill but never broke downriver.

"Papa, Mama, duckies!"

Against this perpetual motion mess a mother duck and two ducklings paddled hard. The mother duck tried to lead her two ducklings, dark with fuzz and with stumpy unfledged wings, away from the whirlpool of current, but the roiling water tossed and ducked them all.

The two families watched the ducklings surface and paddle frantically to stay close to their mother, who, being stronger, could ride the current to rest herself and then swam against it. The ducks struggled, sliding under waves and moving parallel to the spillway, moving forward and being pulled back to the place where the current was strongest. The mindless race of the river didn't distinguish between living birds and the clots of toilet paper dragged across dead branches. The river swept the ducklings apart and banged them together, pulling them back along the seam of water no matter how hard they swam.

"She's going to leave them," Marisol said. "She will fly."

"Papa," said Piper, "get them out!"

Jerry looked at the women. He looked down at the ducklings. The river ran high, and he knew better than anyone what it could do. A huge tree, torn from the banks by the current, hung over the spillway. Objects danced in that limbo of water. The mother duck flexed her wings and rowed herself into the air. Free from the pull of the water, the duck gained strength and flew above the breast of the river.

"NO!" Jill shouted, turning to follow her flight.

The ducklings were two small shapes in the water.

Then mother duck swooped once, low, above her ducklings, quacking in distress. Then she turned and flew high over the bridge and away.

"Papa, get them out!" Piper wailed. People passing gave them curious looks. One cyclist paused, looked down at the ducklings, and shook his head.

"Fuckin' spillway," he said. "But you can't fight Mother Nature."

The river rolled the ducklings like dice.

Jerry considered the water.

"Don't even think about it," Jill said.

When they reached their house, Marisol Guzman headed for their door like she lived there. Jill stopped her.

"You have to go home now," she said as sweetly as possible. "We're all a little upset. Piper needs a nap. I'm sure Manny does too. And my husband and I have things to discuss." Then, because Marisol looked tired and lost, "I'll call you."

"What time, please?"

"I'm not sure."

"What time, Jill? Six o'clock?"

"Well, that's usually when we—"

"Of course," said Jerry. "She'll call you at six tonight. We had a lovely time. See you soon."

"See you soon, Cherry!" She walked off as cheerfully as possible.

"Thanks a lot, Jerry," said Jill, tearing a Post-it off the pad and writing "Mrs. F__ing Guzman, 6 pm" on it.

Marisol let herself into their tiny, dim house. Even if she left home for only a few hours, the smell on returning surprised and dispirited her. She swung Gracie off her back and set her in the playpen, where the baby cried. She dragged Manny into the bathroom and sat him on the toilet, knowing already from the heavy droop of his pants that she was too late, the farmer's market had been too much.

She hoisted Manny into the tub, letting him splash in a safe two inches of water. Standing over the sink, rinsing the brown muddiness from Manny's pants, Marisol thought of the mother duck, how her blue side feathers had flashed when she finally took to the sky. She had called Héctor "El Pato" because he walked like one. Where was her husband? She looked in the mirror above the sink. Her face was so different here, her American face. Haggard and ugly. Even with lipstick. With lipstick her mouth just looked old. Héctor. Dear God.

Marisol had thick black hair with a vitality that shot sparks when she brushed it, which wasn't often, and yesterday afternoon the baby wound her fist in it and pulled and wouldn't let go so she hacked it free with a breadknife and left the baby, bewildered, gumming a clump. She hauled open a drawer and unsheathed her sewing scissors and considered cutting it all off, but she remembered how Héctor loved her hair, how he loved to wrap it around his hands and bathe his face in it. So she walked around lopsided, picking up toys and chucking them in the crib, piercing a bare sole on a red plastic block that Manny had left on the floor. There weren't enough hands.

She had begged Héctor to stay.

"It's too hard without you!"

"If you can't accept what is hard you make everything impossible," he said. Disappointed, furious. He insisted he find her father for her, though her husband was the man she needed. Héctor was always striving—reaching, he called it—toward hope and action. He was her strength; he mustered some instinct in her that she lacked when she was left alone. That curling of the spirit around life, like the first grip of a baby's fingers on your own. The desire to make contact with life was so profound that it began as a reflex. Most fingers were born knowing how to hold.

But Marisol always let go. She had fought to hold on to Héctor and had not been strong enough to do that, either. The civil war weakened her. When they took her father something in her shattered and she could not get up out of bed for a week until Héctor made her laugh—who knows how? Sometimes all it took was a look in his eye, the quirk of an eyebrow, and she returned to life. But she could only do so if he was beside her.

The dirty water from Manny's underpants ran over her fingers. She rubbed and sloshed and watched the waste creep into the creases of her knuckles. She hadn't been sleeping. She could feel herself ebbing, logged and heavy with milk but so tired that the slightest thing made her snap and terrible things came out of her mouth—cruel, evil things, calling Manny stupid, cursing the baby; she was demented by a tiredness so huge it amounted to wickedness.

Héctor preached not resignation to suffering but the healing of it. He shouted at her—Why do you accept so little? Why are you so meek? You must insist on more—not the greedy *more* that demands satisfaction, but the *more* that reaches, that demands the light. I see how you miss your father. Why won't you let me reach for him? What you call resignation, I call despair. A sin against God, Marisol.

She turned off the sink faucet, wrung out the underpants, and draped them over the rim of the tub. Manny splashed happily. She soaped her fingers, rinsed, and pulled him to a standing position. She washed his bottom and his legs. In a few hours Jill would call. If only her English were better. If only she could explain herself to another wife-and-mother, be recognized and forgiven. She was so afraid. She felt close to Jill after their morning together. Jill would listen. And people could help one another. La Negra's song promised it. Unless the song was really about fear, about the fear of losing one's humanity—the fear that a person could be so crushed, so tired, they would no longer be able to help, or care. Marisol shivered. No. The song was about hope. She could make it through four hours. She dried and dressed Manny and fed Graciela, and when her phone rang early she picked up excitedly.

"Jill?"

But the voice spoke in the familiar accents of home and gave her the news that Héctor had been taken, that, for now, at least, he wasn't coming back at all.

Jill didn't call. Marisol waited. Finally she dialed the Ferrell house. She listened to the phone ring while Manny threw his nightly tantrum. When he was finished she changed his pants again, fastened him into his harness, tucked the baby into her stroller, and walked down the street to the yellow house that would smell like pancakes, where a man and a woman and a little girl lived and loved each other and were safe.

She knocked on the door and no one answered. The car was in the driveway. The evening light played gold and rich on its windshield. Mosquitoes materialized and started to bite. No one answered. She put her ear to the door and heard the little girl and her mother reading a book inside. A frog and a toad were going swimming in a river? She knocked harder. A mosquito sucked at Gracie's eyelid. Another trembled on Manny's broad forehead. Soon he would be bites all over, the size of pesos.

Marisol knocked again.

"Jill?" she called. "It's after six o'clock! I have waited!"

She pressed her ear to the door, heard whispers, a giggle. Then: "GO AWAY." The little girl yelled it with delight. "GO AWAY!"

Marisol turned and herded her children away. She crossed the highway and pushed the stroller on the path alongside the deep surge of flooded river, hauling on Manny's lead when he stomped puddles too hard or hooked himself under the river fence. The river lapped the sidewalk, soaking her shoes. She kicked them off and continued barefoot. The river water felt gritty underfoot, and she stepped on a piece of broken glass. Bleeding, she crossed the street and headed for the Kum and Go, a gas station lit up more brilliantly than any church. Inside, the air conditioning chilled her—she felt wet all over. But she wasn't ready to go back into the house whose colors hurt her eyes—the shrieking shades of Manny's toys and the bathroom tiles that wavered in the stink of dirty diapers piled in the pail.

"Miss," said a red vest from the cigarette kiosk, "you can't come in here barefoot."

Marisol wound the aisles, leaving pink smears on the linoleum. Her foot stung. She loaded the stroller's back pouch with cheese crackers, a bottle of water, some apple juice. Manny broke for the sunglasses rack. He spun it so enthusiastically that sunglasses flew out of their slots and cracked on the floor, then he tacked left, hard, and she snagged his harness as he stumbled past and brought him to heel beside the stroller. He pulled for the candy aisle and she stumbled, treading on a pair of sunglasses and popping a rainbow-shot lens.

"You'd better pay for those," said the red vest and visor. "I could call security. Do you know you're bleeding?"

On buses in Colombia you could hand a strange woman your baby if your arms were full and she would hold it for you, but the one time she tried that in America the woman had recoiled and glared at her, and so she had shouldered her baby and gripped Manny's hand and prayed he wouldn't have one of his fits until they got home, and then the bus took a sharp corner and all the groceries spilled and only one person bent to help her pick them up, and that was Jill, who was riding the bus with her little Piper "to keep her from driving me crazy," and Marisol had felt better for a moment.

That bus ride was a year ago. Jerry persuaded the church to donate her a car, thank God, but she still felt so tired. There weren't enough hands in this country.

She had thought when she and Héctor finally made it to America that she would find peace and safety. She hadn't expected this terrible loneliness that was worse than anything. But Manny came out wrong and then she was pregnant with Graciela and Héctor had returned to Colombia, which they both knew would be dangerous, and now he was taken, too.

At the checkout she asked for three miniature bottles of whiskey. She paid for everything; Manny wore the broken sunglasses.

The wind blowing off the river was warm, but even so it flayed her. The wind here all the time so rough and pushing. She wanted to slap it. In some places in the world, where the wind blew constantly like this, people shot themselves just to make the wind stop.

The river lapped over the sidewalk. She pushed the stroller through it, leaving a wake. La Negra sang to her. She sang of the loneliness of leaving one's country, of the hopelessness of the ones who had to live in a different culture. Let me not be indifferent, she sang. Once Marisol had thought this was the best, the only prayer. She had been strong and believed that she was the one who would help others, save them from drowning, being trampled. Now she felt the indifference filling her lungs and pulling her down. There were never enough hands.

Marisol stopped at a picnic bench by the Optimist's Club's empty lot. They sold Christmas trees there in winter, but right now it was vacant except for the enormous red and green sign. She nursed Graciela. The baby sweated against her bare breast. Gracie's eyes fluttered as she gave in to sleep, her lips loosed the nipple and it sprang free, leaking beads of milk. Marisol kissed the baby's damp scalp and eased her onto the grass. She gave Manny apple juice spiked with whiskey and he drank it thirstily. The river reflected mountains of cloud. It pushed hard against the bridge, running so rough and deep that it seemed to stand still. On the railroad trestle overhead a motionless train chuffed to life and thundered away. The river rippled over the path. She tucked her other provisions into Manny's knapsack and buckled him, unconscious, into the stroller with his sister balanced in his lap. She steadied the sleeping baby with one hand and pushed the stroller carefully through the floodwater.

• • •

Eventually, she knew, Manny would start crying. His tears were stronger than sleep. She wasn't worried about the children. They would be received in loving arms very soon. She unlocked her car and slid into the driver's seat. In the windshield she saw La Negra's face round and strong, billowing around her hawk-shaped nose; her eyes beaming wise and beautiful through curtains of rain-black hair. She watched La Negra walk above the river, spreading her arms to include the whole world, with her body like a mountain, the source of that voice dark with compassion. La Negra strode the river, singing. Marisol backed out of the driveway and drove to meet her.

Early Sunday morning Jill was mopping up the streaky remains of her daughter Piper's blue period—that is, the blueberry yogurt that she did everything to but actually eat.

"Haiylp!" called Piper from the bathroom.

Lately Piper had taken to calling out for her in the languishing tones of a southern belle whenever she needed the littlest thing. Jill knew if she didn't move fast those genteel tones would turn to death-metal screams. The Irish didn't invent the banshee, thought Jill. They just had lots of children.

The radio quacked. Jerry always left it on too loud.

"Jerry, turn that down! And hurry up—you and Piper will miss church."

He didn't answer. Where was he? Fucking NPR. Jill couldn't stand it, no considered voice of inquiry please, and especially not first thing in the morning. Lately everything indicted her—telling her that she was no longer interesting enough, curious enough, concerned enough. Jerry loved NPR. She suspected he had a little hard-on for Terry Gross.

"It's important to keep up," Jerry always said. He had so much energy; he could pull her like a caboose. Before she had Piper, she loved it. It was why she'd married him. She'd been your basic liberal arts dreamer, directionless, passionate, interested in the interior life and the human condition. What luxury, looking back! Jerry, solid and (so she thought) practical, promised to give her the kind of shelter where she could think and savor life, stay home, be a mother, take her time. It all turned out wrong.

Long ago he had told her that his favorite word was *genki,* the Japanese term for being in touch with your original energy, the energy you were born with, the energy of a child. Once, this had seemed very spiritual, and significantly possible, but lately she'd come to believe that Jerry had recovered so much energy because he refused to be introspective about anything. He told her that "Why?" was the most useless question ever invented and that it wasted time. The right question, the only question, he said, was "How can I help?" and she had glowed with love at that. But now she wondered if that kind of denial was really helpful.

"You know what I love about you?" Jerry told her a few weeks after he returned, before his night terrors sent them to separate beds. "You never ask if I killed anyone over there."

"What a question!"

"A lot of people ask. You didn't."

No need to mention that she'd always just assumed.

"You know you can tell me anything, Jerry."

"Some things," he said, "can't be told."

His sorrow was so huge that it walled him off from his own family. And La Guzman—she'd just stepped through those walls like they weren't there. But maybe that was because she lived inside the walls already. Jill had Googled it—civil war, Colombia—and after clicking three links had snapped the computer shut because she was weeping. You could do a lot to people without killing them. Fingernails. Testicles. Decades of anguish and bloodshed in a country Americans barely thought about. Generations of it, with no hope that it would ever come to an end. No wonder Jerry and Marisol understood each other. Shut out of their sorrow—Jill should thank her stars. She and Piper were equally naïve as far as Jerry was concerned. They were on the other side of the wall.

"Haailyp! Haillyp!" cried Piper.

"Jerry, can you get Piper? Jesus!"

Between NPR and Piper Ferrell, her nerves were shot and she'd only managed two sips of coffee.

She unpeeled Jerry's hasty note from the lintel of the doorway.

on a dive—sounds bad. back when I can. (heart), J.

Beside it, her own stingy reminder fluttered.

Mrs. F__ing Guzman, Saturday 6 p.m.

The Post-it reproached her. Her tongue stuck in her throat. A small, cold voice, a voice she had only heard once in her life—when it had told her she'd conceived Piper, this small voice, absolutely calm and absolutely certain, told her now that Mrs. Guzman was in the river.

"Hailyp, hailyp!" cried Piper from the bathroom.

"Coming, honey," said Jill. She scrambled to her feet and went into the kitchen to shut off the radio—as if whoever it was could see her and know that if this was what she feared, it was all her fault.

Late in the afternoon, when Jerry still hadn't come home, Jill walked to the river. Bystanders congregated along the bridge, peering down at the dive boat. Jill parked Piper in her stroller beside the spillway and looked down into the water. She could just make out Benno in his orange parka, monitoring the lines. Jerry was down there right now, with his towlines and markers, wearing his harness and diving into the jackpot of the spillway.

She imagined the river was cold, and heavy, and inevitable, closing over what had entered it with only the token protest of a splash. Jerry told her that a corpse diver works in total darkness, using only his sense of touch. Any light would just star out in fractured rays and blind him. He would see fingers of light parting the water, but not the movement of his own hands. Not the bodies waiting in the river. He had to hold it all in his mind's eye—the victim's position, the body bag, the search line, and the closest up-and-down line.

There weren't enough hands. Marisol Guzman wrote her accusation on the water. Not enough hands, she charged, and swung the wheel. Jerry told Jill that the river never paused. You had to be like the river. You couldn't hold back. But not everyone had his energy; his secret of continuous motion, motion that worked with life.

Now Jerry was diving down to the wreck in the dark, placing marker buoy lines around Guzman's drowned vehicle. Now he was busting her windshield and swimming in. Now he felt for her seat belt clasp in the dark and the cold. Now the river rolled her into his lap. Her long hair swarmed over his hands as he zipped her into the bag.

On the boat, Benno waited. Jill ached for Jerry to surface. She imagined the strong muscles of his thighs seizing from the cold and the strain, imagined him locked and rigid, trapped in the dark and the water.

Jerry's head broke the surface and he swam the body in its bag over to the side of the boat. Benno hauled Jerry over the gunwale and he collapsed into the boat. The bagged body nestled against the towline, bobbing in the water.

Hours later, she heard the shower running and knew Jerry had come home. She felt the steam creep into the bedroom. She turned over and hugged a pillow. Had he found the children? Or had his hands simply closed on slimed branches and plastic bags clotted with mud and duck feathers?

"What did you say to her yesterday?"

The room was dark and Jill couldn't see him well, but she felt despair and rage playing off Jerry's bare skin. She should hug him. Reassure him. But she was afraid.

She snapped on the light and sat up.

"What are you implying, Jerry?"

"Yesterday. When you called her at six o'clock. What did you say?"

"I told her to go jump in a lake, Jerry. Is that what you think?"

"This isn't a joke. There's stuff down there, don't you get it? Things I never tell you—"

"I overhear you and Benno."

"Benno doesn't know. The one time Benno tried to reclaim a body he panicked and now he doesn't do anything but vehicles, evidence, and personal effects, okay? Benno is full of shit. There are no words for what it's like down there, and honestly, Jill, there shouldn't be. So shut the *fuck* up. I might still love you, but I need you to shut up."

She looked at the familiar freckles on his wet shoulders. Something in the curve of his spine reminded her of Piper.

"I fished her out," he said. "And I dove for those kids."

"Jerry," she said. "I never called her. I forgot."

He didn't answer.

"Jerry," she said again. "Goddamn it."

She crossed the bed and put her arms around him. "I'm sorry," she said.

His heart beat wildly against her and he smelled like stress sweat. She felt the anger trembling down his arms as he hugged her back, gripping her a shade too tightly, so she didn't know if this was a hug or harming, and she let herself be gripped, her own adrenaline clanging, until they both turned sore and stiff. They were lying that way when Piper shuffled in, dragging her stuffed goose.

"I'm scared."

"Hop in," said Jerry. He let go of Jill.

Piper climbed between them.

"Manny's in the basement and he's crying," she said.

Jill stroked her hair and settled the goose under Piper's chin.

"Manny's gone, honey. He's not here."

"But you're safe." Jerry kissed her.

Jill reached across Piper's body for Jerry's hand. He pulled away from her, turned his back to her and tucked his hand under his cheek. She stared at the ceiling. The rain started again. Jerry dove into his exhaustion and disappeared. Piper whimpered in her sleep. The rain surged, spilled countless nails on the roof.

Jill lay still, listening.

She rose as if stung, pulled on her robe, crept downstairs and through the kitchen to the door that led to the basement. The dog shivered in front of it, scratching at the wood and barking abrupt, urgent barks. But he would not budge out of the way when she reached for the doorknob. Jill nudged his brisket sharply with her knee, an old training trick, but he only barked again at her and would not move. She couldn't bear to move him, couldn't see pushing or hurting another creature today. All her choices had been wrong. Heart pounding, she backed away.

Jill let herself out the front door into the rain, flinching in the downpour, teeth chattering, although the rain wasn't cold. She went around the side of the house and yanked open the gate of the tall backyard fence. Standing in the backyard, she faced away from the house and peered through the curtains of rain. The yard yielded nothing to her view but the tall sugar maple, the usual litter of Piper's toys in the grass, the dog dish, the clothesline hanging slack. Beyond the tall uprights of the back fence, the dripping gables of the house across the alley.

Jill leaned against the gate and let the rain soak her terry-cloth robe until it was wringing wet and heavy and clinging, afraid to turn her head, to approach, even with her eyes, the back door of her house. She stared ahead blindly, at the wet brown puddles rain-pricked in the wet yard, at the wet green leaves whirling down from the wet tree, at her own raw, wet feet, streaked with wet blades of wet grass. At the corner of her vision there was a bright red shape she could not bear to look at straight, a red blot that insisted she turn. Her feet carried her toward it, forced her few steps from the fence to the corner of the house, from the corner of the house to the outer basement door.

Parked there, a shitty red umbrella stroller, wet, red, rusting at the hinges, with shitty candy-cane handles, so low-slung that even a woman shorter than Jill would have to hunch over it when she pushed. The shitty red stroller's rain-speckled nylon lap cradled a cell phone, a broken pair of sunglasses, and a single key. The rain fell hard, and from the behind the basement door came the windy sound of children crying.

SUNFISH

Hardly anyone let anything die of natural causes. Carline saw this time and again. Jobs, pets, parents, relationships—people were either cling-ons or castaways. Cling-ons believed in prolonging an insufferable existence at any cost; castaways jettisoned it at the first whisper of a blemish. To allow for a natural lifespan, to neither hold on nor let go—who could do that? It was a fantasy, like dying in your sleep.

Carline's cousin Daniel, bless him, was a cling-on. Love's biggest fool.

Daniel had summoned Carline over the mountain to Santa Cruz as he did periodically to celebrate some new romantic phase or to bail him out of some new trouble—and often the two were identical.

"Carline, I've met someone," he had told her, calling her up from his Mickey Mouse table phone, twin to one he had in the seventies.

"We're moving in together."

How was it men always met new women so easily? Carline hadn't even had a date in three years. And she was barely older than Danny. Well, women's years were like dog years. If Danny was forty-five then Carline was Methuselah.

Somewhere along the way Carline had been relegated to membership in the Greek chorus of Danny's drama. She existed now to receive his lover's confidences—a bit player to his Romeo, the lugubrious friar or Juliet's menopausal nurse. Worse, in the absence of more fulfilling attentions, she was getting hooked on playing benevolent and wise. But why did Danny get to be a piner eternal, Lancelot by way of Peter Pan? She wanted some love and stupidity for herself. Making herself accessible as an advisor was just a fancy way of being a snoop. When had she and Cissy become so alike? Not that Cissy would believe in this new Carline, thrust into the peanut gallery—one of life's onlookers. Cissy still thought that Carline gloried in the spectacle that was Carline, and that even with a hamper like Sonny she did all right with men. Carline couldn't possibly be lonely. That was Cissy's job. Cissy believed that no one who had been pretty was ever really lonely. To Cissy, Carline's loneliness was just another glamorous cosmetic.

"Come meet her, Carly. Bring Sonny. We want to start a family."

Whenever Daniel said the word *family,* Carline could hear his mental genuflection. Worse, when he said the word *family,* she genuflected too—some reflexes didn't dull with age.

"Since when have you wanted a baby?" Carline said, dumping her tote and Sonny's duffel under the sunflowers in front of Daniel's garage.

"Since always."

"How long you known this chick?"

"Since always," he said.

Anyone who'd been married, really married, heard that kind of talk and just felt tired.

"Her name's Maizie," said Daniel.

"Short for Margaret?"

"Short for *amazing*."

Danny's one serious girlfriend had left him twenty years before; since then he dated a parade of inappropriates, but the relationships never took. Maybe it was because no woman could compete with his hoard of childhood memorabilia—old toys and gadgets, nothing more recent than 1978. Nostalgia was his besetting sin. (How, for example, had he hung on to Daddy's javelina?) His place was a time capsule. Scratch that—time machine. Setting foot over his threshold transported Carline into a younger skin—a shame-filled skin, flaming with grief. God, it made her itch, and not just because every surface in the place cringed beneath the drifts of dog hair.

Carline and Cissy had tried to define the feeling of Daniel's place. Shrine. (Photographs of her mother, his mother, facing off, effaced by dust.) Diorama. Window display. Cissy hit it: secret hideout. Heaven knew how many hours and dollars he spent rummaging the barrows of eBay to obtain objects or their facsimiles from the shared Bowman past. Maybe it was because he never had kids. Though Daniel would beg to differ on the last point. He called his ratty old dog, Miss Mona, his daughter. This irritated Carline, because she had a son, a real one, a galumphing prepubescent enigma, and she knew that no matter how much you loved a dog, it wasn't the same.

Daniel and she argued this—hell, eleven years ago—when she had Sonny at the tit and Miss Mona was old already, or getting there. Daniel sat in his smoking chair feeding fatback to Miss Mona off the tips of his fingers and doting on Miss Mona's intelligence, which Carline translated as plain canine greed, though Miss Mona did have a delicate way of lipping the bacon without snapping or grazing him with her teeth.

"You love your daddy, don't you?" he crooned.

"She's not your whelp," she countered. "You aren't a dog."

"She's my baby," he insisted.

He was as partial as a parent, but that was the only way he resembled a father. He had a streak of willful blindness, and considering that he was a Bowman male, Carline couldn't blame him.

There were some things in their shared childhood Carline wished she could unsee. It went like that in families. Daniel shut his eyes and hid. Her sister Cissy would say that Carline fell into the mirror and stayed, but she was wrong. Cissy wasn't the only one who noticed things. Their poor mother—who knows what she knew? *A lady never tells.*

Mona was some kind of collie. Most of her teeth were rotted out. Daniel wouldn't let his vet pull the remaining few. In Carline's opinion that vet was a criminal for prolonging Miss Mona's life past its expiration date. But she couldn't say that to Daniel without risking one of his rages.

Daniel clung. She'd never known anyone who clung as hard, whose temper broke when you tried to pry him from what he made his through love or the sheer force of delusion. And he was deluded about this dog, from start to finish.

Maybe Carline could use his new girlfriend to convince him

to let Miss Mona go. Sex had a way of persuading people. Unless the girl was still too uncertain of her power to use it. Most young women were. By the time they knew what it was, they'd lost it.

Carline paced the garden with her phone pressed tight to one ear. The connection was terrible, she was probably zapping cancer straight into her brain just like Daniel claimed, but Cissy had texted her for details and Carline was feeling claustrophobic in Daniel's Cub Scout love nest. Besides, if Carline was honest, ranking on Daniel held her and her sister together. It always had.

"The girlfriend's how old?"

Only Cissy could make a gawk so audible.

"How come he never dates a peer?" said Cissy.

"People who believe love conquers all inevitably choose partners who guarantee that it won't." Carline shrugged.

"Or they hold out for the right person," said Cissy, meaning, obviously, herself. "What does she think of the house, Carline?"

"She's 'into vintage.'"

"Well, apparently. She's moving in?"

"I think she really likes him, Cissy. She's sincere. Not Danny-levels of sincere—he's so sincere he sails right around the world and lands back on the continent of Full-of-Shit. But she's in it for real."

"I'm perplexed," said Cissy.

Cissy never felt mad so you'd notice—she took after their mother that way. The strongest negative emotions she permitted herself to feel were puzzled or perplexed.

"Honey, a man can have a mean temper, a drug habit, and a limp dick and he'll find someone to marry him."

"Danny's not that bad," said Cissy.

"He landed you with his dog. Six months dog-sitting a paralytic flea motel."

"He was having a hard time."

"Nothing he didn't bring on himself, Cissy. Drunk driving."

"We all bring things on ourselves," said Cissy, reasonably.

"You can afford to be reasonable. He never makes you come up here."

"Some of us need to work, Carline."

"If you'd ever married you'd know just how hard I worked for my alimony. And I'm paying for my freedom with every minute I spend out here."

Cissy sighed her gusty good-sport sigh, the sigh that let Carline know that Cissy was only giving her sister the last word as an act of patience and charity.

In the morning, Daniel fed Miss Mona wet food out of his palm—probably why her teeth went in the first place. Miss Mona's most recent ailment was on her rump—the skin looked charred and raw—a burnt piece of toast with the carbon scraped off.

"What happened to her?" asked Sonny, who never bothered with anything as subtle as a whisper.

"Mange. Her immune system's shutting down. Poor darlin'," said Daniel, scooping her up. Her back legs were entirely paralyzed, and they dangled from her body. Daniel rubbed diaper ointment onto Mona's cracked hindquarters while Sonny looked on in fascination. He hadn't shown this much interest in anything since he discovered extension cords. Miss Mona wheezed and stank. When she licked Carline's wrist her tongue felt lank and apologetic.

Miss Mona's cataracts put Carline in mind of the comic nightmare of a sunfish she saw years ago at the Monterey Bay Aquarium. The massive scarred-up body, the cloudy eyes, every bit of it battered and grayish. How something could be so huge and so absent chilled her. It swung through the water like an animated dead thing, oblivious to the world beyond the glass. Miss Mona's eyes were like that. Blind and drowned, sad and cold, alive and dead.

"Daniel's always been crazy about animals," Cissy reminded her on the phone that night.

Carline took a bored drag on a cigarette. "Emphasis on *crazy*," she said.

"You like horses," said Cissy.

"I put up with horses like I put up with a pair of high heels that hurt like hell but did wonders for my rear end. I look good on horseback."

"So this gal's really only twenty-five? Lard, he must be terrified," said Cissy.

"Not so you can tell," Carline said. "But who wouldn't be?"

"He drinking?"

"You know how it goes. He falls in love, he cuts back. County didn't scare it out of him, but we'll see."

"I miss Mother," said Cissy, surprising Carline.

Carline's mind went entirely blank. She panicked. Every time she ran out of things to say to Cissy, she worried that she didn't really love her.

"I'm going to euthanize Miss Mona."

"You say that every visit," said Cissy.

"Who ever heard of a pro-life veterinarian? It's just a way to milk sentimental folks for cash."

"Try telling that to Danny."

Carline heard the rustle of cellophane and pictured her sister scrabbling for the last Oreo in the plastic tray. She could hear the crumbs dropping as Cissy chewed.

"Danny's loyal. Mother always called him staunch. Look at how he's hung onto us."

"Taking hostages isn't loyalty," said Carline.

They all sat around on milk crates in the dooryard: Carline, Sonny, the new girlfriend Maizie, Danny, Miss Mona, with the sunflowers nodding and tongues of dust wagging on the ivy that strangled Daniel's redwoods. Daniel's guitar sloped against his shins but he made no move to play it. Carline shifted her behind, which the milk crate grid was turning into an unfortunate denim waffle.

"Can't you get you some chairs, cousin?"

Daniel grinned. "One of these days," he said, looking at his girl.

Maizie was all of twenty-five, closer to Sonny's age than Daniel's. Her hair, eyes, teeth, and skin were still bright. Carline's own teeth had been so perfect at Maizie's age that they'd been featured on a box of Close-Up toothpaste. But age had edged them together. Now when she brushed her teeth (stained every shade from ivory to ochre) they were all huddled up against one another like they were afraid they'd catch cold. She was too vain for braces but not vain enough to put that vanity aside for the long-term benefit, and besides, who was she going to smile for these days?

Maizie tried to talk to Sonny, who felt left out, Carline could tell. He played with his favorite extension cord, the fat orange one as thick as his thumb. The girlfriend, for a joke, plucked a blade of grass and stuck it in the slit on the female end of the extension.

"Mini ikebana," she said, smiling at Sonny.

Sonny blew the frond of grass away, but didn't protest. He liked Maizie. Not that Sonny was any kind of judge. He was like a cat—shined up to some, but mostly lazed off in a world of his own. Daniel off-gassed another one of his stories, and only Carline listened, and then only with half her mind, because honestly, after a few too many jugs of wine he eclipsed the world with his mouth. She and Cissy liked a cocktail or three, but neither was a real drinker. Cissy in particular was proud of this.

"Sheer dumb luck," Carline insisted. "We took after Mother. Codependents. Just as bad."

Carline had this theory that we all get stuck at certain points of our lives, that they come to define us and exert a kind of gravity. Most of Daniel's stories orbited around his momma, a woman who never was, if you asked Carline. In his head Daniel was still ten years old. Though now he was adding tales from the Farm to his repertoire. Just like Daniel, to turn a pathetic stint in County for one too many DUIs into something romantic and glamorous. Like he was Cool Hand Luke. Please. She envied Danny's power to change mistakes into myths.

And Carline, she guessed she was stuck circling the years before Sonny came and his father left, when she still had a shot at her life. She knew it drove Cissy wild, how she still talked like a teenage beauty queen. But if Carline was honest, the only abilities she had ever developed were the ones she had as a mother. Just now everyone was hungry, but she was the only one who could see it. It was distracting how single people forgot the basic functions.

"Maizie was being harassed by a rooster down in Big Sur. It wouldn't let her get to her car. Cujo with tail feathers. Seriously, the spurs on that thing. It rattled around in front of the driver's-side door, flapping its wings and stretching out its neck like a T. rex. Flapping its comb like a greaser. She stood there shaking her keys at it and saying 'shoo.'"

Carline snuck another peek at this Maizie. Daniel claimed he could talk to animals. But anyone could talk to animals as he did. (If she had a dime for every time he held up a conversation by sidebarring with a squirrel.) His girl had the wit to look mortified. God help her, because Daniel could be a torment to any woman with a grain of sense. How had Carline never noticed before, how much he was like her daddy? Chilled, she shifted her milk crate into the patch of sun that had migrated over to the doorway.

"I hypnotized it by singing 'Old Man River' in a Foghorn Leghorn voice."

Maizie inhaled like she was going to say something but Daniel never gave her a chance. He just kept rolling along. Daniel did possess a splendid baritone. Golden and beautiful. The first time she heard it was at her daddy's funeral. Danny's voice broke early, and it was uncanny, those deep tones rolling out of his fifth-grader's body. Danny stood by Cissy at Mother's piano, pouring himself into 'Amazing Grace.' Cissy poked dutifully at the chords with numb fingers. Daddy's den stank of flowers,

which in Carline's opinion smelled like an old lady's under-
drawers. Carline cast herself onto Daddy's lilac-strewn coffin lid
and scrubbed at her masca-racooned face with a scrap of blue
nylon—they all used handkerchiefs in those days, and yes, it
was dramatic, but considering? Come on. Their mother rubbed
Carline's back absently. Even through the runnels of mascara,
Carline was struck by how grown up Cousin Danny looked
when he sang, and as fearless as an angel. He could grip your
heart, no doubt.

Even now. He was singing "Old Man River" in, yes, a cartoon chicken voice, and she had goose bumps.

"I think the rooster would have gotten bored and wandered
off eventually," said Maizie with an ironic smile. Mistake. You
didn't want to contradict a Bowman male. Or use irony. Bowman males did not recognize irony, but it enraged them none-
theless.

"He was hypnotized," said Daniel. "He went and lay down
in the lupines like he was going to hatch a clutch of eggs. I convinced him he was a biddy."

"I love to hear you sing," said Maizie. She put her hand on
Daniel's knee. She knew to do that much. Or was learning,
poor thing.

"If it weren't for me," Daniel said, "you'd still be stranded
there on that dirt road."

The girl hugged him so fiercely, Carline could see that that,
at least, was true.

Maizie and Danny were raising a pumpkin for Halloween. They
hoped to raise a child. Danny said the pumpkin would be good
practice. Carline noticed that Maizie winced at this—the cor-

relation was too fanciful—a nursery rhyme, not a fairy tale. To make amends for the wince she rhapsodized—she was thrilled to have a garden! She moved around so much, growing up. And yes, a pumpkin would be good practice. A pumpkin was very like a baby. Carline rolled her eyes. Poor girl was learning to shack up in symbols, since they were where Danny lived. If this girl wanted to be rescued, she picked the wrong knight. Danny was more of a dashboard Jesus, with fuzzy dice for testicles. His every sentiment was as flimsy as a greeting card, as slick as a stick-on star.

When Carline, Maizie, and Sonny dug up Danny's garden plot, iron nails, bent and rusty, caught in the tines of Maizie's fork. Daniel had sunk them in the ground years ago, to amend the soil. Watching Maizie work barefoot, Carline thought, *tetanus,* and she pitched the nails into the trash, let them clatter among the glass of all of Danny's wine bottles. Danny fished them out and forced them back between the earthworms flickering in the disturbed earth. He couldn't part with so much as a nail.

Later, Maizie wandered enticingly among the sunflower stalks like a Gauguin maiden, a basket of iris and sunflowers hooked over one elbow, a few irises threaded in her cloud of hair, but Danny sat on the porch and lifted the jug, and stoked himself with smoke, and didn't look her way. What was beauty without a witness?

Brushing her fingertips over the heads of Danny's roses, tracing the circular scorch marks that Carline knew were blight, Maizie, her face strained with sincerity, explained to Carline that Daniel's neglect was a form of trust, which was a form of love. If neglect was trust and trust was love, then everything was really all right. He loved her. If he would just look up. Maizie brought the roses into vases indoors, her fingers sticky with pale green aphids.

What was in this for Danny? He had the story that he told, proudly—their chance encounter, the rogue rooster, the instantaneous connection, the glory of love. Their story was all. He polished a tale that went no further than him lifting Maizie over his time-stuck threshold. And Maizie? Maizie had made the mistake of thinking Danny was a destination, a place to settle, come to rest. Carline knew what lost looked like. People that lost went looking for something to lock them in. The poor girl was determined to have an ever-after.

"You done a toothpaste check yet?" Cissy asked Carline that night on the phone.

Carline clicked open the medicine cabinet. Enshrined between a jelly glass crusted with dried-up scotch and a few pellets of Viagra sat that damned red box printed with those white teeth, the cardboard a little crumbly with age but the tube inside plump, unsealed, and perfect.

"Shit-you-not, his little girl found it and tried to throw it out! She was cleaning, being all wifey on him, and she found it and saw how old it was and dumped it in the trash with his eighty-seven kinds of ketchup. He went apeshit."

Carline ground her cigarette out in the sink. She always started smoking around Daniel, and she called Cissy more during one visit to Santa Cruz than she did in the normal course of a year.

"He made her cry. Then he made her put it back."

"God, he can be son of a bitch."

Carline slid the toothpaste back into the box. She never threw it out herself.

"Can you believe Daniel's still hanging on to this shit?"

"Nostalgia."

"It feels like an accusation."

He knew damn well those teeth printed on the box were Carline's. Everyone knew. It was the only modeling job she'd ever booked on the strength of her capped teeth — an expense their mother had always held against her.

"My smile was on the box. That's what gave me the confidence to try out for the commercial!"

"Dan didn't blame you, Carly. And Mother understood. It was a big audition."

Cissy sounded mechanical. Well, this conversation had worn a twenty-five-year groove.

"I was a shoo-in!"

Carline couldn't stop herself. She had to play it out, every single line.

"You couldn't have predicted," prompted Cissy. "The doctors swore Mother would hang on for weeks."

"It was Tom Selleck!"

"A national," Cissy catechized.

"A national. That could have been me at the fuse box, Selleck's nose in my neck."

"No one blames you. Mother didn't."

"She loved his mustache!"

"Everyone did."

"And my agent goes and tells me they didn't cast me because I looked too much like Sharon Tate. But she was beautiful!"

"She really was."

"Patty Hearst, I could understand, but Sharon Tate? I still can't believe I didn't book it."

"Your smile was on the box."

There was a long ritual pause at the end of which Cissy inflected softly, as she always did, with a reverent and tender hush in which the love and patience hung irritatingly palpable: "There was no way you would have reached Mother in time."

Carline had never gone to that audition. Her agent had told her that there was no way she was ready to make the switch from print modeling to television. She made a big deal out of going in for the commercial because it was easier to let Danny and Cissy believe she cared more about a job than her dying mother. Better to seem that kind of selfish than to reveal how truly selfish she had been.

Before the audition that never was, three days before to be precise, she'd had a little procedure—necessary, no regrets, but still, it hurt. The cramps and the bleeding were bad and the dull ache in her chest was worse, and on top of that to go see her dying mother, whom she hadn't told because what if her mother's dying wish would be to insist that the little fish in Carline's body become her first grandchild? Carline flushed the little fish, no regrets, but it was selfish; she knew her mother would say it was selfish.

She delayed rushing to her mother's bedside; instead she dawdled away a whole afternoon in Monterey, pretending she was at the casting call. Really she just sipped Chardonnay from an aluminum flask and looked at fish in the aquarium. She couldn't face their mother's final moments when she herself was still bleeding.

Carline changed subjects airily.

"So do you think this time he'll let me put her down?"

"The girlfriend?"

"The *dog,* dum-dum."

"I hope so."

"I'll just say to him, Danny, when your dog's older than your girlfriend it's time to let her go."

Miss Mona had a seizure. Miss Mona had a fit, which was like a seizure but lasted longer and scared Sonny so much that he went down into the basement and hid with the old trophy animal heads for the rest of the day. Miss Mona had to wear a doggie menstrual diaper that couldn't contain the gallons of green foam coming out of her, so Daniel pinned his best white heavy bath towel around her rump. Carline and Maizie scrubbed the oriental carpet—Mother's gift to Daniel when he left for college—more than Mother had done for either of her own kids.

"Daniel," Carline said, bagging the green stained paper towels and plumping the bag in his overflowing kitchen trash, "she's suffering. Isn't it time?"

"She knows she's loved."

He gathered the dog defensively in his arms and took a deep whiff of her skull just between the ears. He scooped her into the old double-hooded baby buggy he'd picked up at a flea market, covered her with a blanket, rocked the buggy experimentally. Miss Mona closed her eyes and sighed.

"I'll wheel her outside when she needs to make. It's what you do for family."

Pointing out that in most cases he wouldn't notice or even reach Mona in time to wheel her where she needed to go would have led to nothing but a scrap, and Daniel had grown more out of touch and touchier in his unadmitted middle age. The dog's stomach gurgled. Daniel pushed her out to the yard in the buggy. Her sharp arthritic whine when he hitched the baby carriage over the doorsill did Carline's head in. Lard, they both irritated her.

Daniel hated to let anything go. But who didn't? He acted like he and his were some special case. The fuss he kicked up over Mother when she was dying, when she was ready, eager to die. Insisting on more poison, more treatment, when anyone with eyes could see that Mother was done. You had to face things. Carline learned that young. She learned it over and over, with every humiliation, every failed audition, with Mother, with the little fish that wasn't, with Sonny's father, even with Sonny. You just had to rub your own nose in the mess because nothing else would teach you. Daniel was no parent. And that dog was no better than a ruined potato. One injection and she could cross the rainbow bridge into doggie heaven, where the rabbits were more numerous than virgins and every bone Mona ever lost was waiting for her, grimy and game.

"You should have put her down when he was in County, Cissy. You had the perfect chance."

"Don't you blame me for Miss Mona," said Cissy with a rare flash of spleen.

"The animal's in pain, Cecilia Marie. When she breathes, she sounds like a broken squeezebox. Like zydeco in hell. Remember how Mother was, at the end? How if you even rubbed lotion into her hands, she turned white and cried? How she said even her hair hurt, and she didn't have any left in the first place! Six months you had Miss Mona. Why didn't you just get it over with? Lie and tell Daniel she passed while he was gone?"

"That dog was all he had to come back to," said Cissy in her brimstone-and-treacle voice. "Not everyone's as quick to burn bridges as you, Caroline Louise."

"What's that supposed to mean?"

"Calm down," said Cissy.

Carline hung up instead.

Maizie knocked on the door. "Carline? I need the diaper pail."

Carline dashed tepid water on her face, wiped the streaks from under her eyes with the world's flimsiest toilet paper, shook herself all over, and opened the door. Clearly Maizie had heard everything. She wouldn't cross the threshold—she leaned in and dragged the pail toward her and threw Miss Mona's latest accident inside.

Silver liners, the smell.

"*You* could do it, Maizie."

The girl whipped up so fast, Carline stepped back and collapsed onto the toilet lid.

"He won't even let me throw out *toothpaste*, and you think I can persuade him to put down his *dog?*"

Maizie reached out a foot and stomped the mound of diapers down.

Maizie stepped into the garbage can, settled all her weight in the pail. Red in the face. Stomp stomp stomp like she was crushing grapes.

"He's had Miss Mona for practically as long as I've been

alive. Known her. Loved her. I can't compete with that. Don't you get it, Carline? If love means knowing someone, and most of knowing is time, I will not be lovable for a very long time."

Jesus. The child had a point. Mona held, more than any other living creature, two decades of Danny's past. In Miss Mona were his hopeful twenties, his bitter thirties. When she died, what would die with her? No wonder he was afraid to find out.

Sonny wore a dust mask he unearthed from Daniel's tool-shed and elbow-length green rubber gloves he called his Hulk Hands. She could get Sonny to do anything so long as he wore his Hulk Hands. Sonny swooped Mona up into his arms. Carline steadied the dog's head. Mona whimpered, from pleasure at the unexpected attention or in protest—Carline couldn't say. On the couch, Daniel lay passed out, empty wine bottles at hand, *Casablanca* fizzing on his tired old TV. Maizie sat on the floor beside the couch, an old photo album open on her knee. She peeled back the crackling plastic overlay and pried up a photo of Danny as a youth. He frowned out at her over the hip of his guitar like a bereft Adonis. Maizie's gaze softened and she stroked the photo tenderly; behind her, on the chesterfield, Danny snored off his wine.

Maizie held the door for Sonny and Miss Mona, but Carline couldn't convince her to help them beyond that.

"You know this is the right thing to do," Carline said.

Maizie nodded. "But it's still wrong."

"He's too old for you," said Carline, "you know that, right? Something happens to single men in middle age. They live alone too long, they get—stiff. Don't smile like that. I mean inflexible. Men get brittle, women get chin hair and opinions. And no matter what you both may believe, you can't sexually transmit youth."

Maizie's small pile of belongings slumped pathetically beside their Gigi's enormous antique breakfront—still filled with the heirloom Dresden figurines their grandmother cherished, irksome cupids mostly. Nothing Maizie brought to the house could trump Danny's heirlooms with their luster of long association. It isn't her fault that she can't rouse him. Sex, after all, has less power to move a man than Carline's been led to believe.

"I am so tired of making mistakes," said Maizie.

Carline shouldn't have antagonized her. Maizie wasn't bad. But really. Being that young was unforgivable.

Carline and Sonny hurried the dog out to the car. Sonny's protuberant blue eyes watered above the white muzzle of his mask. Carline had given up taking this as a sign of emotion a long time ago. Sonny's tears, like his laughter, flowed detached from any cause she could guess at. Miss Mona licked her nose, nervous swipes with her tongue. Carline hated that dog, how used up and pitiful she was, hated Daniel for keeping her, hated the disgrace of it. She looked awful, like she'd been through chemo, which anyone in the family could recognize—and Carline wouldn't put it past Daniel to have given Mona chemo and lied and said it was mange.

"Is this stealing?" Sonny asked. He slung his seat belt too hard across his chest and it hitched up short. She waited with a pretense of patience while he loosened it, her foot mashing the clutch.

"Kidnapping, at least. It's kidnapping."

"You remember when you were little and Miss Mona could still walk and run?"

"I threw her the yellow ball."

"And she could see, and she could chase it, and she was happy."

"How do you know?"

Sonny always asked this. She ignored it, because attempting to answer it led to an endless chain of explanation that left her feeling groundless, exhausted, and feeble.

"Remember how you fed her under the table even though I told you not to?"

"Bacon," he said happily, "and mushy carrots."

"Well, back then she was all dog. Now she's mostly pain, with just a little bit of dog. As you get older you lose parts of yourself, parts you need. It's like someone turns out the lights inside you, one by one, until there's nothing left but pain."

(Jesus, was this what happened to her father? Here she thought it was Mother who suffered, but maybe her father had reasoned his own exit this way.)

"When there's nothing left but pain, it's better to say good-bye. Miss Mona, the part of her that is still a dog—wants to say goodbye."

"How do you know?"

"I can see it."

"How come Uncle Dan can't see it?"

"Because he loves her."

"How do you know?"

"Pain is bad, okay? It's just bad."

"But you said she's part dog and mostly pain. And if she's

mostly pain, then the dog part doesn't hurt. Maybe the dog part feels okay."

"It doesn't."

"But how do you know?"

The vet, a small gingery man with the close-clipped hair of the prematurely balding, wore a white coat that looked too big and borrowed, and it billowed when he bent to examine Miss Mona. His fingers, tiny and deft, lifted her lips, angled her chin, stalked down her spine and finally chucked her behind the ears in a caress. He listened to her heart. Funny how redheads didn't age, they just pickled up or faded.

His voice piped reedily; his eyes were as bright as a squirrel's, and shrewd, taking Carline and Sonny in.

"You say your cousin sent you?"

"He couldn't make it. He's working a lunch shift."

"I didn't know he worked Wednesdays."

"New schedule since he got back."

"You realize," he said to her, "Dan named one of his nigiri specials after me? The Little-Red-Albacore-Vet."

"He does that for people he likes," she agreed.

"The point is," the man said, "I know your cousin. I know where he stands with this dog."

"She'd have died years ago out in nature."

"We could do dialysis again."

"Christ!" Carline said. "Just send her!"

The veterinarian's face shuttered; any pretense of polite attention drained away.

"Miss Bowman, if you don't mind my asking, whose suffering are you trying to end?"

This was why she hated Northern California. Everybody dispensed their dime-store enlightenment. If you want to be that on the nose, Carline thought, just get into rhinoplasty.

"Bastard," she said to Sonny on the way to the Pacific Grove Target. "I can't believe he charged me for that. I bet he's in love with Daniel."

That was the problem. Everyone loved Daniel. But nobody did him any good.

In Target she picked out one of those body pillow covers in a bright blue plaid, big enough to sleeve poor Mona. She bought a length of garden hose and some duct tape and she let Sonny take two packs of Twizzlers at the checkout, although he'd never grasp the concept of a bribe, and watching him gnaw on the red ropes bothered her some way she couldn't put her finger on, his chin slick with pinkish slaver and his canines shiny in a grin.

She stopped at Daniel's favorite liquor store and bought three fat cans of Guinness stout. Two for Mona and the last can for herself when the deed was done. She served Mona the beer in a yellow basin. Mona lapped it cozily enough. Carline microwaved the pillowcase so it would feel warm, like a womb. Maybe if Mona felt like a puppy she'd slip backwards without regret.

Carline had gone about it all wrong with the vet because she was basically honest. Their mother had cursed them with knee-jerk candor. It was a definite handicap. Carline had practiced for years and still couldn't think tactically, or deceive. She was, let's face it, a shitty actress. But she could at least have summoned the Cast-Iron Bitch. Carline loved the phrase *cast-iron bitch*. She liked any descriptions that made women into metal—but *cast-iron bitch* was her favorite. She'd always felt, deep down, about as durable as a ballet slipper—just papier-mâché with a skin of pink satin scraped over it for decency. But a cast-iron body, black and heavy, greasy, stone cold or red hot—how useful that would be.

When her mother was dying, Carline became Cast-Iron Bitch, up against the doctors and lawyers with whom Danny and Cissy were too fragile, too young, to contend. She may have stopped visiting their mother's hospital bed, but that was because she was busy hammering out the business end of Mother's death. Back then Cast-Iron Bitch surrounded her feeble glowworm of a heart with dense molecules of metal.

Now she let the iron flow down her arms, making them heavy and deadly. She felt her torso go molten and then cool into something hollow. Her legs rang like gongs when she took a step. Her head was solid iron, her eyes blank casts. She trudged, like the statue in *Don Giovanni,* and the earth shook where she trod. Cast-Iron Bitch's black unbreakable fingers could, if they wanted, pierce flesh like awls, and they felt nothing but their own strength. She bent heavily and picked up the dog. The dog's cries rebounded off her iron ears. The dog's smell wavered around the iron nose and fell back from the strong blood-rust tang of metal.

Cast-Iron Bitch stuffed the dog into the pillowcase and hooked the side slit over Mona's snout. Now the dog was just a wheezing plaid pupa, heavy and peaceful from the beer. Cast-Iron Bitch dragged her out to the driveway. She reeled out the hose in one savage yank and stuffed one end into the tail-pipe of her car and tucked the other end in the pillowcase. She stomped to the front of the car so she could let herself in and idle the engine.

Once she was in the car, iron inside iron, her head ached and her iron ribs felt like they were puncturing her lungs. Sonny crammed himself into the passenger seat, set his big feet on the dash, and sat there twiddling his packet of licorice laces. Cast-Iron Bitch twisted the key in the ignition and the car shrugged to life.

"What if she really is, though?" Sonny asked.

"Is what?"

"Uncle Dan's daughter."

"She's not."

"How do you know?"

"She's just a dog, pup."

And there it was.

Long ago, before she knew anything was different with Sonny, when he was still at the chubby infant stage where they remind you of every baby animal in creation—duckling, chickie, lambkin, cub—he was her pup. Is it any wonder people get dogs and children mixed up? Those trusting eyes, the way they come to you for comfort when you've hurt them. Babies and puppies both round bottomed and bumbling, slobbery, prone to gnawing and nipping. They even smell similar—that sweetish dusty milky smell at the top of the skull that you inhale until your eyes roll back in bliss. How could she have forgotten? When Sonny was learning to crawl he arched his back and strained on the carpet just like a fat seal perched on a rock.

And the noises he made! Waking to him was like waking to an entire pet shop.

"Goddammit, Sonny."

Why did the past always have to step in and clutter up the present? Trembling, the bitch switched off the car.

"What's all this?" Daniel asked. He padded out in his sock feet, finger in the neck of a wine bottle, his cheaters slipping down his nose. He looked like a confused old woman.

"Oh, I thought we'd slipcover Miss Mona," Carline said, giving him a scrap-metal smile. "Beautify her mangy behind. Doesn't she look pretty?"

Daniel set the bottle on the pavement, adjusted his glasses, and glanced at the coil of hose that Sonny was looping into running knots. The stink of exhaust hung in the air. He looked at the yellow bowl laced with beer foam, registered Mona's rubbery belch inside the pillowcase. Carline caught a flash of comprehension, fleet as a fish. Pain hovered in his eyes and then spiraled back down into the depths where he drowned things. He nodded at Carline, smiled a trembling smile, and hunkered down to scratch Mona through the plaid.

Shame should be heavy, but this feeling was hideously light, a gauzy unraveling that left Carline tiny and exposed, less tangible than vapor.

Danny unfolded from his crouch. She heard the bones in his knees click. (When had they all gotten so old?) The dog breathed, farted, sighed from her depths.

"Sonny," Carline said, "lend me your Hulk Hands."

She shucked the drunk dog.

• • •

"They're trying for a baby," Carline told Cissy.

"The way he smokes? I doubt he has any sperm worth counting."

"Ew."

"You brought it up, Carline."

"It would be a disaster."

"He's always wanted a family."

"Okay, here's the thing." Carline closed the bathroom door and locked it. "I can give him Uncle Jeff's address."

Cissy's silence was as pointed as a question.

"Mother had it all along. The address, I mean. She gave it to me when she went into the hospital. Told me she kept Danny's real daddy's whereabouts quiet because she wanted Danny to have all the advantages."

"I thought we'd found out everything there was to know about Mother," murmured Cissy.

"I was as shocked as you are. I stuck the address card in my navy blue Coach bag, the hobo bag, you remember how darling? I meant to give it to him but with one thing and another, there was never a good time. And then you know I went on my leopard-is-a-neutral kick and phased out the navy purse—stuck it in a closet and forgot all about it. Don't sigh like that, Cissy—I aced Psych 101 last semester. I *know*. But it was an oversight! And then when I got into that vintage perfume racket, selling Mother's collection, I thought, why not offload my old handbags? I was cleaning them out and posting them and that's when I found Uncle Jeff's address."

Carline peered in the mirror, pocking her chin with a grimace and searching for stray hairs.

"The phone number's still good. I talked to Dan's dad. Well, to the wife, because as soon as Uncle Jeff heard it was me he handed the phone off."

"You can't. Danny would never forgive us. He'd hate Mother."

"But it might distract him."

"She's his sainted aunt. Literally, Carline."

"He always persuades himself that these strays are soul mates. Remember when Mother was dying, when Danny was convinced he was gay and wanted to come out to her and "make things right"? All because of that boy Andrew in the hospital ward? Said Andrew looked deep in his eyes like he was peering into his soul. And we said to him, Danny, you mean Andrew with the Coke bottle glasses? *That* Andrew? His eyes don't peer into your soul because he's in love with you—it's because he's more myopic than Mr. Magoo! And this poor girl's mistaken Danny's musty-ass heap of heirlooms for a solid home. Cissy, I kind of like her. She deserves better. You know Danny doesn't really want to be a daddy. He just never got over not having one of his own."

"Spare the dog but euthanize the relationship," said Cissy.

What a coward she was, in the end. In the end she iced the address onto the surface of Danny's speckled bathroom mirror with ancient dentifrice. She was her mother's daughter, neat-handed and precise. She forced the tube flat and rolled up her former smile until it was just a curl of empty plastic. Who was to say anything was for the best? The wrong things hung on forever, and the things you cared about refused to stick. Probably that old sunfish was still alive too, still circling in its glass halls, dead-eyed and incurious, waving daggered fins with a slow, chilly pulse, plump as a boulder, denser than lead, cruising around like a planet among lesser satellites in all that water.

Outside, Maizie, barefoot in the pumpkin patch, wandered among the small, eager vines that were unfurling their green cords and reaching out for something, anything to twine to.

A NEIGHBORLY DAY FOR A BEAUTY

When did sixteen-year-olds get so young? Danny's always dismissing Maizie as just a kid, but the girls in here look like infants. Yet these fetal teens appear far more blasé than Maizie feels. Chewing their gum and communing with their flip phones. Are they faking it? Is she the only woman in the place whose buried Catholic conscience is mortified to find itself here? The boy looks uncomfortable, at least. He pulls off his carelessness less believably; slouched in his chair, he doesn't know what to do with those long legs, those big feet in their enormous shoes. His mustache has yet to take on any real muscle, and he has no idea how touchingly young it makes him look. If she were his mother she'd tell him to shave it.

Staff swim in and out of view behind bulletproof glass. Maizie feels drowsy. If it weren't for the creeping snail of fear currently gnawing her mental cabbage, she'd actually doze off. And why is every single magazine in this waiting room fixated on celebrity baby bumps? Regressive choice for a Planned Parenthood clinic. She flips through an article on single celebrity moms in the latest September *Us Weekly;* though "single" hardly describes it. They're phalanxed by posses of nannies—it takes a village, after all.

Maizie fills out forms. She pees in a sample cup and puts it into the gloved hands of a lab tech. A medical assistant shuts her in a tiny exam room, leaves her to sit in the queasy glare of fluorescent overheads. She flicks at the white paper girding the vinyl exam table. The gray metal stirrups have been left half-cocked. She considers pushing them back in, but she doesn't want to touch them. There's not much to else to look at. She read somewhere that some people find medical scenarios erotic. Translucent plastic sharps container for bloody needles. A cylinder of swabs on the counter. She'll pass. In all that white and beige and gray, the exam room's few splashes of color shock her—electric blue latex gloves peeking up from their boxes, candy-pink antiseptic soap in the dispenser over the sink, a glossy red can marked BIOHAZARD.

She pulls a paper towel from the dispenser, pleats and unpleats it. Maybe the time is done for dreaming. Whatever else is true, none of this is what she dreamed. She considers calling Jill; surely Jill, who has been through worse, will tell her what to do. But one of Maizie's current disciplines is to be an obeyer of signs, and that one above the table says NO CELL PHONES. To distract herself she plucks an STD pamphlet from the wall rack and flips through. The scrupulously diverse pictures of chlamydia victims and herpes sufferers fail to distract her from the betta fish that darts in her stomach, changing colors: dread, excitement, excitement, dread. She should have eaten first.

• • •

A nurse arrives and reads from a checklist without looking at Maizie.

"Single?"

"Living together."

"The father?"

"Doesn't know."

"Do you consider yourself to be in any danger in your home?"

Now, there's a question. Aberrant behavior can be rationalized as romantic, at first. The little incident with the toothpaste alarmed her, but she told herself it was proof of how hard and how truly Danny loved. If he felt that strongly about a tube of expired toothpaste, imagine what passion he would lavish on her. When Carline saw the Close-Up Maizie had thrown in the trash, she squeezed Maizie's shoulder and whispered, "God help you, I never had the guts."

After that, anytime Maizie put a foot forward in her own present, she stepped in Danny's past and it stuck to her shoes like dog dirt. But no one can say she hadn't been warned.

The nurse asks if she'd like to see a social worker. Maizie says no. The nurse asks Maizie if she has understood her options for termination. Yes, she understands. Vagabond Maizie has picked up a little hitchhiker of her own. She has a few miles to make up her mind, but she'd better commit to a destination pretty soon; hesitate and she'll fly past all the exits.

The nurse hands Maizie some pamphlets. Domestic violence. Depression. Parenting. Abortion. Adoption.

Back in August, Maizie and Danny tried raising a pumpkin for Halloween, feeding it milk, which was Maizie's idea. Their pumpkin grew a little—it plumped to the size of a softball. Then, stingily, it refused to swell. Danny blamed the milk, and by extension, Maizie. Furious, he dragged her out to the garden and asked her why she'd filled his momma's best Fiestaware bowl with rotten milk.

Pine needles drifted in the yellowing milk. Ants struggled on top of its floating skin, and curds had formed along the wick that fed into the pumpkin. Danny made her fling the whole mess over the fence. She was so frightened, she knocked the bowl on a picket of the fence, breaking it in two. While Danny raged over the broken bowl, Maizie scried the hieroglyph that the ants and milk made on the pavement. It screamed *Go*. Instead she swept the sidewalk clean and stayed. A few fights later, when gophers severed the pumpkin from its stalk and dragged it underground, she did nothing to stop them; she knew at that point nothing could save it. The sod burped and settled and eventually the vine died.

According to Babycenter.com the *morula* is the size of a *poppy seed* right now. Why not compare it to something more parasitic? A flea. A nit. Then again, poppy seeds always fetch up in her gums between canine and incisor. You can't tongue one free. They're tiny, but they embed themselves

in the lush lining of your uterus.

They stick. They rankle. They're as small as atoms. *Thou minimus, thou bead.* Is there a little angel inside her dancing on the head of a poppy seed? *Though she be but little, she is fierce.* Maizie feels sick.

By the sixth week, Babycenter.com tells her, their fertilized germ will have developed an *epiblast* and a *hypoblast*, which sound like core workouts at an adamantly upbeat gym, and will be the size of a

   lentil.

Almost a palindrome, *lentil*; a legume Maizie detests. The food of her anarchist squats and ashrams, mushy in the mouth, the flavor of ashes and misplaced aspirations. It's early enough, there would be no scraping, no aspiration for this little lentil. She could take a pill instead. Why don't they tell you, *Right now your embryo is the size of the pill you'll need to set it free; problem and solution are equal in size, do it before the blastocyst becomes a*

   kidney bean,

that symptom of steakhouse salad bars, that can-flavored blot in the three-bean salad. She has always scraped them off with the flat of a knife, buried them under a napkin, which is what she probably will do to their kidney bean. Sooner rather than later. Because if she waits until the ninth week she'll have a

   grape

plumping in her, a stubborn little Dionysus (why a *grape*? why not *your alcoholic boyfriend's bloodshot eye*?), and the week after that the embryo becomes a full-blown fetus, the size of a *kumquat,* at which point its *hands will meet over its heart* like a fat little friar.

These lyrical greengrocer's lists range from the toothsome to the absurd—how can a fetus be a *fig* one week and a *pea pod* the next? Babycenter.com should diversify their descriptions—why not compare the fetus to a packet of cigarettes? Right now the volume of your child's blood is equal to a pony of bourbon. It is the length of a corkscrew. It is the size of the fist of a man who raises his fists only when you provoke him.

• • •

Halloween night, she sits across from Danny at his antique din-ing table. Danny deals them each a scarred-up cutting board, a steel paring knife, and serrated blades to carve out the pump-kin caps.

"This one looks pregnant," Maizie says, hoping he'll catch her hint.

"All pumpkins look pregnant," Danny says. "That's why people like them."

Maizie smiles, and hope rekindles in her, briefly.

Danny's hands are fast; before Maizie's finished scooping out her pumpkin he's carved a perfect jack-o'-lantern.

"It's beautiful."

And it is. Danny's good at many things.

She hacks into hers and the knife slips and her pumpkin's nose caves in.

He tries to console her.

"Yours will have homespun charm, Maizie," Danny says.

"It looks like one of the Children of the Corn carved it."

He laughs, and for a moment it seems possible for them to be happy.

But the guts smell sour when Maizie slops them into the garbage, and some fiend, perhaps the little imp they've kindled in her guts, prompts her to say over her shoulder,

"Basically carving pumpkins is like giving them a D and C."

"What's D and C?"

"Dilation and curettage. Old-timey abbreviation for abortion."

"Christ, you're morbid," says Daniel, showing wine-purple teeth.

"Halloween is morbid; kind of the point," she retorts.

"Not true—Jack Pumpkinhead is smiling."

Danny blusters on about the Halloween when he met his cousins, a familiar story that normally she'd let breeze past. But Danny's words are wind and her news is a candle inside her. She has to shield its tentative flame.

When the pumpkin shells have dried, Danny lowers candles into their deep wells and the heads glimmer to life. He explains to Maizie that he is moving back home, back to Texas, and that it is over. The pumpkins gape at him like incredulous children. The news she's been shielding inside her flickers briefly and gutters out.

Maizie drives up Highway 9, parks, ditches her shoes at the top of the trail, and wanders along the riverbed. Her joints are sore, her feet feel huge. The fetus is triggering changes on the chemical level or the level of dream—phantom thickening, phantom pain, movement that isn't yet movement, under layers of fat in the dark. Are her feet growing or does she just dream they've grown, and what on earth is she going to do?

The river steps down a waterfall with giant's strides, white where obstacles shatter it. She rests beside a miniature tumble of cairns and caves. When she bends to pick up a rock to skip, she startles a snake. Startled herself, she staggers, drops her stone, and sees that dozens of snakes bask on the rocks, testing the air with coral tongues. She mistook their green curves for ripples on the water.

The snake she startled slips a quick figure eight, but miscalculates, and the current whips it down the falls. Other things give way to the current: an ant, a leaf. But the snake, swept in, struggles against the current. It is pure muscle, a winding thread of will in the water. It knifes the current and gains rock.

Then it slips into a crevice and disappears. And all around her the snakes abide in their stillness, and their stillness is strength, a refusal to be buffeted.

It is November 1. Day of the Dead. But she herself is quick. Quick. Quick.

Dear clusterfuck,

Because that's what you are—a cluster of cells from a— I thought he loved me.

Dear blastocyst,

Jill tells me I have to start over and use the correct terms. I said clusterfuck is the right word but she says it's too hostile. I have to use the right terms—zygote—except you're past that—or gamete? All scientific words for clusterfuck. It isn't too late for me to pretend you don't exist. Jill is reading this over my shoulder as she drives. She says it is.

Fine.

Dear embryo,

I don't rightly know how to describe your Aunt Jill's part of the country. It's nothing but roads and sky. I could call it Middle America—you see all the flags? Or God's country—see all the steeples? In the main it's just roads and sky and the occasional hill that Jill says lifts you up so gently you wouldn't even know you've climbed. Maybe people built the roads to get away from the sky, or maybe to meet it; the sky doesn't care. The cars look like beetles trying to race out from under its cupped palm. The entire landscape is sky. Sky for an

ocean and corn silos like sandcastles at its edge. Clouds
for mountains and great biblical lakes of light poured
out among them. The sun throws down ladders of light
and maybe one of these days we can just climb up out
of the corn and strike into those thunderheads and find
the throne of God Almighty and ask him why any of us
are here.

On the last stretch of Highway 80 they pass a billboard bla-
zened with a blue-eyed baby's head and a speech balloon that
proclaims, "I'm a child, not a choice, Mommy."

Jill flips it the bird. "Presumptuous little squirt."

Jill bumps Maizie's rolling suitcase over the curb and leads
her toward her high-shouldered, big-hipped white house. Jill
and Jerry have converted the downstairs of their rickety Victorian house into a daycare; emptied its generous square rooms of
furniture so children can scoot on tricycles or bound on smiling
rubber horses. Jill's achieved all this in a few short years.

"Necessity," Jill says, dismissively, "it rides me like a hag."

Maizie climbs the wet steps and Jill's foster daughter Kyla
runs down to greet them, demanding to see the *dardoll*. Maizie
can barely decipher her speech. They pay their respects to the
potbellied resin gargoyle hidden in the rock wall and then climb
more steps along the garden, where the last golden sunflowers arch as high as MGM blossoms in Munchkinland. Two cats
slink down the staircase and disappear under the tomato vines.

Jill conducts her through the coatroom rubble of tiny shoes
and boots, into an inferno of child-noise. The front room boils
with children. Children of indeterminate gender twirl on the
scrubbed boards wearing tutus and batman capes. Children

cast themselves onto tiny chairs and weep, or glue tear-stained cheeks to the big windows, crying for parents who amble away and vanish between the sunflowers. Children climb platforms and slide down futons and roll on mats in the echoing dimness. Everything is shabby and well-used; even the notch-eared cats looked comfortably grubby and resigned.

Jill threads her way through the chaos, stopping to hand a crying child to one of the teachers—all of the women who work here look like roller derby queens slumming at a day job—peeks into the kitchen to greet some volunteer parents prepping the day's lunch, sweeps a gaggle of children toward the tiled toilet area, where yet another derby girl diapers a squirming toddler on a plastic fiberglass changing board. Bare-bottomed boys mill by the tiny sink, hobbled at the ankles by their shoved-down pants, washing their hands and waiting their turns to be diapered. A little girl sings to herself as she pees.

"We put the toilets in this open space in the back so little kids can watch big kids and learn how pottying works," Jill explained. "I hate the use of *potty* as a verb. My vocabulary was the first thing to go when we started all this."

She'd borrowed the daycare center's design and philosophy from her favorite architect, Christopher Alexander. In *A Pattern Language* he mapped the perfect village, and it included this neighborhood drop-in childcare house.

"It's daycare as a second home, as an extension of the home—a place as stable and open-ended as a family house, where parents can drop their children off anytime, night or day, as if we were extended family. Kids can play here, eat meals, do homework, sleep, live—and move fluidly between this space and their homes. Parents come in and have lunch or dinner with us; if a single mom gets sick she can drop her kids here and know they'll be cared for."

"Sounds like a hell of a lot of work."

"Driving west to pick you up and transfer Manny and Gracie to their father is the first break I've had in five years. But we had to make some kind of money when we took the kids. God, it's still the nineteenth century. What are the options for the liberally educated poor gentlewoman with no connections? Governess, housekeeper, schoolteacher, nanny. Nurse, I suppose. So. Home daycare. It's a nightmare. We're constantly in danger of being shut down, losing our nonprofit status. I can't pay people decently. We need to convert the basement into a real tornado shelter. The legal issues alone—I don't do it gracefully."

A child flits past wearing a bread bag over her hair. The bag stands up like a chef's toque and rattles as she runs.

"Lice," says Jill, her mouth twisting. "They're little germ vectors. This place is a petri dish. In spite of our best efforts."

She touches Maizie's thick braid of hair.

"You look good."

"Hormones."

"Cherish them. After Piper was born my hair fell out in clumps."

Jill rakes her fingers through the new white hairs that kink around her temples and cowlick the crown of her head. She shakes a blurry tangle from her fingers onto the floor. Similar hair clouds, linty and buoyant, scud in the corners of the hall.

"You don't enjoy it."

"Oh, 'enjoy.'" Jill waved her hand. "I wish joy—enthusiasm—were gifts I could give. I leave that to Jerry."

"It doesn't seem fair."

"Oh, 'fair,'" says Jill with the same inflection. "Want to see the backyard?"

"And, Maizie? I'm glad you're here."

Every night at three a.m. Maizie wakes up in a sweat of dread. Sometimes she vomits, and sometimes the water in the toilet splashes back in her face, baptizing her. At these times she thinks of the maids she's had, Mrs. Cho, Neepa, Cevriye, Gvantsa, spat on by steam from cooking pots, mop water seeping at their feet, or tiny drops of water flicked in their faces by the toilet brush. She thinks of Jill, always up to her elbows in piss and tears. How many times are women baptized? Especially mothers? Every single day of their lives? Baptisms both slapstick and tragic: no restrained sprinkle from fingertips dipped in fount. It's no graceful immersion, cool water enfolding us in flowing robes—when two masculine hands force a woman's head down for the most part it isn't to dip her in a river—sweet honey in the rock though she is exhorted to find.

No, mothers are baptized by a child's artless vomit, by their tears and blood. She still can summon the shock, intimate and hot, of the moment a baby pangolin let go all over her thigh, the scalding warmth of its urine. The trail of snot a comforted child leaves on a breast, or in the crook of a neck. The blissful (or regrettable) creep of a lover's semen down one's thigh. There are her own seepings—blood, desire, even a thought can cause a woman to deliquesce.

Life itself knits in a tide of slime. Saliva. Tears. Particles of gold in seawater, and a thousand single-celled creatures that dart and—if they could—would sing. Hosanna to the filthy mother who we wash away with tears. The germs swarm over us and claim us. Name us Mother. Lover. Every woman a Danae under a shower of gold.

She feels as huge as a landscape at times, as generous and all-receiving as the earth, at times as oppressed. Women catch every pang of lust or ecstasy or pity or terror of hunger or pain, catch it with their bare hands, if need be. Defiled or anointed? And baptism begins deep in the body—in the fluid-filled sac. We're born baptized and baptized we continue to be, sprinkled and enjoined to the mess and fuss and pure liquid expression of humanity. Barely a dry hummock of repose between spurts. Spilled milk and crying. The buttery infant shit spun from liquid gold; the unexpected spire of breast milk that jets when a baby cries. Men do not get half so wetted, except, perhaps, with blood.

She misses being a virgin.

Jerry and Jill's spare room smells of their former dog. When the heat shuts off, the faint (imaginary?) piping of frogs rings painfully cool and sweet at the edge of her hearing. It's times like this Maizie wishes that her vague belief in God did more than conjure some pervasive maleness—to whom can she pray? And for what? Babycenter.com informs her that by the time her baby turns into a *large mango* it will be too late, she'll have no medical or surgical option and will have to allow it to become an *ear of corn*, a *rutabaga*, a *scallion*, a *head of cauliflower*, a *large eggplant*, a *butternut squash*, a *cabbage*, a *coconut*, a *jicama*, a *pineapple* (as it pitches its hammock and turns her into its personal tropical island). Finally, when the clock of its conception strikes, the child will turn into a *pumpkin*. At which point, even if a prince does show up bearing her glass slipper, it will no longer fit her foot.

If Danny loved her it would be different. If Danny loved her, Maizie could be that Babycenter.com still life; how oil-daubed and luminous, how well brushed would she be! She would have the luster of a crystal decanter, she'd be a goblet, gemmed and lucid, a fallen tulip petal still a-sway on a tabletop. The lush lining of her uterus would be the oriental carpet, its crimson piled up in folds around a single jewel of an apricot—not an it but a "you." Yours the tender skin with the blush at its crease—yours the radiant flesh. You, her heap of peaches. You, her bowl of eggs.

But Danny does not love her. So sense dictates that she must make you the dead hare, the half-plucked pheasant, the gaping flounder, the slivers of flesh carved from a blood-red joint of meat. And soon.

Jill is no help.

"Assuming I let this thing stay. What if it's a girl?"

"Decent odds."

"What if it turns out to be a feckless alcoholic?"

"Chances are."

"What if it hates me?"

"Also possible."

"Or it's a serial killer?"

"Could be."

"Likes Danny better?"

"Might do."

"Blames me for parting them?"

"Probably will."

"Born with only a brainstem?"

"Not impossible."

"It could be the Antichrist."

"Don't flatter yourself."

"Jill, you're not helping!"

"Love set you going like a fat gold watch."

"Mother of God!"

"Sorry."

"I feel like I'm staring into an abyss. It's monstrous. Doing that to somebody—giving them life? Or undoing a life before it's done?"

"Welcome to motherhood."

"I feel lonelier than God."

"You've *eaten a bag of green apples. Boarded the train.*"

"God you're glib."

"It's because the shape of my own life is hardening off. I forget what it's like to agonize."

Maizie can't make a decision. She doesn't know what to choose for herself, for the question unfolding in her, multiplying its cells, developing its doors of perception and a heart that beats. She's afraid because once she chooses, the shape of her life, and the (just say it) baby's life will be that much closer to setting. She could get stuck here in the middle of nowhere, dependent on the kindness of her sister, living among a passel of other people's children.

Jill insists that Maizie walk every day with her and the nursery-schoolers.

"Caring for toddlers is like living in a perpetual haiku," Jill says as they scramble up the road to Benton Hill Park. Jill's new foster daughter Kyla brings them a caterpillar to admire. Maizie loves the orange bulb of its head, those fierce mandibles writ small. Even the tiniest beings are perfected and complete.

Jill hands Maizie a fallen walnut, still in its fat tennis-ball rind.

"Take a whiff."

The green rind smells nutty and lemony both. It actually counteracts her nausea.

The park on its hill feels as remote and hushed as a temple. Wind sweeps through the walnuts and the catalpas, and there's a sea-roar from cars rushing down Benton, and the sharp cheeps of birds in the bushes. Jill shows Maizie the treehouse—just a platform circling an oak. Climbing up, Maizie is tempted to check the oak's branches for photographs, for prayer flags, strands of silver beads.

When she was a kid in Thailand, she couldn't imagine why mothers chose to leave their children with the nuns. But choice is more of an illusion than her younger self would have believed. There are forces she has always been subject to without being aware of them. She is swayed by pressures she never could have dreamed—the heart had its tides and there were undertows that dragged at the will. Money. Biology.

Maizie and Jill collect walnuts with the children and roll them down the steep incline that winds toward the street. Their hands are stained with walnut ink.

"Kyla's on a linguistic bobsled lately," says Jill. "I say a word and she has it."

Kyla looks up and, as if to prove Jill's point, says, "Wa-nut."

Kyla gnaws on a walnut fruit and then cries because it is bitter and cries harder because Jill takes it away.

"No, Kyla, yucky, ptah!"

She looks at Maizie sheepishly. "I've become such a prig."

"How are things with Jerry?"

"The Guzman kids catapulted us into middle age. But according to Jerry I never really joined the human race until I got thrown over the castle walls. You know. We rub along. I have a feeling that as soon as Piper turns eighteen Jerry's going to pull a Thomas Merton. The only thing holding him back right now is the question of whether or not monks have to pay child support."

"Do monks have to pay child support?"

"Neither of us wants to find out."

Jill catches Maizie's thought and shakes her head.

"Jerry and I are together on this. We want to help you, whatever you decide. And the marriage—we're together, we're doing this—and I think it's a good thing. It's almost enough, Maizie."

Jill takes Maizie to Hy-Vee grocery to buy frozen blackberries. She swears they will help with the nausea. Seven-year-old Piper, as thin as a spider monkey and wild with excitement, drags her Aunt Maizie away to the fish counter, ignoring Maizie's feeble protests. Maizie is too weak with hyperemesis to fight a second-grader, and Piper's fascination with live crustaceans brooks no denial.

Piper presses her face to the tank to watch the scrum of shellfish. It is charming to see her niece crouch before the vat of dungeoness crabs and green-brown lobsters, to admire Piper's reflected face on the glass of the tank, her gappy grin pumpkin-wide and missing its two front teeth. But behind this beaming face, a banded claw bumps the glass, a broken feeler twitches. A crab drops a foreclaw before Maizie's eyes—its big fiddle arm just falls right off and sinks among the lobsters. Maizie's skin creeps. The lobsters at the bottom of the tank have folded into themselves and don't move, and most of the crabs at the bottom of the tank have also given up, but the ones on top are huge and beautiful and lively, creamy-aproned, with violet shells. Their frilled gills work frantically. They cost nineteen dollars apiece.

In the next tank three tilapia swim—big cat-faced dove-colored fish with pearl pink lips and tame gazes. One tilapia is clearly not long for this world—it lists sideways and fins frantically to right itself. Whatever has life wants to live.

On the drive back from California, Jill insisted they stop at Point Lobos so Maizie could say goodbye to the ocean. Maizie perched on some rocks above the lagoon. Wind tangled her long skirt around her ankles and bannered out her hair. Jill stared down into the water, her eyebrows thick in a frown. Jill, intent and fierce, completely unaware of how beautiful she is with the sun gilding her hair. Love for her flooded Maizie, and gratitude. Jill put a finger to her lips and pointed down at the lagoon.

In the clear green water, a sleeping harbor seal drifted. Its eyes were closed; it sank to the shallow bottom, lay without breathing for long minutes. Then, slowly, like a plumb-weight, it surfaced. It floated, an upright buoy, still asleep.

Is it snoring?

The seal sank again. Jill nodded at Maizie, beaming. She puffed her cheeks and raised an imaginary cup of tea. Maizie took a sip. In Thailand they emptied their lungs and sank to the bottom of the compound pool. Tanned skin in blue water. They tucked up their feet and bobbed against each other like unborn twins. Open-eyed and smiling, they blew long silver strands of bubbles that caught in their long blooming hair. They crooked pinkies as they raised invisible cups. Toes gripped tile. Lungs bursting, they pushed off and exploded upward in tandem, laughing and gasping in the sun and air.

Wind shuffled the sunlight on the surface of the water and obscured the submerged body of the seal. The wind died, the ripples cleared. The seal, completely at home in its element, lolled elegantly against sand and stones on the bottom of the lagoon.

Did she just feel the baby flit?

Maizie leans against the fish counter for support. On the other side of the glass, a dead rainbow trout glares up at her from its bed of ice.

> Dear Parasite,
>> Why should a dog, a horse, a rat have life, and thou
>> no breath at all?

Your hostess will seat you now.

"Do you remember Mrs. Cho?" Maizie asks Jill during a naptime lull.

"You don't have to whisper—once they're asleep we could vacuum the floors and play the Hallelujah Chorus and nothing would wake them," said Jill.

She and her sister sit in the darkened front room, surrounded by children laid out napping on their little mats.

The smell of sleeping skin and breath creates a gentle fog that Maizie has to resist sliding into. Her stomach is a small bulge now—she's in the cute phase of pregnancy—she's rounding out and glowing.

"I remember Mrs. Cho's food," said Jill. "I got so fat."

When Mrs. Cho made fried chicken, seven-year-old Maizie and nine-year-old Jill camped on the linoleum floor of their kitchen in Seoul and listened to the drumsticks whispering in their grease. Maizie mapped the veins in Mrs. Cho's swollen ankles. Jill picked bits of crackling from the frying pan and fed them to her kitten.

"She was the first adult who ever made me feel loved," said Maizie.

Mrs. Cho wore a polyester housedress cut like a nurse's uniform. It was white and striped with fine horizontal lines of blue and pink. It was not a beautiful dress but Maizie could never see those particular colors without feeling a rush of longing. Mrs. Cho left the dress hanging on their laundry room door when she went home. Sometimes their mother left them locked in the house at night, alone, and Maizie would stand under Mrs. Cho's dress and thread its thick, stretchy hem between her fingers.

"She didn't love us. Mom paid her."

"What about Mustache? Of course she loved us, or how else would she have known?"

After a particularly awful first week of school, Mrs. Cho met them at the door beaming. She told Jill she had a *splice*. Jill, her face still screwed into the scowl she used when she held back her pickle vat's worth of tears, tried to push past Mrs. Cho, who was blocking her path to the cookie jar. But Mrs. Cho took Jill by the hand, repeating *splice, splice for you*. She pulled Jill into the box room next to the washing machine. Maizie, munching a cookie, followed.

How, Maizie wondered, had Mrs. Cho known that Jill had always wanted a kitten? Their old apartment from their real life didn't permit pets, so Jill had never had one; she'd entice stray cats to their patio with slices of olive loaf. None of the cats liked her for it.

Jill's new kitten had black ears just coming unfolded, tiny transparent claws that Jill could extend by pressing his knuckles, and eraser-pink pads on his paws. Above a pointed white chin he sported an ink-splotch mustache like Charlie Chaplin. You could hear his purr even over the thump of the dryer.

Beaming, Jill lifted the kitten to her neck.

"Mustache," she said.

Jill had dimples. Maizie had almost forgotten.

"Mrs. Cho loved us," Maizie insists.

Jill rises, lofts a fallen blanket over a sleeping child, strokes a few sweaty curls back from a forehead, pats the rump of a restless boy who is whimpering in his sleep.

"You can't help but love the people you take care of—your hormones trick you into it."

"I used to think Mrs. Cho was a guardian angel."

"Oh, lord, if I hear domestics compared to angels one more time, Maizie. I just. Don't get me started. I guess it makes sense. Children belong to the supernatural, so it follows that domestic help must be divine. Divinity is such a convenient trait to find in an employee—no crass human needs, no grubby sense of self. They work like drudges but that's okay because they're either better people than we are or they're magical. Look at Mary

Poppins. She was a demigod who cleaned the nursery using telekinesis! And Maria from *The Sound of Music*? She was a nun. Those are our ideal nannies. No wonder childcare workers are paid so little."

It is like Jill to intellectualize. And maybe they had idealized Mrs. Cho as a way to deny her as a person. But it was more than that, Maizie hopes.

"But she knew! She knew Mustache was what you needed. That's magical."

"I did have kittens plastered over every single wall in our room, Maiz. Anyway, we were so poor before that. And she was our first maid," says Jill. "Of course she seemed magical."

They'd meet their share of maids and other children's nannies—indifferent maids, resigned maids, bewildered maids, maids who giggled at everything, even when the children of the house hit them or called them names, maids who never spoke, sharp-eyed maids, impatient maids, syrupy maids, unhappy maids, efficient maids—

"Mrs. Cho was different," Maizie insists. "She wasn't just a maid."

"None of them were just *maids*," says Jill. "Terrible word. So virginal, so Olde Englishy. As if the maids ran off to Sherwood Forest at the end of their working day and drank mead. Sorry. I just—being on the other side of it now—I get ragey."

Jill adjusts the square of cardboard they use to darken the windows. She waves at a tiptoeing parent who's arrived to pick up one of the half-day kids.

"Anyway, I hate to think about all that. Maybe she loved us, but she couldn't stop us from moving to the Philippines. She couldn't stop Mom from making me ditch Mustache because she wouldn't put him through an island quarantine. That horrible family and their two boys—remember how Timmy always had his hands down his pants? When they weren't up his nose? And Mrs. Cho had to go work for other people, and the cat ran away and turned feral."

"Mom says Mrs. Cho still fed him. For years. She loved us," said Maizie. "Mom told me she gave up a baby. A little girl. She gave it to her sister, and her sister made her promise never to tell. Her daughter never knew who she really was."

"Maizie. This isn't Korea. Or the 1950s. You're not a pregnant widow with two little boys to feed."

"I know." Maizie feels irritated. "I just wonder how she felt. How could she endure something that sad and have been so kind to us."

Mrs. Cho had arthritis, and her knuckles stood out like polished knots; she rubbed them with Nivea when the fine, stretched skin cracked into chilblains. But did her hands remember, did those deep aches from weather and work and age also contain the ache for her renounced daughter? When her daughter was born did Mrs. Cho's heart snag on her little umbilical stump and did the child's cries send her frantic to scoop her up, hold her to breasts that buzzed and let down milk? Did her hands reach out to smooth the infant's hair, did they ache to hold her?

"When I first had Piper I thought I didn't love her. I was too beset. And Jerry was just—well. She took everything I had and made me realize I didn't know jack shit about love and that everything I ever did or felt before having her was just . . .

sentimentality and selfishness. Love is fucking hard. It's filthy and boring and never-ending. I never understood Jesus. I'm like Pilate, washing his hands of suffering. I say pass the soap.

"So I don't know. I don't know how Mrs. Cho kept her heart open or how she survived that kind of sacrifice and was able to work for us brats and tend to us brats and never hear her own daughter call her 'Mother.' Maybe having your heart broken breaks it open. Maybe hers was always open. I have begged the universe or Sunny Jesus or Buddha or whoever to split me like an atom, make me explode with love—because any other state is unbearable—but I got bupkiss. And then last year . . . Okay, can I tell you something dumb?"

"Always."

"I had a conversion experience. Via YouTube. Okay, you can't laugh. You promised not to laugh."

Maizie looked at Jill.

"With Mister Rogers."

Maizie's mouth quirked.

"The man saved me. I know Jerry wants his church to take credit for the changes in our lives, and bless him, he has no idea. When we first had to take care of Manny and Gracie I'd sit with them and watch Mister Rogers feeding his fish and singing *Everyone makes mistakes oh yes they do* with the tears just stream-ing down my face."

"The Gospel According to Fred?"

"No one ever called him *Fred*, Maiz. That was his *point*. He was Mister Rogers. Kids need someone to be in charge. He was an adult. So. Mister."

Maizie still feels like a teenager herself. Who in the world is in charge of her?

"I read about him—you know, interviews, everything I could. He spoke to everyone he met like they were children, with the gentleness most of us reserve for babies, and newborn babies at that. He looked into every single person he met and saw them as shining-vulnerable responsible-capable-innocent-necessary-divine. To him each person was his neighbor—and a terribly young, terribly vulnerable, terribly worthy soul. He saw people the way I suppose he believed God sees us. That level of tenderness, Maizie—how is it possible?

"I couldn't believe in God, but I did believe in Mister Rogers. I would talk to him, in the bathroom, with the door battened against all those kids—I still pray to him. And when I did, I would hear him singing—you know what he always sings?

"You can never go down, can never go down, can never go down the drain.

"And it saved me. Because, Maizie, it's true!

"I took on those Guzman children but I couldn't love them. I tried. I'm the one who convinced Jerry to remortgage the house so we could bring their father home. Everyone says, oh, you're so noble, caring for those children, moving heaven and earth to return them to their father—even Jerry thinks so, but on the inside, Maizie, I knew I wasn't noble. I just wanted to be rid of them. The guilt was killing me. So I'd put on *Mister Rogers* and try to cope.

"Forget the Land of Make Believe. I'd ride that trolley to the ends of the earth just to see the man take a seat on that padded bench in his entryway—his goddamned seventies entryway done up in muddy turquoises and greens. He'd come in whistling and he'd change his shoes! I just marveled. A tie with a sweater, Maizie—who could be bothered? As a kid I took all that for granted, but when I watched it as a grownup, well, even the way he parted his hair blew my mind. Everything he met he cared for. He treated all of it—objects, people, his fish—with such tenderness, such exactitude. His very presence implied that taking care of anything brings it to life.

"And I knew it was okay. It was okay if I didn't love those Guzman kids, as long as I was taking real care of them. Maizie, kids don't see a difference between love and attention. What matters is if they're cared for. If they're attended to. Maybe Mrs. Cho loved us. Maybe she didn't. She cared for us. We were attended to. She brought us to life—and isn't that all anyone can do?"

Dear Baby,

I still don't know if I am going to keep you. My mind is blinking like a turn signal, indicating a turn, indicating, indicating, but I can't make myself swing the wheel. I'm falling in love with couples on adoption sites. They're all so scrubbed up and solvent. Like Edward and Elsa, an alliterative Anglo/Argentine duo who pull crackers at Christmas and raise horses and could offer you grandparents in Cornwall and Buenos Aires. They aren't intimidatingly good-looking, either, baby, so you wouldn't have to face that pressure. Edward has a lazy eye and Elsa is plump—the kind of plumpness that will nourish you, the kind of plump a small child can trust.

I could choose you a childhood. Imagine. Scratch that—what I really want is to have chosen my own childhood. But no one gets to do that.

I wish I could consult you.

Spring rains dominate Maizie's third trimester. Dust-blue clouds clap a blackboard sky. Maizie loves how trees tune up before a rain, how they bow and rustle in expectancy. Jill and Maizie walk the nursery-schoolers, a row of rubber ducks in their raingear, to Brookfield Park in a gentle downpour. Rain sweeps a hand over the children. The children's bright jackets are soaked and the colors grow more vivid. Maizie tries to shield Kyla with a purple umbrella, eventually gives up and lets her walk bare-headed. By now her belly is so heavy that she walks with a toddler's mosey herself—that drunken sailor waddle.

In the park the children pull the fetlocks of a willow to make drops fall. They try to throw stones into the creek, but most of them lack the motor skills so the rocks bounce off boot tops or roll harmlessly into the grass. Rabbits browse among the tuffets of creek-grass. Sparrows settle in the beams of the picnic shelter and shrug off the drops of rain.

On the way back they are trapped at a railroad crossing by a heavy train storming past. It frightens some of the children, who hold their ears and cry—the thunder of its weight, the unexpected whistle. What is it about trains that these kids fear? The size? The duration? But it must be the noise, that gnashing of brakes and track, shattering the regular doo-wop of wheels and car-sway. A slowing train sounds like iron teeth grinding in pain.

"Where train going?" Kyla asks Maizie.

"To Illinois," responds Maizie. She always sends trains east, the direction of the morning. Though Kyla has no concept of Illinois or east—hell, Maizie barely believes in them herself.

"Train get you?"

"No," explains Maizie, "they're on tracks." Though *track* is only slightly more comprehensible than *east*.

"Train won't get you," says Kyla now, as the last car winds away.

Down in the park the creek is overflowing and turning the park to a paddy where hidden frogs are singing. And the rain falls not too hard.

Dear Baby,

When asked, Midas tells Dionysus that the best thing in life would be never to have been born at all. You will have to make up your own mind on this. You will be human, and it will hurt. The shifting algebra of love will wreck you; you will learn to balance its equations, or you won't. You will settle into a life you can bear, perhaps even a life you love, or you won't. You will find someone who loves you, or you won't. If you do, you will lose them eventually. Many things will come as a surprise, not all of them unpleasant. There may come a day when you inform me, or some other mother, in rage or despair, that you did not ask to be born. You will want an answer to your cry, Why am I even here?

I might tell you this: You are here because two people riding carpets of magical thinking blundered together. You are here because for a few brief moments your mother thought a handful of stories could make a life—and it did. It did. I could say, You are here because your father lost a dog when he was little; you are here because he taught your mother to skip rocks by the San Lorenzo River long after your mother had given up ever being able to learn such a childish skill; you are here because your mother thought this meant your father would restore your mother's childhood always and for all time. Instead, and this is better because it must be (reality is too strict to fight forever—it is a wall you will break yourself against if you gainsay it), they made you.

You are here because, like many of us, your origin is rooted in misalliances so perfectly meshed that they are little miracles. You are here because your mother believed in saving helpless creatures and you were one your mother finally could rescue.

You are here because just before their love broke like a wave and receded, your mother woke your father up with gentle kisses and announced she had an inspiration. Your mother curled herself around your father and asked your father, did he trust her? The sun came in the window, yellow-blue September air, sharp and clear as a Golden Delicious. Your mother drove your father up to San Francisco, out to the Presidio, where they parked below the bright orange vista of the Golden Gate. Behind them, white barracks stood in parade rest against a dark backdrop of cypress, redwood, and pine. Nearby, Crissy Field lay washed in fog. Your parents caught glimpses of Marina beauties walking French bulldogs, and children flying designer kites in the white. Over the water, the fog was beginning to lift.

Your mother hoisted a backpack and took your father's hand. They hiked oxbow roads, and your father grew impatient, but your mother squeezed your father's hand and smiled.

"Trust me."

Finally, your parents stumbled down a hill toward a towering cluster of dark evergreens. At the bottom, your mother yanked aside a little iron gate and led your father under an iron archway into a clearing. The clearing, under a canopy of fir, smelled of warm pine needles and cool black earth. Small arched tombstones, all froggy with moss and the size of croquet hoops, dotted the glade.

"Look." Your mother knelt and scraped at some yellow-green lichen gilding a rock.

"It's a pet cemetery."

The graves stretched in irregular rows, some nestled in the deep shade thrown by the cypresses, others leaned crookedly beneath the kaleidoscope of sun and fog that revolved in the grove.

"They started this in the forties, and shut it down in the eighties, I think. Now it's illegal to bury stuff here. It's where navy officers and their kids buried their pets. I love how the names change with every decade," your mother said.

Daisy. Fido. Rex. Patches. Schnapsie. Buck. Missy. Sandy. King. Commander. Walter. Lulu. Fifi. Spike. And farther down, Brandy. Misty. Lucky. Heather. Casey. Alf.

Your mother chose a declivity well guarded by the giant trunk of a redwood and unpacked a blanket, a split of wine, some bruised tomatoes, Brie. Your mother fed your father the soft, slippery tomato and buttery cheese, and let your father drink most of the wine, and then your mother pushed your father back against the redwood, settled next to your father, and asked your father to just breathe. But the stillness of the place welled up inside your father until he felt like he was going to lash out or die.

The pine boughs waved. A crow swooped over them with its heavy shot-silk wings. Your mother kissed your father, unbuttoned his shirt and parted it. Your mother put her tongue to your father's navel.

"Shhh!" Your father shook your mother and she sat up.

Two rows down a brother, a sister, and a father stole through the ferns. On hands and knees the children searched for a clear spot in the bracken. From their shelter in the lee of the tree trunk, your father and your mother watched the little sister remove a zipper-lock bag from a backpack. Inside the bag, your parents saw the stiffened form of a reptile—a small lizard, leopard gecko? chameleon? The brother and sister dug a grave with plastic spoons while their father, in a bored way, stood lookout.

The children patted down the grave and the brother arranged a halfhearted cross made of popsicle sticks loosely bound with a rubber band. The brother was obviously humoring the sister, who lay some frowsy dandelions and a red construction paper heart below the cross. The sister wrote on the crossbar in marker, the silver glitter kind. The brother snatched the marker from the sister and added to her inscription. The family stood a minute, the sister obviously trying to summon tears, and then all three turned aside. The family left the creature's zipper-lock shroud gaping on the grave.

Your mother darted over to examine the cross.

"'RIP Clyde'! Only the brother crossed it out and changed it to 'Stubbi.'"

Your father needed to smoke, so he sauntered among the graves, the silence buzzing in his head. He chained a couple of cigarettes and crushed out the butts next to an elaborate altar. The sun had finally unpicked the web of fog and it glinted off a dull, convex mirror set into the headstone.

Your father squatted to pick up his butts, and read the inscription painted in fading purple lettering around the mirror.

"Liberty. 1966–1975."

The mirror was a hubcap. Your father's heart thudded. He saw floaters as he leaned in.

On the lap of the grave, a Polaroid preserved behind a cloudy plastic sleeve.

"Maizie!" he shouted. "Come here!"

Your mother ran over. Your father slid the faded snapshot free. The picture was sunbleached, the figures nearly washed out. A rail-thin officer. A longhaired woman. And an almost imperceptible dog, lowslung, chunky-bodied, lop-eared.

"Orla."

"Honey," your mother said, "the photo's so faded. That could be a beagle. Even a corgi."

"No," he insisted, "it's her."

Your mother squinted at the picture, holding it tenderly between her fingers.

Your father snatched it back. Your father wanted to chew it up and eat it. Christ, it is Orla. She is here. He never lost the precise memory of the velvety nap of her ears between his fingers. It is Orla, all right, and it is made right.

Joy he didn't know he could feel seized your father, and your father seized your mother and crushed
her against his chest. Your father kissed your mother
fiercely, shotgunning his joy into her. Your mother
drew back laughing, and he bear-hugged your mother
because *Orla* and they put the picnic blanket to its in-
tended use after all.

You are here because even mistakes have their moments, and now that you are here I'm not even sure
I believe in mistakes; their symmetry contradicts the
whole notion of error. Welcome to the world. I'm sorry
for what you won't have, and for the ways in which I,
and the past that created you, and the world we can't
escape, and you, yourself, will hurt you. I'm sorry and
I love you. I still don't know if I have the courage, or
the selfishness, the lack of foresight or the blind faith to
keep you. I don't know if I can bring myself to tell your
father about you.

For now I will eat frozen blackberries with you
tucked like a flaming star inside me, and we will sit in
a row on the couch with your aunt and your uncle and
your cousins, and we will all watch Mister Rogers and
drink the blackberry thaw straight from the bag. Such
clear, cold juice, dark as blood, but sweeter. Whatever
becomes of you, baby, when everything is said and
done, all that really matters is this: You are here.

GRACE

A lone bull elephant seal lives in a small cove at Las Piedras all year round. Some instinct is broken in him. He never ventures out into the deep water. He never grows a heavy mat of fur and flesh over his summer skin. He remains smooth-coated as a garden mole, haunting the beach, a one-eyed anomaly. The scientists (I asked) don't know what to make of him, but following some biologist's prime directive they never interfere, never relocate him. They tagged him and stand back to see what, if anything, he will do.

The bull does nothing. He does even less than the usual run of elephant seals, and these are not animals renowned for vigorous activity. He swims a little, in the shallows of his cove, but he doesn't ever venture into deep water to hunt for food.

Who or what sustains him? He must eat somehow, the biologists insist, measuring his undiminished bulk. Otherwise

when they came to the beach to collect samples from the an-
nual catastrophic molt, they would find nothing but bones.

I could tell the biologists, the bull knows me. I've received
whiskery caresses from that Cthulhu snout. I could tell them
that for his unnatural presence in the cove, as for so much else,
I blame my mother.

I have been alone for a very long time. Never married. Never
had kids. Wanted both, first complacently, idly, then as more
years passed, sharply, with increasing anguish. With the passing
of more years the anguish receded but took hope with it. Hope,
that little-discussed STD. How distracting! How inconvenient!
It's a distant itch, most of the time, and then when things start
to go right, it breaks out in a rash over everything.

Carline says I have the most boring job on the planet, but
she doesn't complain when I prepare her taxes for free. Yes, I
work in an environment of unflattering fluorescence and pro-
tective-coloration taupe, but it's an environment I chose. She
calls it terminally bland but I like environments that have no
history. And surely I am not the only person on earth soothed
by office supplies.

Even preparing taxes has pitfalls for the fanciful mind. Tragedy lurks in the numbers—divorces, deaths, debts, disasters.
A life rendered numerically is still a life, and after twenty-five
years in the business I can infer enough from a straightfor-
ward 1040 to concoct a Russian novel. When you're wandering through the wastes of receipts and spending you learn to
track the footprint of desire and necessity in the sand.

But I didn't mean to sell anyone on tax preparation as

divination. I only mention my job because that is how I met Héctor Guzman, resident legal alien, fifty-six, self-employed contractor and Mennonite minister—qualifying widow(er) with dependent child(ren). A flurry of forms 2441 and 8812, schedules SE and EIC, and the bones of his life, his fate, what he achieved and what he was up against, all lay inked neatly in boxes on my desk.

I might have fallen for him based on his tax information, even if I hadn't looked into his face and found it was like opening a door in a wall and arriving unexpectedly home. A recognition: he knew something that I also knew; he knew something I thought belonged only to me, the thing, in fact, that made me feel alone. And the shock of feeling *known*—in an office deliberately chosen for its neutrality—abashed me so much that I dropped my eyes to his paperwork and my voice stuck in my throat.

He brought his children with him into my office, and they were so brightly colored and oblivious that it broke the spell. The little girl (Graciela Marisol Guzman, five years old) herded her brother (Manuel Mauricio Guzman, eleven years old) like a sheepdog. She crackled with authority. A cowlick poked up out of her bob and trembled like an antenna.

"Manny, sit," she said to him, and he dropped to the carpet happily.

"He has special needs," she said in that pompous manner particular to five-year-old girls. Manny, a sturdy boy in a Ninja Turtles T-shirt, trawled his fingers through the carpet shag and netted a fallen staple.

"Pretty," he said. He handed it to his sister as if bestowing a jewel. She took it gracefully, unbent it, and pressed its points into her thumb. Then she placed it on my desk.

"They are okay with you?" Héctor Guzman asked.

"More than okay," I said.

They were both whole and alive in the way that only children and animals seem to be.

Graciela rifled through her pink backpack and pulled out a marine life coloring book. More fishing dredged up a single red crayon nub, which she handed to Manny. He ground it into the outline of an otter. I gave Héctor Guzman schedule SE to fill out and stole peeks at him under the pretense of sorting through his files.

Now that I know him better I can tell you that Héctor is one of those people content with being a blur. He's like a star—look at him directly and he's hard to see, but glance with your peripheral vision and he flashes brightly. He seems as innocuous as a diner coffee cup—he's short and sturdy-built, with a little belly, and he's bald except for a crescent of hair around the back of his head and over each ear. Most people wouldn't look twice. But if you do you realize he's not a coffee cup at all—he's a Toltec jug. And my God, he inspires similes.

He caught me looking and grinned. I blushed.

"You sister was very kind to refer me to you."

"How did you meet Carline?"

"She was at your brother's house—"

"Cousin."

"Your cousin's house. When I arrived to meet my children. The woman who cared for them drove them out to me. She had also a sister, living in your cousin's house?"

"You mean Maizie's sister, Jill?"

"Such a drive. My children have seen more of America now than I have."

He reminded me of someone I couldn't place, someone I had loved for a very long time, ever since I was a girl. When he turned his head and pulled at his mustache, it came to me.

"Mr. Waldenstein!"

"Pardon?"

"Sorry, I was thinking of a book. It's not important."

It was important. Some girls sigh over Gilbert Blythe, or want to pound mud on the moors with Heathcliff. When I was ten I fell in love with Mr. Waldenstein, Ole Golly's late-in-life suitor in *Harriet the Spy*. From very early on Mr. Waldenstein was my ideal romantic hero. He's dapper, he's gallant, he's brave and humble, he can pedal the hell out of a delivery bike. How I wanted to be Harriet, tucked cozily in that dark carrier basket on DeSanti's bicycle, but even more to be Catherine Golly perched in ridiculous dignity on George Waldenstein's handlebars, squired up the hill and so improbably, so rightly in love. Catherine Golly Waldenstein, who isn't even real, but who taught me more about parenthood and integrity, and romance, than either of my parents. Catherine Golly Waldenstein—it's because of her I still held out hope. She looked like an oak-carved effigy of an old maid, hawk-nosed and plain; she supported a simple-minded mother, and worked as a domestic; but she was loved, loved ardently. My whole life I hoped to find Mr. Waldenstein: a mild, decent man with a mustache, a man who invested his deep heart in the person of an upright spinster, a hatchet-faced, compassionate, Dostoevsky-quoting nanny.

It is dangerous to identify with fiction too closely. But with my family, what else did I have to go by?

"You've missed a couple of exemptions here," I said. "You could be getting money for your son," I stopped, unsure of how much Manny could understand. I showed Héctor on the form—dependents with disabilities. Then Manny stood up and bumped against my desk and spun a dish of paperclips off the edge. Héctor Guzman rescued it neatly before a single clip could spill.

"Pretty!" Manny grabbed the dish of paperclips again and this time he spilled them on the carpet, where they schooled and glittered like minnows. Héctor said something in Spanish, blushing furiously. He stooped and swept the clips into the dish.

"Don't bother," I said. "Here." I hunkered down next to the children and strung three clips into a little chain. "You can play with them. They are pretty."

Graciela strung the paperclips into a long garland. Manny played my stapler like castanets. The tinselly paperclips trembled in the drafts he raised. Héctor frowned over his paperwork; he nibbled his borrowed pen.

"Your perfume," he said, "what do you call it?"

We think we're all alone—it's easy to believe, in the long dark corridors where we barricade ourselves—but we're connected, all of us, real and fictional. Watching the man fill out forms, with his two children playing at his feet, I wanted to shuck my cold-bearing fur. I wanted to pare off all my heavy, horrid skin and emerge softer, sleek and clean. How long I'd been alone in the cold dark sea.

• • •

I told Carline about Héctor Guzman, about George Waldenstein, all of it. She was skeptical.

"You must have seen the resemblance, Carline—why else
would you send him to me?"

"Is that why you inked all those hearts in my copy of *Harriet the Spy*? Honestly, I was too busy dealing with Danny's stuff
to really pay attention. Danny just ditched everything when he
went to Texas, you know. I'll be eBaying his crap for years.

"Anyway, it was a rare impulse! A momentary lapse into
kindness. Maizie was a wreck when Héctor Guzman showed up
and Jill had the kids to unload from the car, so I made awkward
small talk with the man for about five minutes. Found out he
wanted to set up a nonprofit down in Pasadena, so I sent him
to you. I didn't expect him to turn your head.

"You know you're just projecting right now, Cissy," she said.
"You can't tell if someone's good or not based on their tax return and a fleeting resemblance to a minor character in a children's novel."

"Do you know any good men?" I asked Carline.

"Mother was a good man."

"Come on."

"She was. All the best men I've met were women. Louise
Fitzhugh was a lesbian."

"So?"

"So probably her fictional good men are thinly disguised
women."

"What makes women good?" I asked.

"We've been trained up so long that assessment's meaning-
less," said Carline. "It's like asking what makes a dog loyal."

"Tell me that Danny at least took the dog."

"Of course. Goddamned Danny," said Carline. "He's 're-turned to his roots.' Says there's a whole side of him that we kept in shadow—'you Bowmans,' he calls us now like he isn't one of us. The loon."

I was stung—for our sakes, for our mother's, even for Mai-zie's. Had we been so stingy with Danny? Leagued against him?

"How do people do it, Carline?"

"What?"

"Turn on a dime."

Were all the duties and preoccupations, the web of friend-ship and custom, nothing more than marking time for some people? Were they really just hawks, hovering, hunting their real life like a rabbit in the chaparral, and was it only when they dove that you realized you were just a speck in the landscape of their discontent?

"He's integrating, Cissy. *Finally.*"

"Don't you feel a little bit guilty? On the girl's behalf?"

"I did them both a favor. People just drop you on your head when you put yourself in their thrall. She needed to learn that. Anyway, they were doomed. None of us is any good at adult relationships."

"I've noticed."

"In a way, Danny's defection gives me hope. What's that Tom Robbins quote? 'It's never too late to have a happy child-hood'?"

"That's drivel."

"Don't be bitter, Cecilia. You've met your storybook prince."

• • •

After we'd been dating for a few months I proposed a family visit to Las Piedras. I wanted to show them the elephant seals. I needed to pit Héctor against the spectacle of the seals' suffering, or my own history. Plus it would be fun for the kids.

"Cissy, you're setting up a palimpsest," said Carline when I told her. "That's a fancy way of saying you're trying to rewrite the past."

"Thanks, Psych 101."

"I wouldn't go back to see those critters if you paid me."

She paused.

"Is it the inflatable dong faces? Because, Cecilia, there are subtler ways to let a man know you want to sleep with him."

When confronted with a herd of flop-nosed Cyranos, what would Héctor say? Would the piggy eyes, the flapping proboscises, revolt him, and would he be moved by the mute appeal in the unadorned faces that the females and pups turned up at us? I hoped for some subtle response to these least subtle of animals.

I told Héctor his kids might like looking at the weaners. Then I blushed and clarified, the seal pups that stay behind after they're weaned, they teach themselves how to swim, they play in the tidal inlets, prepare for a long life at sea. They're cute.

"You like weaners?"

He smiled, poked his tooth bridge out at me, sucked it back in the blink of an eye. When either of his children was hurt or distressed, the other called, "Take out the bridge!" and he palmed his false incisors and turned to them and grinned. The wide smile, its total lack of vanity, revealing that naked gap of gum, transformed his saturnine face into a Halloween pumpkin, made him five years old again, whole and unharmed, his mischief intact, and his sense of glee.

When I asked, he told me, without elaborating, that the guerrillas who held him for ransom in Colombia had knocked out his two upper front teeth.

"I was very fortunate. Many more received worse."

I wanted to press for details. I looked it up instead. Héctor was right. He had been treated with the merest kiss of violence.

"I don't know why," he said. "I don't know why I was spared."

The bridge was meant to be temporary, but he couldn't afford the dental work to get the hole permanently fixed.

"Doesn't it bother you?"

"The teeth help when the children cry—and they cried so much when they first came back to me. Gracie barely knew me. Manny remembers, but in truth, I am a new father to them. So it is good to be able to do this."

He poked his tongue through the hole again. You have no idea how the hole in Héctor's teeth distracted me.

"I quit drinking Diet Coke for him, Carline."

"Seriously?"

"Yeah. He told me it's basically like drinking blood. I bought Manny a Coke once, to be friendly, and he poured it on the ground."

"Weird."

"Not if you don't want to subsidize death squads."

"Dammit, Cissy. Are you sure you want to be dating someone with so much baggage? I mean, you can't even enjoy our national beverage in his presence without having to think about human rights violations."

"He can quote Emerson. From memory. In English and Spanish."

"But he has yet to kiss you."

"I told you about his teeth. He's shy. And there's always the kids."

"Those kids! Traumatized up the ying-yang."

"I never should have told you that, Carline."

"We were little nightmares after Daddy popped off. And isn't the son— Look, Cissy, do you know how hard that is? Even if a kid is normal, it's hard. And when they're . . . you know, not neurotypical."

"You always swore Sonny was worth it."

"He is." Carline sighed. "But there are days when I know I simply have to tell myself that because otherwise I'd lie down in the carpool lane and hope for a quick death by SUV."

She sounded wistful. Middle age had finally erased the little penciled-in differences between us, blurred the individual territory we had staked as children of pretty versus plain, of lovable versus obedient. But now that I was dating Héctor, Carline must have felt left back, just a little. I would have, in her place. God knows I have felt that way my whole life.

Life isn't fair, our mother always snapped at us when we cried *No fair!* Spoiled, she called us, entitled little madames lacking the gratitude God gave a flea.

"If you're going to date this guy you're going to have to learn to be very fucking valiant, Cissy."

"I can be valiant," I said, miffed.

"I'm not sure you can, honey. It's harder than you think. We Bowmans are not known for our valiantry."

"Valor," I said.

The moment the car crackled into the parking lot at Año Nuevo and Héctor pulled the hand brake, Gracie announced she didn't intend to get out. The wind carried the unnerving sound of the newborn pups' cries, eerie, Orc-like, high-pitched and yodeling. Farther out, frustrated males gurgled and kathunked like possessed plumbing.

Startled by the din, abashed by the multitude of huge animals in the distance, Gracie refused to budge. Children are so exhausting.

"But you have been excited to visit the sea elephants," said Héctor.

"Elephant *seals,*" she corrected him. "Their noses are yucky."

"Yucky!" echoed Manny happily.

High-handed little chit, wasped my mother. *Whale her butt,* drawled Daddy. *Don't stand for any back-lip.*

"*Defects are ascribed to divine natures to signify exuberances,*" said Héctor. "Emerson."

Gracie stuck out her tongue.

"*Wherever is danger and awe and love, there is Beauty, plenteous as rain, shed for thee.* Emerson again," Héctor said. That earned him the full raspberry.

"*Momentico,*" said Héctor to me. He crawled in the back and settled beside his daughter, speaking in low and urgent Spanish—I caught *porfa* and *listo* and a string of endearments that melted my blood with desire and envy.

"Speak English, Daddy," Gracie whined.

I was ready to love this girl but I itched to strangle her.

Pretty much, Carline put in. *Welcome to motherhood.*

Héctor caressed Gracie's hair. He caught my eye over her head and blinked, grimaced, shrugged. What-can-you-do?

You have to be valiant, Cissy.

I ratcheted a smile and rallied. If I was sick of always coming in last, then why did I choose it so consistently?

Outside, an indifferent sea wrinkled against the horizon. Seagulls wheeled. A family burst from their Prius like dancers leaping out of a cake, the older child helping the younger hoist her bright red backpack, the brochure-blonde mother swigging elegantly from her blue enamel water bottle, the father, wearing a sun-hatted baby in a chest carrier, snapping shots of the kids with his phone.

The car heated up. I felt prickly with irritation and foggy with defeat.

The ocean was so near that I could have magician-whisked it off the planet like a loaded tablecloth, wrapped myself in it, let it whirl me away, *no fair, I'm not playing!*

Mother, how do I do this? But her response would have been to draw a paperback from her pocketbook and bury her nose.

The other family launched a bright purple jellyfish kite, trailing leagues of pink neon ribbon across the sky. The baby commanded the wind by clapping his hands while its immaculate mother stretched her calves in warm-up for a walk on water.

Manny hauled on his door handle, but Héctor hadn't released the childproof locks, so Manny satisfied himself with kicking the back of my seat. Gracie still wasn't budging. So Héctor continued to soothe her in Spanish.

"*A la orden. Listo.*"

How could he take this child so seriously? Clouds smothered the sun and we plunged into shadow. The kite pitched headfirst into the sand.

Valor, Cissy. Only craven ingrates compete with little kids. You don't need to.

And it was true. I watched Carline with Sonny. Although she loved him completely, epically, her heart ached toward adults; her love for Sonny did nothing to diminish that yearning. I had to fight the voices, those old self-wearying furies who insisted that if Héctor loved his children he would have none left for me.

"I need some air," I said evenly, and flicked the locks. Manny erupted from the car and went bowling toward the stretch of beach packed with beta males.

"Gracie, stay with Cecilia!" said Héctor, and gave chase. They disappeared among the dunes.

A kittenish little salt wind flickered into the car, rasping at my eyelids. Guilt and panic always leave me listless.

"You let Manny run away," said Gracie. "It's your fault if he gets squashed."

"No one's getting squashed."

"We *always* keep the doors locked."

I dug my knuckles into my eyes. "I forgot, okay? Shit."

"You said a bad word," said Gracie.

"I *know.*"

I craned around to face her. She glared.

"God hates you," she said. "My real mother never said any bad words. Or my foster mom."

"Neither did mine. The f-word was *fudge*. The s-word was *sugar*. It's an insult to candy! Bad words for bad feelings are better."

"My real mother is dead," she said.

"So is mine."

We sat some more.

She turned her face to the window, searching for her father, her brother, for any bright motion against the pale monochrome vista of dun-colored seals on dun-colored dunes. I wanted to dump out the entire beach like an overflowing ashtray.

"They look like monsters," she finally said.

"Oh, honey." The tremor in her voice stung me. "They're only seals. Monsters aren't real."

She flinched as if the lie would smirch her.

"Okay," I said, "you're right. But I've been right up close to one of these guys. And it wasn't a monster. Up close everything is less scary."

Another wishful fib. I just couldn't stop coining them. In Gracie's fierce little presence whoppers dropped from my mouth as if I'd been enchanted to spout the proverbial snakes and toads.

I tried facts.

"Elephant seals can dive under the water longer than any other seal—did you know that? They live most of their life deep in the ocean. We're lucky to get to see them out here. Most of the time they're underwater."

"Like my mom," she said.

"Who told you that?"

Héctor had impressed on me that while each child knew their mother was in heaven, neither had knowledge of the itinerary that sent her there.

"I don't know." Puzzled, she sucked in her cheeks, picked at her seat belt.

"What makes a monster, anyway?" I asked her. "Maybe monsters are just creatures who don't share our element? Who thrive where we would die?"

She rolled her eyes.

"You know what I do when I get scared?" I changed the subject. "I get nosy. I try to find out as much as I can about what scares me. Some monsters change shape when you get to know them."

Ignoring this piece of tepid consolation, the little sorceress absented herself from the conversation entirely—simply vacated her body and slipped away someplace where the fumbling logic and half-truths of my adult explanations could not insult her.

Héctor hiked up carrying Manny, both of them glistening and winded. Gracie reanimated with a galvanic bang, unbuckled her booster seat, slid from the car, and ran to her family. She tilted her head to catch Héctor's smile, and gathered herself into a performance of excitement, shimmying and hopping, pulling at his shirttail, tugging him toward the path. Children take advantage of our need to believe in their innocence, their resilience. Children lie to us too.

"Let's get out of here. We'll go find my mother's seal," I told Héctor. "He'll let us get right up close."

We drove to the little cove a few miles down the highway

from the herd's haul-out. It was just a curve of coast, a few dunes quilled with pampas grass.

Héctor and I sat down on a salt-whitened driftwood log trenched in the lee of the dunes. Plovers were inoculating the sand with hypodermic beaks. The ocean had cast huge mats of seaweed, tangled with bulbs of kelp and jumping with sand flies onto the beach.

The day had turned painfully beautiful, with blazing clear skies and that distilled California light that makes everything look like a new-minted platonic form. Héctor pointed out at the distant water, where two bulls collided in the surf.

"I'm sorry about Manny," I said. "I never dreamed he would run off like that."

The bulls smashed together as sharply as waves breaking against a rock, sounding their trumps, noses lifted, tusks bared. Waves bowled against torsos and blood pinked the water.

Nearer by, Gracie untangled a rubbery flex of kelp and skipped rope with it. Manny crouched in her shadow filling his pockets with sand. I loved to sit at a distance and watch Héctor's children. Their gestures and movements fell into such blameless order. They bounced around each other like diatoms. Get too close and I lost perspective; the pointillism of their personalities obscured the wider impression of their innocence.

"Every bit of violence I witness reminds me of their mother," Héctor said.

The clashing bulls opened wounds in one another with their tusks. Blood surged and spouted, crimson gouts that broke in bubbles on their shoulders and chests.

"When I was taken by the guerrilla, our church would not assist us, the NGOs refused because they will not fund terror-

ists. The neighbors who were raising my children made a second mortgage on their house to pay for my release. I cannot
repay my debt to them. And yet I blame them—they should
have nailed my wife to the earth! I owe them my children and
still I resent them."

How could hides that tough split, how could they bleed
when their blood circled so deeply beneath fat and skin, beneath hides that were so thick?

"You shouldn't have to see this. Christ, I'm a boob."

"Boob?" he said with a sudden gleam of teeth and a glance
down at mine.

"It means 'idiot.' I should have taken you someplace peaceful. The Mystery Spot. Or to see the butterflies in Pacific Grove."

"Marisol said water rewrites the world."

"When my daddy killed himself," I told Héctor, "my mother
had no language for it. None of us did. She took all our shock
and rage and moved it to California. But the ocean didn't rewrite a thing."

The surf sizzled around the bulls' raw hamburger wounds.
Their blood, so scarlet-bright and unreal on their bodies, turned,
in the spray, to a soft pink mist.

La vie en rose, I thought.

"Mari wanted to live near the ocean. Instead, I brought her
to Iowa. Locked-land! She did not complain. Only once she
begged me, and that was to stay with her and our children. You
must know this of me, Cissy. I was arrogant to insist on finding
her father. If couldn't make my country whole, I determined to
unite my family. And so I left them."

The younger bull was tiring. The alpha male lunged and
harried him out of the surf.

"I thought she would be safe in America. Instead, she found the water.

"Cissy, I didn't know that a person could be demolished by being taken from what is familiar. I am not such a person. I blamed my wife for being less able than I. I survived the guerrilla and she couldn't even survive America?

"People still ask me, how could a mother not choose life? But perhaps in Marisol's case it was the other way around. Perhaps she felt life did not choose her. Because I did not choose her. I was not generous with her, or with my children."

The younger male shuffled backwards onto the packed gravel at the tide line, streaming blood, small in his defeat. He beached himself on a warm patch of sand and immediately fell asleep. Satisfied, the old bull lumbered out of the surf and back to his harem, where he mounted the nearest female and pumped away at her, triumphant and bleeding.

Watching this, Héctor's face unclouded and he laughed.

"How peaceful your seals are, Cissy. There's no malice. Even in their violence, how generous they are—and whatever is generous has beauty."

"My mother said these animals were the ugliest varmints in God's creation."

His hand fetched mine and he pulled me to him.

"What is it with you, Héctor? You always seem so happy just to exist."

"I'm not happy. I'm delighted."

His arm slid unhesitatingly around my waist. His palm burned me and I recoiled from it like a snail, trying to draw in the excess flesh, the years that age and solitude had solidified into fat.

He squeezed me.

"All this is delight, Cissy."

I sucked in and pulled away slightly before his palm could nestle against the fold of skin that rippled above my waistband no matter how high I hiked my pants. But his hand refused to retreat.

"What do you see in me, anyway, Héctor? Why did you even notice me?"

"Your perfume, first," he said. "Then all of you."

Sudden light caught the Vaseline-gold of Gracie's strand of kelp as she whipped flourishes into the sand. She skipped in a widening circle around her brother, who heaped sand into hills that fizzed and swirled apart in the wind. She skipped down the length of the beach, capering like a spider. She reached an outcropping of barnacled and gull-beshitted rocks and let the waves crawl over her feet. Then she disappeared between the boulders. Manny abandoned his sand piles and followed her. Minutes spun. Neither one of them emerged from the outcrop.

Héctor shot me a glance recognizing that silence is more suspicious than screams, and we ran together into the nook between the boulders.

My mother's seal lay between the rocks on a pyre of gravel. Gracie and Manny were wreathing it in snakes of kelp like an orphic egg. The old bull's monumental stillness flooded the cove and called on the ocean to cease its whispering. Light lapped the animal's wet fur and turned it to shining pewter. The barnacles on the rocks shut up their houses; even the drift of anemones in the rock pools stilled when confronted by the unstirring sierra of his body. The bull was so profoundly asleep that he might have dreamed the entire world, dreamed the beach, dreamed the four of us who stood at his side.

"Go wait on the log," Héctor said to the children.

Round-eyed, Gracie took Manny's hand and they scurried up the beach.

The bull's snout lay in a straight line on the gravel, the vacuoles sealed. His good eye was closed, but the blind red socket stared up at the sky.

"This animal is dead, Cecilia."

"No," I said. "You don't understand. This is the one I told you about. The one my mother left to me."

I knelt close to seek the movement of his huge heart, scanned the slope of him for a twitch of muscle, a swell of breath. I held my hand in front of the bull's nose but felt no marshy vapor. I tickled one finger, tentatively, down his flank. Nothing.

"He's alive. He has to be."

I grabbed the seal by the ruff and shook his loose skin. His fur felt desiccated and cold. I dug my fingers into it, trying to find a pulse, some heat or life to contradict the marine stink of half-rotten fish rising from his unresponsive folds.

"He can't be dead. He's mine!"

I didn't realize I was crying until Héctor pulled me away from the seal.

Héctor poked out his tongue and dislodged his front teeth. But before he could palm them the teeth shot from his mouth and fell into the dark slab of shade beneath the elephant seal's body, where they disappeared between the bits of gravel.

I pelted the dead seal with loose pebbles, frustrated and weeping. Sand fetched up in the lines in my palm as I dug. It slipped through the cracks between my fingers. Heavier elements, crab shells, sea glass, nestled briefly in my cupped hands, but I threw those, too, at the dead seal. Finally, my fingers scraped the sand's wet brown-sugar layer and I scrabbled there in the seal's shadow like a demented terrier.

Héctor pulled me to my feet.

"Let it go, Cecilia."

"But your teeth!"

"*No me importa.*"

"Héctor, how do you stand it? All of it? Any of it?"

"Because I was spared. I have always wondered, why did the guerrilla do so little harm to me, to me alone, among all the other men they held? Did they see in me their own violent righteousness? They are pitiless men. Did they recognize their arrogance in my own certainty? What was it they saw, that they should call me brother? I have to live with this question. What, in comparison, are teeth?

"My pain is so huge," he said, "my body, my heart, everything tender and bruised. But I discovered when I was captive that I could look for the comforts. Tiny places on my body that did not hurt. I could concentrate and feel not the rope abrading the torn skin, but the tip of my tongue where there was no pain. The relief of my eyelids smoothing over my eyes. That is how I survive. What choice do I have? I am here. I am alive. Life chose me. I have been broken open where I wanted to fall apart. Now everywhere I go, I seek out softness. The generosity, the places that offer comfort. This sand, your skin."

Reader, I kissed him.

All of us mammals are born breathless, like free divers, or sounding whales. We must plunge, sealed and stifled, in order to breach the world and its light. The transition from placental breathing to filling our lungs for the first time is a crisis humans resolve with an outcry. Not the clamped cord but that first breath parts us from our perfect union.

We breathe; we are divided.

Only in elephant seals, those sadhus of the sea, does the newborn mammal's tolerance for asphyxiation increase with age. Their tonnage is so immense that they can shut down heartbeat and breath for extended periods of time. In order to hunt in the deep waters, to seek and devour enough food to live, they must know how to die. Even now seals are foraging in the sea, breath suspended, heartbeat stilled, dangling like needles from the reverse of a half-finished tapestry, trailing their faint thermal threads. Ashore, too, they will lapse into corpses and revive.

Héctor and I dove deeper into our kiss; we didn't need to breathe. As my tongue raked the warm naked gap left by Héctor's teeth, our dead seal shuddered, took a breath, rolled upright, hove his body into the water, and swam out past the breakers.

Finally, he plunged.

Héctor closed the three of us in the car. Manny breathed on his window, drew squiggles, lightning bolts, and hearts. I sat in the back with Gracie. I brushed the sand from the soles her feet.

"Shall I tell you, Gracie, about my mother? Shall I tell you her name?"

She nestled tentatively against me as though perhaps I was not a monster, perhaps none of us were; perhaps we were not even unpredictable animals, cold and starving from long years at sea.

Acknowledgments

Special thanks first and foremost to my sisters Katherine Parker Bryden and Michele Parker, staunch supporters, tireless and insightful readers of countless drafts; Katherine, you came in like the cavalry; Michele, you let me borrow more than clothes for this one.

To Chris Kearns, who taught me to read and write.

To my editor, Jenna Johnson, without whose vision and deftness this book would not exist, and to Pilar Garcia Brown—both of you pushed the work to better places than I could have imagined; and to my agent, Ellen Levine, who stuck by the book in its messy teething stages.

To Sarah Weintraub for her friendship, and her passion for Colombia; to the members of the Tassajara writing group, where this book began (Michaela Bono, Lea Seigen Shinraku, Everett Wilson, Caitlin Gildrien, Dave Rutschman); to Ken Yoder, who pestered me to keep up the work; to the teachers and sangha at

Tassajara Zen Mountain Monastery and Green Gulch Farm, for their patience and support, in particular Linda Ruth Cutts, Jiryo Rutschman-Byler, Jeremy Levie, Marsha Angus, Arlene Lueck, Tenshin Reb Anderson, and Bryan Clark.

Thanks to Myo Lahey for gently nudging me off the priest track and telling me to go write instead.

I owe an immense debt to the Iowa Writers' Workshop— teachers, peers, and friends; especially Sam Chang, Connie Brothers, Jan Zenisek, Deb West, and Marilynne Robinson; particular thanks go to Kevin Brockmeier and Michelle Huneven, wonderful writers who put up with more first-book panic emails than anyone should have to bear.

To my son, Bruno, who helped me to find the courage to try. To Patricia McGuire Stigliani and Bruce Parker, founders of the Benton Street Fellowship. Thanks mom and dad.

And to David Graham.